IMMORTAL NORTH TWO

— • —

A NOVEL

TOM STEWART

LUCKY DOLLAR MEDIA

Lucky Dollar Media

luckydollarmedia.com

luckydollarmedia@gmail.com

British Columbia, Canada

Cover design: Katrina Johanson

Paperback ISBN: 978-1-7772211-5-7

Ebook ISBN: 978-1-7772211-6-4

"Immortal North requires an emotional investment from a reader, but if you are willing to give Stewart your time, he will give you a piece of the trapper's and the boy's hearts. And you will find by the midway point that you have given them all of yours. Very highly recommended. ★★★★★"
—Jamie Michele, Five Star Readers' Favorite

"Immortal North is one of those classic works best savored slowly. I was so immersed in the wonders of the natural world and the mysteries of human love and existence that I wanted the story never to end. One of the finest examples of true literary fiction I have ever read. ★★★★★"
—Marcus Lynn Dean, Author, *Thermals of Time*

Books by Tom Stewart

Immortal North: A Novel

Immortal North Two: A Novel

Under Big-Hearted Skies: A Young Man's Memoir of Adventure, Wilderness, & Love

Collected Works: Short Stories & First Chapters

Author's Note

When I finished writing *Immortal North* in October 2021, I had no intentions for a sequel. Yet, here we are. The tale felt unfinished.

Reading this novel without having first read the original *Immortal North* would likely be a mistake. If you choose that path, I hope at least it's an interesting one.

—Tom

DEDICATION

To the North, of course.

A RED FOX HUNTING in the night.

Coat like a Russian princess, coat like a fashion trend she started, burnt-orange looking like she could set the night on fire, turning the head of any rabbit she didn't see first. Elegant stockings blacker than the space between stars and that space is very black. Shining eyes bejewelling her handsome face.

Overhead, arched branches hold skiffs of snow, the forest decorated in strung garland for the nightly gala of winter survival, the high-stakes dance of predator and prey.

To appease the sky's heartbreak losing its sun, a god blows from its palm a little pile of stardust that bespeckles the gloomy firmament with incredible starlight. The sky is much appeased, and below, the red fox walks in her winter ball. As if the Earth's turning were a slow waltz to court this red queen. Hardly a wintry night more regal.

Her ears swivel forward. She slips her black stockings into the snow—the drifts themselves should be so lucky. Stops. Three legs sunk in the snow, one bent above where a paw hovers the surface. Her eyes so fixed on what she can't see they admit to her awareness nothing else. Eyes locked just ahead, a foot, maybe two, not more than three. She can't smell it and doesn't need to. Few others besides her and the wise owl would know of this poor mouse. Her head lowers. Her head raises back up. Her head rotates a quarter turn. Dials back to twelve. She's pinpointed the mouse and her eyes widen.

The mouse stops scurrying its tunnelled paths. Probably its jaws full of some seed or wild grain. Could have sensed the predator above. Maybe felt the delicate weight of the fox stalking in the snow. Now both of them motionless, these two in a blind standoff.

The fox rocks back onto her haunches to load up her hind legs, then she springs into the air. Midway through her arc, her snout points like a spear at the unseen rodent. Paint this thin porcelain moment onto the side of a china cup.

She'll drive down through the snow and clamp her jaws, powerful for their size, into the soft grey body that'll emit just a tiny squeak. A little tragedy to be chimed by the night's smallest peep. She in the air with her hind legs kicked out and her big tail behind her. The white tip of her tail like a struck match before it burns and the sky all aglitter like that's where past tsars chose to store their jewels. Everything dressing up someone's death so pretty here.

Then, big paws so wide.

Those big paws so wide that as the lynx closes the final distance sprinting she doesn't even break the snow's surface. She isn't totally silent like owl flight, but those padded paws, how they puff up the snow in little donut clouds with her every running step, how she runs over the snow not through it, how she travels so like a ghost that the poor fox entranced with her own prey never hears her. Never even hears her. Imagine jumping and never coming down.

The princess protests. The night's lament: a squeal rather than a squeak. The princess protests no longer. A royal cloak stolen by a cat burglar: a fox in the jaws of a lynx carried off in the night.

The North doesn't play favourites.

Welcome back to the North.

WOODS

WHEN THE TRAPPER WAS young he was told a story of a mythical arrow shot from a mythical bow. For *that* arrow to reach its target, it had to cross half the distance. Then it had to halve that distance again. Then again, and so on. Of course *that* particular arrow never reaches its target because it never crosses all those infinite halves. How could it? That still made some sense to him. Turns out *this* arrow is not *that* arrow. A part of him was surprised.

Jacob had been watching through a hole in the window broken by a shovelhead. He saw a shirtless man holding in one hand a knife, and in the other a rope strung over a rafter and noosed around his friend's neck. The jagged hole in the glass and the angle through which he gazed only allowed him a target of that wild-looking man's head. So half-drunk and adrenaline-jacked in that northern morning, that's what Jacob sighted for. Pulled a bowstring for. Then, a man who was no archer, loosed an arrow.

He watched it graze the head of a man you'd rather not graze.

The broadhead so pretty and dazzling in its flight as it sliced through that spectrum of morning light. As if the blades were reflecting the shining state of lovingkindness that for the last few moments had entranced the trapper enough for him to lower Dave down from the tips of his toes to flatfooted.

The blade slit the trapper's ear then cut across his temple and sliced his eyelid. Its sting came before the blood and the blood came quick. His head reeled backwards and the blade must have nicked a vessel because there sprayed a thin arc of blood. The arrow thudded hard into the cabin wall and the trapper, wounded, looked from Dave to the window. A man outside the glass frantically reloading a bow. *His son's bow.* This hand plays itself out.

His knife already gripped prompted his next action. An *instinctual action*, a defence lawyer might say. Entirely justified given the circumstance. A trial lawyer might implore to the court: *Could you imagine a clearer case of self-defence, Your Honour? He was even bleeding from an arrow while watching another being loaded.*

The trapper had lowered Dave from his dancer's pose but hadn't yet let go of the rope. He gave his knife the smallest vertical toss—the quickest one-handed way to swap his grip from handle to blade, as that's how you throw one. He caught the blade with a light grip and pinched the metal with the cutting edge facing outwards between his fingers. His remaining nails, those he hadn't lost digging in the clay the night of his son's burial, were blackened underneath with grave soil.

He was losing vision in his right eye and that blood was colouring his world a rageful red as he watched a man who just shot him reloading his dead son's bow. That earlier tide of lovingkindness was out and the flood of mean intentions was in. The trapper so recently overwhelmed by total compassion now had the instinctual switch of self-defence flicked in his head: thoughts gone from light to dark. He squared his body for the throw. *Aim small, miss small*, that maxim in his head. He focused his one clear eye at the semi-circular hole in the window featuring a man's face. That face a small target and built with bone to withstand blows and deflect projectiles. He knew a head was a poor place to try and stick a knife. Just above the lower rim of broken glass was a softer, fleshier target. The trapper drew his arm back while sighted on an Adam's apple to cleanse this man of his original sin.

Jacob had unclipped a second arrow from the side quiver and with shaky hands managed to get it nocked. He was drawing back an arrow already aimed at its destination.

The trapper had his arm cocked and knife high for the throw. He tried to blink his nicked right eyelid and clear his view but it only partially responded and the blood flooded the bank of his lower lid and trickled out, he looking like some hell-beast weeping blood. The rope in his other hand he released his grip and started his throw and Dave lunged at the trapper while yelling out hoarsely, "*No!*"

Dave hurled his body into the trapper who'd halfway taken a step to put some weight behind his throw. Dave knocked him off balance before either man could loose their weapon. They hit the floor and Dave with his wrists still bound came down on top of him and he tried to stay on top to at once keep the trapper grounded while also using his own body to prevent Jacob from finding a clean shot.

Jacob outside the window floating that sight-pin trying to find an entry point for his arrowhead. Searching for a patch of chest skin not covered by Dave. He held and he was starting to shake from the pulled weight of it and couldn't find a home for the dart without risking arrowing his buddy.

Dave yelling coarsely, the noose which hadn't much slackened continuing to strangle his voice. "Stop!" Exasperated pleas to stop. "It's over!"

Had Jacob even found exposed skin over vitals, for all the bow now was shaking he might've missed anyways.

Dave still yelling to Jacob, yelling to the man below who wasn't struggling, maybe yelling even to his own rattled self in sounds of strung out and scratchy pleadings, "It's over! It's over!"

The trapper from his fall had banged his head off the floor. His dazed world resounding with ardent calls for truce may have restrained him more than the weight lying over him. From where he lay he watched Jacob draw down the bow.

Heavy breathing. A strange calm.

Dave hadn't even reached to slacken the choking noose. His mounted position over the trapper may have been one of pretence, given that his hands were still bound and the trapper's greater physique. But Dave still kept his hands placed over the man's chest, uncertain what would happen if he took them away. In a voice barely louder than a whisper, Dave said with such desolate finality you would certainly never start even a sad folk story with it, and likely those words too bleak to even end one, "It's over."

Jacob lowered the bow but his heart's tempo didn't follow suit. His breath in the cold air hardly showed gaps between the plumes, train steam not pipe smoke.

Dave said in the tone of a snake handler about to unhood a viper, "I'm getting off."

Slowly, they both sat up on the floor. Then all three men took turns looking at one another, in what seemed to be a tentative armistice coming at the end of some strange and small, though still tragic war.

Dave couldn't see the bow Jacob was holding outside the window but he told him to put it down and just come in here.

Jacob was listening to Dave but looking at the trapper. Trying to assess the man's commitment to this new peace. A man with a scarred up chest all pockmarked, wild hair, and bleeding rather profusely is not the most convincing picture of trust. But when Jacob came in he left the bow outside. He watched the trapper and in the trashed cabin, he righted a chair across from him without taking his eyes away, and then he watched him some more.

Though any of them could have spoken first and had grounds to—questions, accusations, apologies—nobody seemed eager. Dave's nerves were spent and if he was relieved from having not been hanged to death and then laid down into a cold grave already dug just outside the cabin, he didn't show it. Maybe he figured the reluctant role of conflict mediator was up to him, as he was the first to finally try to put some words into the cold cabin air.

He started to say something to Jacob but choked on the first word. The rope looking like an elongated necktie he grabbed the knot and loosened it like one. He told Jacob that he was okay. He lifted the noose up over his head and then held the stiff loop in his hands and looked at it. Like it framed a dark hole and luckily today he had only had to glimpse where it led. "I'm alright," he said again, whether to Jacob or himself. He turned to the man who'd put his head through that hole, that rope.

The trapper had his knees bent upwards and his wrists overtop them where his hands hung limply. Dave watched him bleed. Rivulets ran down the trapper's face and dripped onto his crotch while he looked at the floor.

Dave got up and stepped carefully among the wasteland of clutter to the kitchen. Came back. "Here," he said.

The trapper didn't look him in the eyes he just took the towel.

Jacob said, "What the fuck is going on?"

Dave looked around until he found it. Laid it on Jacob's knees.

Jacob held it up, turned it. Stuck his finger through a small hole. Dave told him the awful significance of that tear in the small bear hide. Then he started telling Jacob what all had happened and he didn't start it from the afternoon in the lodge when he was abducted by a six-foot jackrabbit, he began it from the day they pulled the trigger. He said, "We."

The trapper listened to the details and didn't look up once.

Jacob even while holding the hide, even with his finger poked through the hole like one of the worms no doubt curling through the boy's lying body, even with the boy missing and the boy's bow recently in his hand and a bereaving father and an imploring friend—*No way*, said his disbelieving mind motivated for self-preservation. It began conjuring up any and all plausible counter-explanations, a mental factory manufacturing shadows of doubts, however faint, to refute or undermine this dreadful story and stop a word that already chimed in his head without anyone having yet said it.

Murderer.

But preparing for the defence of that charge meant acknowledging such an accusation had been levelled against him, and some part of him, maybe the emotional and spiritual core inside him people call a soul, got the first intimations of that weight: of potentially, even just potentially, being a killer of a little boy. And the weight of both its guilt and repercussions—legal and social—was already drawing him into a deep pit. He shook his head, not vigorously, but deliberately enough it looked like he was trying to rid himself of that word through each of his ears.

Jacob put the bear hide aside. He made his defence to the room while speaking at the floor. "No way. I saw a bear. Unmistakable. I clearly saw a bear through the scope." His head down. "Say what you want. I know what I saw." His lips tightened.

Dave was seated directly on the floor and his lower position allowed him a look up into his friend's downward gaze. Jacob's eyes weren't tearful but when next he spoke Dave hadn't heard him use that voice since his wife left him. If voices had colour this one was all grey.

"It was a bear." Jacob looked at the man sitting across from him. This man nearly catatonic and appearing homeless and beaten—beaten up, beaten at life. The spiritual dejection told in his face that after his assailant had finished physically assaulting him, he or she had then taken a bat to his soul.

Jacob repeated the words his hunched body and now pleading voice weren't selling. As if his back had been broken in a deadfall trap and though the rest of his body was convinced of the new paralysis, his voice was yet outstanding. Again a lame plea, "It was a bear."

As subtle as it was, immediately following those echoing words you could see the trapper's next breath drew deeper. Like those words had drifted across the room and the trapper inhaled them and their insolence swelled his chest. The cabin so quiet and his breaths a half-beat quicker were a half-decibel louder. His good eye squinted, now matching the other that was narrowed from the cut. His hand that recently held a knife twitched where it rested on a knee. Then curled into a fist. His other hand that pressed the towel to his head lowered down at the same time he raised his hellish eyes. The one red enough that it might have, for the length of time it took to bring Jacob up to speed, been dwelling on some burning otherworld. He set their anger on the speaker.

Dave watched the leaking blood that the towel had slowed, unslow.

"I saw a bear." Incredibly Jacob said it again and he may as well request that epitaph for his headstone.

The trapper dropped the bloodied towel and clasped his hands together and they turned white and looked like he was trying hard to restrain something, perhaps struggling very hard to not go down a particular route that a certain part of himself had a proclivity to travel. He looked like he was about to lose some inner battle.

"*Stop!*" the peacekeeper interceded, his arms outstretched to them both. "Stop." This time quieter to de-escalate even himself.

Jacob was looking back and forth between the two pairs of eyes locked on him. He wanted to ask for proof. *Proof of the body.* That the bullet matched his calibre. That's not an unreasonable request and he knew that and of course any court of law would require the same. Could be he finally saw evidence enough across the room from him. Whether he was looking at pure hate, pure loss. Whether he realized his next words were likely to pull a hair trigger to those double-barrelled boreholes of violence fixed on him. He must have got the satisfactory proof he was reluctantly seeking—slow to get there but he got there—because he stopped turning his head from one man to the other, stopped his requests to see the body, stopped shaking his head, and just hung it.

The trapper looked away from Jacob and his vision caught the bear cloak and he didn't stay there long. Looked to Dave and for more than one reason was repelled by him also. Saw a chaotic room of broken pictures in broken frames and dishevelled books and lost trinkets and each in turn he averted his gaze 'cause he saw nothing worth seeing. He just closed them, tried to, the cut eye not heeding his will. The towel once again pressed to his head. He looked like he had just finished last in some modern game of blood sport, or first in a high-stakes gladiatorial one.

Jacob reached to his inner breast pocket for his flask and unscrewed it and tipped it up and with pathetic patience he waited long enough for the last few sorry drops to drain out from the bottom. Touched his tongue to the metal rim for those clinging laggards. His desert just begun, he should have saved that paltry hydration to slake coming toils. *Murderer* chimed in his head. He had made no eye contact, so when he asked for a drink it was only addressed to the general room.

The room didn't answer.

Like the all-consuming anger that had impelled the trapper to rope a man's neck and hang him from the rafters, like the state of mystical love the trapper recently glimpsed and which had its honeyed spell broken by the immediacy of threat made keen by his own cut skin, the intense feelings of his returned anger receded and his rage was defused. This morning's prelude to violence was silenced by the futility of playing on—*nothing brings the boy back.*

The trapper sat in a room with an innocent man he'd almost killed, with the proof that his boy had been, and with the man who'd done it, who was also the reason his own head stung and bled. The trapper sat there in a plethora of pain in this cabin of shambles.

Life always generously offers a thousand ways to die, and bleeding, scarred and rather wasted looking, it appeared that the trapper had sampled his options before finally electing to just drown in mistakes. But he must have preferred to do so without the company of these violators of his and his boy's woodland sanctuary, because he asked them to leave. His first words echoed Dave's and sounded nearly as hoarse. "It's over," the trapper said. "It's over. It ends here." Then looking between the two of them so as not to look at either of them and in a dead stare, "I want you to leave."

When Dave and Jacob heard that, they thought he meant leave his cabin. Later they'd come to believe that that particular request may have meant something else entirely.

Jacob could have apologized and it did look like he was going to say something. But what does it really matter? What's done is done. Walk into the empty arena where the sand is caked in blood and say sorry, then listen to its lonely echo off the empty bleachers. How much good is that? Good for nothing. Save those words so ineffective at remedy or repair that they could only be taken as further insult. Jacob got up from the chair and made for the door in silence. Dave followed. Saw his shirt and jacket on the floor by the door, his boots. He took them to the porch and into the winter outside.

The trapper put on a coat and didn't zip it and followed them out. Everyone walking haggardly into the morning sun and a world disrespectfully bright. As if in the moments preceding one's death, the only question to ask: Don't the birds know I'm going to die?

Dave limping with his twisted ankle. For the first time he saw the big hole in the ground he'd earlier only heard being dug for him. Heard that soil being pitched up out of the earth and landing with the flat sound of some bedevilled metronome counting off the time he had left in this world. Though he couldn't now hear that metronome, of course it still ticked.

Tick. Tick. Dave looking at the mounded soil beside the pit that would have covered him over. The grave looked about six feet deep. He just shuddered.

"Wait." The trapper said that then went to the shed.

He returned with a pillowcase and handed it to Dave. Dave saw the missing batteries and bullets taken from their cabin. The trapper's face didn't allude to whether he was trying to right some wrong by returning the theft, or if he knew that without the batteries they'd have no other way to power their satellite phone and call in a plane for a pickup. After the earthquake of murder, the small theft of these personal goods was tremorless. Dave closed the pillowcase. He looked into ruined eyes haunting a harrowed face. He didn't see hatred, didn't see spite. But he didn't see goodwill either.

Dave wanted to say something but he wasn't sure what. *Sorry*—but it wasn't his fault. *Take care of yourself*—sounded stupid and cliché and those words inadequate for a man who had just lost a son and would now be alone in the wilderness. *It'll be okay*—maybe it wouldn't be. *Thanks for not killing me.* That's all he came up with and none of them were any good and had he spoken them, their own indelicacy coming out of his throat ought to justify that bruised blue ring around his neck. Sometimes words are useless. He restrained an impulse to offer his hand. Sometimes gestures are useless. They stood a pace away on level ground but unequal footing. Dave was about to turn away.

Then he said, "My name's Dave."

They looked at each other.

Dave walked over to Jacob. They left, Dave with a hobble to his step and Jacob with a ringing in his ear.

The trapper watched them go then listened until he heard their silence. Then kept listening. He hadn't slept in over a day and the last sleep he'd had was short and restless. He was several versions of unwell: exhausted, malnourished, bereaved, spiritually lost, physically injured. He turned for the cabin. He passed the empty grave. Its appeal was not lost on him. Saw his son's compound bow on the porch. Fixed his eyes for the bedroom and tried to pay little attention to anything else and so left snowy boot tracks over the floor and stamped tread marks into the wax pools left by spent candles and he shattered glass already sharded and incidentally kicked assorted treasured shambles. Something broke. But it was just his meaning for life recently held frailly in place by thin threads of vengeance. The noose loop lay on the floor with its long tail still strung over the rafter and as he passed it he pulled the rope and its tail-end slithered up over the beam then came down, landing with a flat sound in a limp and messy coil. He had stopped pressing the towel to his face before they all left the cabin, and blood from his eye had trickled to his chin and dripped to the snow where he had stood, dotting his route to the bedroom. A perfect bloodspot trail so barbarous fate could track him down and finish him off. He wiped his bleeding head and saw the big red swatch on his arm and knew his wounds required immediate attention. He didn't give them that. In that nightmare morning with his distraught mind swelling with loss, he just lay down.

. . . .

It was morning when the trapper went to bed and he didn't even stir until the latest hours of the night and when he stirred he never fully waked. A sickness in the calamity of his dreaming mind. Battles waged and lost. Voices in his skull—some new, some old—fighting for territory; some holding their ground, others giving it up. That mental combat would at times manifest in his body when a leg or arm would twitch or kick or punch in a violent hypnic jerk.

Inside the trapper was a smaller trapper. He had crawled into a small hole that he'd dug into a wall of his mind. A larger trapper tried to reason with him, tell him it's okay. Hey, it's over. The little guy like a soldier still out there in the jungle not knowing the war had ended. Your loyalty is admirable, the bigger trapper said to the smaller, but the battle's over. Come on out of that foxhole, soldier. Let's go. He informs him of the bodies, of the peace treaty.

But the little guy questions his loyalty 'cause he signed up to fight forever. He swore he'd always be there for them. For *him* and for *her*. He pledged it, vowed it. Let the ground rot him away and it would only show that word etched into the lengths of his bones. *Forever.* The little man asks with venom in his voice, *Is forever over?* His greased sarcasm slips through his clenched teeth. His commitment to fighting for wife and son will never diminish and his loyalty is not open to refutation however clearly the facts are presented against his beliefs—in fact, for him, his valour is sized in proportion to holding improbable beliefs. *More* loyal if your convictions don't falter while facing an abundance of counterevidence. That's what he was taught, that's how he was indoctrinated. His essence is family and to that edifice he pledged his enduring loyalty. Any argument to shift him off his foundations sounds to him as reasonable as theories on the dryness of water, the coldness of heat. Pure nonsense.

The big trapper tries again anyways. Look around, he says, it's over. The cabin's empty. He peers at the little guy in his hole. They're gone, man, he says to him. You'll just be guarding a past that doesn't need to be caretaken. The big trapper outstretches his hand, makes a beckoning motion. Come with me, we'll face the future together. It'll be okay. We'll go slow.

That small soldier isn't budging.

Please. Just come on already, it can't be undone. We have to keep swimming or we'll drown. We'll starve and wither in the past.

But now that smaller trapper sees the big one for who he is. He was trained early to recognize defectors, *traitors*—those who used to fight shoulder to shoulder beside him, now gone to the other side. He was told that in the fog of war former friends may become enemies, to trust no one—not even himself—and that the first casualty of war is the truth. Stay vigilant. He knew this day would come and here it is.

The bigger trapper with the outstretched hand. *Come on, bud.*

Then from that foxhole the little guy does lean out—maybe some words got through to him—leans out a bit, just his face catching a bit of mental moonlight, only so far to better direct his aim and like a little hooded cobra he spits in the bigger man's eyes then reaches out just far enough to bat that hand away. He tucks back into his hole and two short thuds echo. His heels digging in.

Kindness didn't work so the big man tries to be tough with him, uses stronger language. Then the big man gets aggressive, levels threats and curses. But his back already up against a wall, the hostile behaviour only makes junior entirely convinced he's facing an enemy, and he volleys back some strong language of his own; for his small size, his voice is not. It echoes off the skull of the man in bed with enough tumult they stir him half-awake. He turns in bed in an anxious haze. Then back again to anguished sleep.

It's a dark corner of the mind where that little guy is holed up so you wouldn't see his eyes narrow, but neither would you if there was light, as the eyes of this soldier of loyalty sworn to defend the present from constant insurrection, temptation, and threat are always narrow. You wouldn't hear him chamber a round 'cause his gun is always loaded when enemies move among you. The little guy is very crafty and fits in tight places and when nobody was looking he'd infiltrated the rest of the mind and wired himself up to it all—the reach of the past now to be found in all kinds of places. If forcefully extracted, he'd just take it all with him. His finger on the red detonator button, the charge live to self destruction. *What's it gonna be?* he asks that slowly. He's in no rush.

So the bigger man who overplayed his hand backs away. Easy there, he says. What can he do? If he can't reason or plead or order or outwit, he must accept that if he's sticking around, that little monster's occasional demands, however delusional—*for that which no longer is and never again will be*—will have to be heard. The bigger trapper leaves him to his small and tortured sovereignty.

TOWN

SHE SAW HIM FIRST. That's a fact and she might tell the story differently but she is no longer around so we'll just stick to the truth.

Her mother had made her wear that ostentatious pink puffy dress—some might call it a frilly monstrosity or ornately grotesque—for the fall dance, and said to her, "I know you're just going to go be a little wallflower so I'm going to make my little flower pop." That azalea's name was Paula, who later for many years would commonly answer to *Gran*.

Before this occasion when she had worn a dress it was for church Sundays or religious holiday dinners, and so it wasn't the case that formal garments were entirely foreign to her. But her wiry body and sorta gangly movements never quite made a natural pairing with any dress. Whether it was the hormonal awkwardness of her first harvest moon dance, or feeling on display in such a loud number, her self-consciousness was coming through in rigid movements that clumsily accented a garment that needed no accent. But the mild embarrassment blended in well with that of many others', and her blushing flatteringly coloured her fair-skinned cheeks. Young Gran's smile like Old Gran's smile modelled charm, and any garment, even had she worn one designed for a coronation and hand embroidered with silver trim and gold lining, should just be trying not to embarrass itself when in the company of that smile.

The small town had come to be because two merging rivers once facilitated the transport of trade goods before the railway was built. The town's oldest roots grew out of the fur trade. There was farmland to the south and big woods to the north. Social occasions of mostly Christian celebrations drew people from the land like worms coming up to wriggle in the rain, lively affairs indeed.

So Gran would tell the story that he approached her stage left of the punchbowl, and he did. So far so true. But truth is in the details. Shortly before that, she walked her white dress shoes (really just simple ballet flats a half size too small with ornamental pink bows stitched over the toes) around the square perimeter of the plywood dance floor, passing the hay-bale benches covered in blankets, passing chairs and round high-tables to stand between the punchbowl and the entrance. That entryway not made of grand oak doors with brass knockers but just a wide gap under an archway constructed by braced two-by-fours supporting a string of white lights strung up like low roped stars. The same lights hanging over the band in the opposite corner.

Someone leaned against the arch and those bulbs swayed like the nurturing dark was rocking the starlight to sleep. Pretty, just like her dress shoes, because cheap can still be pretty.

When she walked from one side of the dance floor to the other, she knew what she was doing. Ask her about it. But don't listen to her answer. Just see if she smiles in denial, if those cheeks gracefully lined with life's indelible markings show proof of love, if those cheeks for a short spell borrow from the memory of that hot azalea mess a pink hue of bashful but most tender denial. Norman, the trapper's granddad, was one of the tallest young men there and long hair back then wasn't so common on men. Ask her about that too.

It would have been jazz in the big cities but here it was the fiddle, two guitars, a piano, and a songstress in the far corner playing mid- and faster-tempo folk and country tunes, some of them old and some of them older, not all of them sung in English. Gran was talking to a girlfriend by the punchbowl but looking less at her than towards the entranceway. Must have been a pleasant conversation, as she was smiling.

Norman made his way towards the punchbowl. He had not yet met her and did not now acknowledge her. And though her flamboyant pageantry contributed significantly to the carnival of the night, the flood of women and colours and music all coming at once as some big fantastic smear made it so she was only one of many bright swatches within it. He was shoulder to her head and about to pass her by, maybe for good.

First words they spoke were hers and came without a smile. "Don't be stepping on my toes, dear." She was seventeen and figured he was at least a year or two older.

That young man looked down to his dad's cracked and polished leather shoes, shoes that had not stepped on hers. First thing he ever said to his future beloved: "What?"

Only now did she smile.

Ask him what colour her dress was. He wouldn't know.

"When you take me to dance. My toes can take it but these shoes *are* not mine, they are my older sister Jane's and you'll have to answer to her not me if you scuff 'em. And she's the mean one." Right there she basically set the tone for their next seventy years.

They didn't dance right off the bat, which could have been due to the hesitation of that young man, who only a few days before had his inauguration into that activity when his mother counted them through some waltz steps. Didn't look like people were waltzing. At times he broke from conversation to watch not the women dance but the young men.

They were talking and Norman had a whiskey. She told him how her father taught at the local school and how her extended family were mostly farmers, cattle and wheat, south of town. He talked about the woods, their trade as trappers. "I have other plans too."

Most of her time was spent caring for her two younger sisters. "When I can I take a book from my father's library. Do you like to read?"

He said, oh I just can't barely keep my fingers from turning the pages.

She knew he was fibbin' 'cause he was grinnin' and that made it not a lie.

"Well sitting with a book and a cup of tea is just about heaven to me. I may sound like an old soul, but I assure you I'm older."

After he asked her to dance he should have taken her hand or put one of his on the small of her back, that would have been gentlemanly. But it was his first dance of his life and only his first whiskey of the night and so that minor gaff of courtship could be forgiven. It wasn't a slow dance, she turned and he kinda shimmied and bobbed. He was about to ask her to the following song but nearing the end someone had walked up to the new couple and rather uncordially asked, by not asking, to cut in. This person no doubt had their eye caught by this standout and wanted their own turn to dance with such beauty. The rival stood there beside them awkwardly and before the last notes of the song carried off into night, said with a blank face, "I'ma cut in now." *Statement.* No inflection at the end. Ruth McDonald was delivering a fact.

At the bottom of Ruth's rather high-cut purple dress were thick thighs built to pull out heifers stuck in the mud. From the dress's cut-off shoulders were arms that won last fall's stooking contest for stacking twenty-four sheaves of wheat into four piles. Time: *one minute, twenty-eight seconds*, no gloves. Even the men wore gloves.

Granddad had one eyebrow cocked taking in this extraordinary purple suitress. He'd probably not describe her as conventionally alluring, but still, not without affecting a certain amount of intrigue. In the way you might not want to mount up on some lively bull, but you might still be kinda curious about the ride. He was smiling amused when he looked over at his dance partner. His smile faded. Girl Gran's thin eyebrows had gotten low and angled and mean.

"I'ma cut in, Paula now." *Statement.*

Gran's eyes were just slits, like a she-cougar at her moose-kill who just now saw a sow bear had sauntered up out of the woods. Bear strong and unyielding. Cougar leaner and wiry and though outgunned, not without her own ferocity. Oddsmakers would do well to take into account the shock-absorbing qualities from the width of Gran's garment. "Ruth you'll do no such thing and you better just walk on back and get yourself some punch before I serve you some."

The son they will one-day have, Charles, will have a violent streak, but Norman did not. He had been in one fight. Another young man started the altercation and Norman ended it. He didn't like the feeling of it and didn't like how the other guy looked afterwards. He'd relocated to a relatively distant location the other man's nose and the gore of it and what seemed the dehumanizing aspect of it wasn't what he wanted to be part of. Didn't accord with his view of the world. After that fight he said he'd do his best to make it his last. He didn't enjoy watching violence either—but, well, who wouldn't be just a little tickled at this arena of flattery being contested in his honour, even if that arena was about to get bloody.

"Paula I'd like to see you try," said Ruth. "But maybe first you oughta ask your fat brother if his pecker ever got straight again after he tried to get fresh with me after the tractor pull." Ruth had one of her mother's earrings in her hand and was taking off the other. The closest dancers didn't break from their embrace on this rare night for romance, the gentlemen just led their ladies and danced away, couples turning as if revolving on an axis of their own private world.

Gran squared to Ruth and Ruth looked happy about that and eager for it.

But then Granddad touched Gran for their very first time. He put one hand over her ear farthest from him, as if to ensure the words he was about to speak stayed only with her. He brought his mouth close and whispered through her dark curls and over her mother's pearls.

Gran looked up at him. Didn't smile. Looked at Ruth. Did squint. Looked back to Granddad. Walked away.

Ruth got her dance. That sow bear for the first half was looking over and smiling proudly at the northern lioness, who had her back turned to the pair. When the song ended they broke. Ruth walked towards Gran who somehow knew she was coming without looking that way because she partly turned. But Ruth didn't stop she just said, "You can keep 'im." She was hobbling.

Gran was holding a drink in a paper cup brought by a new young man named Peter. Granddad approached and asked her for the drink and then not even looking at the boy he handed it back to him. He didn't ask her to dance he just took her by the hand.

The affectionate wind rocked the glowing bulbs strung above the band. A man in black with long dark hair had red spruce tucked under his chin. His fingers on the frets. He had earlier been fiddling but was no longer fiddling. He just drew a first long stroke and turned that fiddle into a violin. The man drawing his bow and the soft wood singing. The man's eyes were closed like they were open to somewhere else. The guitarists and pianist and singer were taking a rest and even they watched him and that instrument that sounds better as it ages, the wood becoming softer and so softening the notes, deepening the resonance, enrichening its song. A violin that before it made its way to where woods met pastures, had for a century lived on the east coast, and before that crossed an ocean leaving former homes on foreign shores. It had a *before that* too and it sounded like it did. A sound that can both break hearts and fill them. It's a strange world where things can be both haunting and heartening. The dark-haired man with his eyes open somewhere else.

Drawing over the strings, filling up the body with melody until that hollow brimmed and overflowed and filled the audience, moistening a corner of a pair of eyes. As if the many horse hairs that strung his bow were crying for all their lost colts.

Love was in the air and couples danced within it. Her thin hand in his. And from that clasp would come other life. Unbeknownst to them, where their palms met roots sprouted. Small vines already curling out between their fingers. The melody was a ribbon that wrapped and tied those clasped hands. Granddad felt it. She looking up at him, her other hand high to his shoulder, his on her waist, them turning like the music's silk had wrapped them up, that ribbon moving off into the night, uncurling around their waists gently turned them. So they turned.

Some reveller still in search of his own romance tripped on the cord of the overhead lights, and for about the duration of a love song, the only illumination came from the candlelit mason jars on the tables, pin-specks of tiny stars from a high sky, and the streaks of fireflies.

Then with the lightest strumming of major chords, two guitars joined that violin. The singer from the band stayed seated and took up no microphone. She sang. Her voice flowing like warm maple syrup to entomb in its resin some sweet amber moment. Singing in a language few recognized, a melody all, maybe all, would.

She sang about love, as if there were anything else. Sang it to the dancers, as if those ears were listening.

WOODS

THE TRAPPER WOKE AT dawn curled up in a ball and partly
from the cold. Nearly twenty-four hours of sleep. His dreams
so very dark that even if he makes it through the day he greatly
fears another night. He lies there as fragile as the dried silk from
an empty cocoon. The heavy blankets kept him from freezing in
a room barely warmer than the winter outside. But the weight
of the wool nearly caving in this husk of a man, emptied of his
core, frail with loss.

His stomach and chest are pits. The endless cavity of the
darkness, of the shape left inside when someone takes a spoon
and carves out those things nearly as important as your organs
and you're left all hollow. A jack-o'-lantern man lacking a smile,
just a mangled eye.

He rolled to his back and his sore head took the pillow with
him as it was stuck to the bloody side of his face. Like he'd
been tarred and feathered, but his hasty persecutors hadn't even
bothered shaking out the feathers. He pulled at it and one cheek

widened, the glue of dried blood stretching the right side of his mouth, the image of half a man whose lack of a groan told he was without a sound adequate to express the depths of his grotesque pain. The airspace above him became obscured by the hanging vapour of his breath. In that godforsaken morning he begrudged the cadaverous mist, evidence of his continued existence. He listened to a silence he'd never heard before. A new type of silence. My, it was stark. As if he'd ported his ear to some perfectly isolated void. He wanted to retreat to whatever tiny hollow inside his heart hadn't been crumpled away, then lie down next to the bones of that former artisan who once tapped at the walls of his heart.

Some part of his fractured self knew if he didn't get up now he never would. It knew the stakes of this morning, that it was vying for its own existence as well that of the whole.

I know this is hard. Harder than words. But just listen. Here's what you have to do. Do this and anything else on the day is extra. We make a list. Then we carry it out. No matter what.

He had as much enthusiasm to humour this voice with its list as he had for the continuation of his pulse.

Step one: Get up.

Step two: Go to the kitchen and drink water.

Step three: Assess your head.

He touched at his head with two fingers and felt the crust and cake of dried blood. He touched at his drooping eyelid. It stung. He winced. He poked it again. It stung again. He winced.

Step four: Make a fire.

Step five: Eat something.

That's it. That's all. For however long, that's your day there. The voice thought steps three and four ought to be switched around and it did so and informed him. Then it said, *Step six: Make coffee. Anything over and above that on the whole day is extra. And the hardest part,* he told himself, *might just be starting it. Just walk a narrow one today. You can do this. Just stay focused. Just do the steps.*

Steps. The seemingly innocent were trip hazards and triggers and he now wished he'd used a different word.

Do not listen for steps coming from the loft, he told himself.

He lay there listening to the space between thoughts filled with different types of silences. The silence of no steps being made by his boy, of a room lacking family voices, of wooden cabin walls without pops from the warmth of a fire lit by a loving, joyful child. No merry kettle whistle, no creak from the hinge of the stove. Various vacancies all dense with loss.

Do not listen for him opening the stove.

He agreed, then used that empty pause that followed the agreement to listen for the squeak of the stove.

Hey. Stay focused. Don't make of him what you did of her or you'll never come back. You feel something meaningful but those memories and those feelings are working against you. If you hold onto them, then when you do want to move on, the past is the one not letting go. This morning matters. A lot. How you frame things. What we do here. This is very important. Now c'mon, get up.

He agreed. Only to make the voice go away. He lay there. He lay there because he knew there were only three options that awaited him. Either he was leaving the bed to enter the ruinous present after a terrible existential shelling; or handing himself over to a prison of the past that he had, after *her* departure, spent time in before; or walking into a future he wanted nothing to do with—like a country whose language he didn't speak, he some ill-fated refugee who though was told he'd found asylum only discovered that the customs of that most foreign land were the sacrilegious opposite of his own sect. He looked for a fourth option and discovered one but when he searched his person he found no blade.

Hey! Focus! If you don't at least try now while things are still fresh, the tracks will become so deep you'll never steer out of them later and you'll just follow those ruts off the cliff. Right now matters. You have to at least try. Take these first steps and leave it all behind.

He lay there and then he lay there. His rotten bones that loss had quickly made porous and hollow, bled of their marrow, had now turned leaden, some form of petrification from sadness and fear. He did not move.

You can't bring them back. No holes inside you get filled with the dust of the past. You buried them. You buried him days ago.

Leave them buried. That'll be you too one day. Save your crying for the reunion. That day is not today. Get up.

He did not.

Get up. Get up 'cause life is and you are. That's it. Soon you won't be. There's your touchstone. It's always been that way. Before her before him, it was that. You know that. That's always been Rock One, your foundation. Right? That part asked that rhetorically and didn't wait for himself to answer he answered it himself: *Yes! So go be what you are. The woods, their beauty. Trapper, pick up the trap.*

He was thinking about his boy.

Fine. Go ahead and dig up those bones. Then go crawl inside yourself and sweep your arms over the soil and cover yourself up just as dead.

He was willing to agree to that.

Your call. Go ahead. Do it now. One small fraction of a multitude dying out in the same instant. That's how much sorrow you're worth. That part was trying anything it could here, borrowing former lines spoken in the most manic of times, as this voice was of course pleading for its own life too. *Go be that sad thing feeling sorry for yourself. Just don't tell yourself it's romantic or loyal. That's bullshit—it's not. It's the easy way out. Yeah this is bad. But it too will be over. Let's have that day not be today. Not today. Get. Up.*

All the silences.

The part of himself trying to rally the other parts was about ready to lie down with the rest of them. In truth, for all its talk, it too was barely hanging on. It didn't want so much to do with the world either. His sharded self was nearly wholly beat.

There came a last attempt: *You're standing in front of three doors. Behind Door One is Death—that's easy, that door will one day open itself. Behind Door Two is a caretaker of the past, which doesn't need a guardian, the night watchman making his rounds at the dead museum of his own memories, obsessed with old things that can't be undone. Keep that door shut. Don't be him. And here's what's behind Door Three: Not that. It doesn't even require any dressing up, 'cause it's just not those other doors. But in fact it is dressed up. It's the unknown. The near and unknown future with its chance for better things—even if right now the chance feels small, even if those better things don't yet look shiny. You can't predict what you'll feel like in even short times ahead.*

Stillness.

Gran once said if you find yourself suffering you got lucky 'cause now you have a chance to bear it well, to put it to use and transform it.

That sounded like a call for loyalty to the past and the small trapper inside the trapper pricked his ears up. Meanwhile another part of the trapper was hating himself for using the past that way, like some grave looter digging up a body to see if it had been buried with gold teeth.

Yeah you were a family man. Took that as your identity and means of orientation: Up is this way. Down is that way. Forward is there. This rallying cry was gesturing inside the man's skull. *Well, what to say? Too bad. One by one those points of orientation disappeared. Black magic snuffing out stars in the night. What else to do? Find new orientation. Be something else. See what that's like.*

That fractured self was kinda mixing messages and trying anything here and the little trapper inside the trapper felt like he might be getting tricked. Rolling his thumb over the detonation button.

Get up in curiosity for the present or hope for the future or in honour or defiance of the past or I don't care for what just get the hell up!

The trapper could have just been repositioning his stinging head or making a futile attempt to get away from his own plaguing voice, but he turned in bed.

Whether or not that movement was actually a sign of life, the rallying cry believed his words were getting through. Hope raised his voice. *Look. We're in a battleground for the present moment. Arm yourself. Pick up anything that looks like something. Some scrap of resolve. A tiny goal. A cup of coffee. The sun. Hunting. A book. Anything.* He thought further and said, *You don't have to like the feeling of that first step—actually, expect that you won't. And the second might not be any better, who knows maybe even all the rest to come—but you won't know until you take them. And yeah you'd go back and do things differently, but that's not how it works. And yeah maybe we screwed up immeasurably and we're sorry my God we're sorry and if we could just atone we would and maybe some things can't be atoned for 'cause some mistakes are too large to learn from because they cut you in half. So we're broken. And then what? Hey? And so what. You're broken. Other people get broken too. Maybe in time to come you won't be. For now then you just be a broken thing that still takes a step. A limp, a crawl, I don't care, anything. Get up. In this paralytic present you go blink out a fucking novel in Morse code if that's all your wounded body is good for. Then you thank your one working eyelid for its efforts—that's valour—getting up is valorous, lying in the bed of your sorrow is not. So get up or don't—and you will get up! No more talks now. Nobody is coming for you. It's just you. The world doesn't care about you, owes you nothing, you're not special to it, there's no light at the end of the tunnel, so get up and adjust your eyes to the darkness.*

The trapper gave a deep sigh.

New plan: Forget steps two through six. Your whole day is step one. Your whole day is one step. Get up!

The trapper sat up. His head hung towards his chest like a puppet shorn of its head-string. He felt nauseous.

Good. Feet.

He put his feet to the floor. Not the cold floor, there was an old matted bear-hide there and though he had set his feet on it every morning for years, the soft curls on his soles caught him off guard.

Stand! That part of himself commanded himself.

He despised the thought. He stood in vertigo.

Step! That part of himself was relentless and cruel.

The man stepped and hated that also.

Go face the battles of the day. That Frankenstein part was almost smiling, like he'd resurrected the dead. All of them.

· · · • · • · · ·

The trapper forgot the plan was to get water and he was so cold he just went to the fireplace. Knelt to it and halfway opened the stove door and it squeaked loudly. As if from out of the ashes some skeleton hand had reached out to drag its nails along the chalkboard slate of his black soul. The screech stopped him. He stayed listening to the wake of its silence.

Squeaks like that when you open it too. A part of himself was already on the other side of a painful memory and it extended a hand backwards to help him along. *Not just when he does—when he did, I mean.* That voice gentler than earlier, whether or not it was the same voice, and maybe there were no distinct selves in the man's head, just one with subtly distinct pitches and cadences to match varying moods and opinions, or if a distinct self-part, whether working with others or siloed off on its own. *So you take things back. Gently. Gently, but firmly. Take things back.* A voice like the one he'd use for the boy, or Gran might've used at one time for him, or the trapper himself in Gran's later years had used for her.

The early sun silhouetted the evergreens. Mist brightened by sunrays steamed off the smoking trees like wraiths caught in the morning light. He saw the ghost-mist as proof there were no borders to the spectral past. Inside the cabin his breath-plumes rose undisturbed. He watched them where they hung above in a consortium of apparitions.

Something moved in the trapper's periphery. The loft, the top of the stairs. He looked. He looked away. Fast. He stared into the empty stove and swallowed hard. He closed the only eye with muscles responsive to his demands. Took a deep breath. Then opened that eye slowly. He looked back to the top of the stairs. Neither he nor what he saw there breathed.

· · · ● · ● · · · ·

At the top of the steps stood a boy. A grey-blue boy. The trapper blinked and because of his wounded eye it was a wink. The boy winked back. The trapper looked back to the unlit stove. "Imagination," he whispered to himself. The word smoked. And of however many internal voices this fractured man may have had, what he'd just seen was clear enough that likely none would be entirely convinced of that categorization. He was facing the ashes but his peripheral awareness was like a radar screen, one with a blip on it. A blip high and right where the loft met the stairs. His whole awareness on that blip. Blip to the top step. Blip now halfway down the old wooden stairs that for the first time made no squeak bearing a descending presence. In not wanting to encourage his delusions or validate his dementia, he didn't look directly at it again. But his hopeful denial wasn't playing out so well. In a compromise he didn't turn his head, he just rolled his eyes towards it.

Grey-blue boy. Moving down the stairs. He cornered his eyes to follow that sinking shape.

It stepped silently his way and he could hear his own heart pounding. He knew that sound wasn't the boy's steps because to match its pace the boy would have to be running. He thought at first the ghost boy was going to come stand next to him on his right side, but he was angling behind him. That seemed worse. With scared eyes fully cornered, he didn't turn his head to follow. Still trying to uphold some tacit agreement with himself to not fully acknowledge his own new insanity—*new* because abducting a man and roping him to a chair then orating a deterministic history of violent millennia before hanging him for accidental manslaughter in which the accused had a plausible defence, could fairly be considered his original insanity.

The grey-blue boy disappeared behind the man. He hoped for good. His eyes on the curled grey ashes in the stove, like the fire had eaten the bones but left the feathers. His palms sweaty. He regained his breath and encouraged his heart to settle. Once in his past he had fought a bear and afterwards he'd looked to his hands to see if they shook and they did not. Now he had his fingers laced to subdue their tremble. The boy had not reappeared.

Calm yourself. Breathe. Breathe again. Imagination.

To his left appeared a boy. Standing there within reach. His body made even lighter by the sun. The luminous opposite of a shadow. The man's pulse returned to jacked.

The boy wasn't looking at the man, he faced the stove. Long johns and a long-sleeved shirt. The man's first thought: *They look a little small on you.* The empty boy knelt to the stove. The kid was looking into the ashes, kneeling like the man was kneeled, like one a shadow of the other. The man's hands clasped together. As were the boy's. The trapper leaned in towards the stove. So followed the boy. The man leaned back and the boy did too.

He's me. You're me, the man thought.

Then the boy slowly turned his head. The child's uncanny gaze stared through him and in doing so raised the small hairs on his nape. The trapper increased his shallow breaths while the boy, looking as if built from one, showed none escaping his blue lips.

For so many reasons, the man turned away from those piercing eyes. From the disbelief his boy was gone, the disbelief he was now here, the guilt and shame and sorrow even more so than the fear of his own insanity, the fear of what the boy might ask and of what he himself might answer, and that staring any longer into those eyes, proof of his paramount paternal failure, he'd have to answer to them. So he cowered his eyes under those feathery ashes, like a bird burying her head in the pit of her wing.

The ghost boy hadn't moved but the man imagined he did—*so now delusions on delusions*. Imagined that his little fingers had to the stove reached out and were gripping the handle. And that he'd have to tell him to please let go before gently prying his tiny fingers away, one by one. That's the worst part, those fingers unwrapping from the stove's handle not all at once but one by one. Having to ask him to please let go. *Please go back to bed*, he would have to say.

Why?

Because you can't come with me, he'd have to tell the boy while very gently prying off the next curled finger.

Why?

Because I made a mistake and now you can't.

But I want to go with you, the boy would say.

I know. I know. There's nothing I want more. That's what I want too. But I made a mistake and now you can't. He'd say that prying off one more cold and curled finger.

Just take the mistake back. Some mistakes you can.

I want to. But some mistakes you can't. This mistake I can't.

Why?

Why. Because life is hard and I'm stupid. That's why. Please go back to bed little boy. I'm sorry. He'd uncurl another finger.

45

Can I come crawl in with you? I'm really cold and I dreamt of the bear.

Of the bear?

Yeah of the bear. He was really scary. He was chasing me.

That might split the man in two right there, or rather, quarter him up as he was already halved.

The man would just whisper to his little ghost, his little god: *Little boy, you're breaking my heart. I'm sorry. You can't come with me. I'm not a father anymore and I barely ever was. I failed you and I'm sorry. Find your mother.*

I don't remember what she looks like.

The man would look around for her picture but the cabin's state was tornadic ruins, he the source of that storm.

Listen for her.

I don't remember her voice.

The man himself almost out of voice, out of words. He would use a weak exhale to try and inflate for the boy a last comforting bluff: *You'll be okay.*

How do you know?

He'd have by now all the boy's fingers pried from the stove and be holding that last little finger in his hand. He'd want to wrap that finger up in his fist and just hold it forever. Ask the boy to please go back to bed and please let go, yet it's the man holding onto him. *Just please let go,* he'd say. Maybe the man would be crying or the boy would be, or maybe ghosts don't cry.

He'd find out soon. And inevitably the boy would ask him, *If I can't come with you then can you come with me?*

The trapper's loyalty to the past. That inevitable question. He was afraid of his answer. Bit less afraid. Not so afraid. Not afraid at all. *Okay*, he might say. *Yes*, he'd say. *I'll come with you.*

He still hadn't looked back to the ghost boy and he waited in patient anguish for the child kneeling beside him who had not spoken, who had not reached for the stove, to do whatever he came to do. And he knew anything the kid did would be alright by him, and anything the kid wanted to say he'd agree to, and anywhere he wanted him to go he would go. Maybe for a prior second he thought he could steel himself enough to tell the boy firmly he had to go back to bed, but now he knew those strong words would never leave his lips—no way would he ever tell the boy to let go. *No way not ever.* This love was a defenceless love. *So be it. I'm yours. Little boy you just hold on as tight as you want. You want me with you then say the words and I'm coming.*

He turned from the ashes to the boy and saw the boy's blue lips. "Are you cold?" he asked him instinctively. He went to take off his jacket and cover the boy, but realized he himself only had long johns and a long-sleeved shirt, and the colour of his own chilled skin wasn't all that different, and had he looked in the mirror he'd have seen his own lips were nearly as blue. He raised his eyes to the ghost of his son's.

Long ago the man had dutybound himself as the keeper of holy artifacts and the guardian of stars: a family man. And though he'd failed at that task, that former definition was validated because the boy's eyes were galactic. The boy's eyes looked like marbles of self-contained universes. He always thought the boy was smarter than him, and maybe that wisdom had been present in that little head from birth, the way a seed contains the plant. Seeing him there in the room, it was as if the grace of the old dirt he was buried in had aged him into the wisdom he'd always had, now told in his eyes.

From what he saw in them he expected a message of comfort to follow, roles reversed and the boy now paternalistically telling the father to keep on, be strong, that I hope what comes to you in life is kind, but I want you to expect at times it may not be. He expected some timeless and caring words, as that's the type of message he himself would have imparted to the boy.

The mist outside the window churned in an eddy of the breeze causing the light inside the cabin to glint off a few particles of floating dust that no matter how quiet the room never do seem to fully settle. The kid's eyes glimmered. The man looking into those whirling universes waiting for his little ghost to speak.

The boy reached a grey-blue finger with smoky skin towards the man. Touched it weightlessly to the side of the man's cut head. Whether or not it was actually there, the man felt it. Then he lowered the finger to the man's chest. His head lowered looking down at it. Little wisps like solar flares, nebulous digit, translucent as a thin cloud. The boy swept that finger up the man's chest to his nose. Then he turned and looked to the stove and so the man followed his gaze because for certain those eyes had things to tell. Quiet grey feathery ash. And whether the ghost boy sunk back into the man's skull or joined the mist smoking off the trees, or whether he curled up among the breath rising in the cabin or slipped into the soil, when the man turned back to the boy, the boy was gone.

TOWN

Poker night at the small-town bar. Loretta Lynn was singing from out of the jukebox some future classic and half the men were having their hearts broken and the other half were falling in love. Four tables of six players. Over the course of the evening, players were busted and eventually four tables became three, became two. Finally one table of six, and one player there with a chip stack so high you could only see his rye 'n' Coke when he lifted it for a drink from behind its little bunker. From the standing crowd of former players and general spectators made up of friends and family, someone whispered that the guy couldn't lose. "Now Charles can just start pushing all-in whenever he has a half-decent hand and he'd swallow them all up."

Later into the evening Charles won the game. He collected his prize of two packs of candy licorice, one black one red, a token for a steak 'n' spud redeemable the following Saturday night, or any Saturday thereafter, and bragging rights until the next weekly game played at the bar. He'd only have use for the Twizzlers, given he was planning to return north by sled to his family's cabin the next day. He'd give the candy to his little boy, who nobody yet called "the trapper."

Most people left after the game concluded. The few that lingered talked about the game, that specific one, as well the general theory of poker, exchanging impassioned beliefs on the importance of *tells* versus an approach founded on pattern recognition and deduction and putting chips behind small but favourable probabilistic odds. Inevitably they took up a deck and moved off to a corner table. This time not a sit 'n' go tournament, a cash game—buy in as you like, come and go as you please. People smoked in bars back then. The haze would hang above the tables.

Plaid and wool and down jackets on the back of chairs, even one jean jacket, though outside it was brutally cold. A few men sitting and watching behind the players. Nobody was bothering with the jukebox, so the soundtrack of the night was no longer Loretta or Kenny or Dolly or Johnny, just the players' voices, chips clacking, cards shuffling, ice clinking glass. A couple hours in to this afterparty, Charles started rebuilding another little trove of other peoples' money. Not plastic poker chips this time—bills and coins, and a wristwatch of moderate value.

Bruce owned the hardware store and said he wasn't going to play tonight but he'd be dealer. He shuffled and bridged then dealt out two hole cards per each of the five players.

Charles had his green flannel sleeves rolled up. His dad's hair was long and his son's was long too. His was cropped short to his head. He reached out over the wood of the table and pulled the two red Bicycle cards towards himself. Squared their edges flush, one card overtop the other, and set his thumb to their closest corners. He brought his right hand over to shield the faces. He went to lift them but he didn't lift them. He first watched the four other players checking theirs. Watched their eyes. Whether they held their breath or sighed, or were novice enough to pretend to sigh, or advanced enough to admit no change—not just in their facial expression but of their whole body. Watched for any perceptible slumping in their seat or squaring of their shoulders, patterns of how they drank, smoked, talked, blinked, cleared their throat, if their nostrils flared, licked or didn't lick their lips.

He pried his top card's corner just enough to see a red Jack. Let it down. Pried the bottom one. Red Jack. Two red Jacks.

Under-the-gun folded his cards with a low spin towards the middle and Bruce collected them and started a pile of discards. The action was to the cut off, the seat immediately right of Charles. That man took a moment. The big blind was a big man and had a sizeable stack of bills and draped over the top, so as to hang facing outwards, was a little gold charm on a thin gold chain.

The big blind addressed the cut off. "Yuri. Those that don't remember history are doomed to repeat it."

Yuri didn't respond to the big blind. He set down a dollar bill. "Call."

The action was to Charles on the button and he didn't waste time and took three dollar bills from his stack. "Raise to three dollars."

The small blind folded.

Peter in the big blind owned one of the lodgings in town, a motel smaller than the hotel whose bar they were now playing poker in. He owned the gas station. He owned two rental properties as well some vacant land. There were a couple people in town who said they liked him, and they were his wife and kid. The cigar in his mouth wasn't lit, just wet and chewed on. He said, "Gentlemen. It seems fair to let you know ahead of time that this pot, based on the cards Bruce just kindly dealt to me," he winked at Bruce, insinuating a favouritism that did not exist, "has the potential to get expensive." He had a gold bracelet on his right wrist and its links were much thicker than that thin chain dangling over his stack. Peter set his thumb to the bottom of his bill pile then drew it upwards crosswise over the bills and they made a small but perceptible flapping sound. "When I looked at these two cards, fellas, the first thing that came to my mind was that if I was in your shoes, that is, if you all were me and I was you, it would be nice if someone would warn me ahead of time. I think that would be an amicable thing to do." He was looking around the table, even at the players that had folded, and the side of his mouth without the cigar was smiling. His eyes rested on the cut off. "Amicable. It means friendly, Yuri."

A spectator sitting behind the small blind coughed a short laugh, punching out a tight cloud of smoke.

Peter lifted his money pile and took out from under it a single hundred-dollar bill. He laid it on the table. "Raise to fifteen."

"I can't change that," said Bruce.

"My mistake. Already breaking the bank here." He picked out a five and a ten from underneath his little gold charm and put them to the table and Bruce pushed the hundred back his way and pulled in the fifteen.

Yuri in the cut off was a logger. When he finished in the black his wife might get a new dress and their daughter some candy or a doll. When he ended the night in the red, he was going back to work anyways. Like most people in town he was a Christian, but he would be leaving materially less of one because a few hands ago, his Hail Mary bluff on the river got called and a little twenty-four-karat Jesus crossed the poker table, walking, as he does, over water, in this case, those puddles condensed at the bases of beer cans, while dragging his gold chain towards a new home.

Peter slid the hundred-dollar bill back to the bottom of his stack while watching Yuri, not the only pair of eyes watching Yuri, waiting for him to fold, call, or raise.

Yuri checked his cards again.

Peter picked up his newly acquired gold charm. Held the chain in his fist such that the little shiny saviour would lie over his knuckles. He most delicately licked the tip of his other hand's pinky finger, then polished the god. Took the chain in two hands and lifted it above his head, then in some kind of self-coronation, let it down around his neck while still looking at Yuri.

Yuri laughed. He said in a thick Ukrainian accent, "What goes around comes back around, Peter." He pushed his two cards away from himself and pushed his chair backwards a couple inches and crossed his arms over his chest and sat back to watch the hand play out.

Peter winked at him and said to the table, "It's a smart man that learns from his mistakes." Bruce swept Yuri's lost dollar to the pot. "Action to the button."

The trapper's father considered a call or re-raise. Fifteen dollars for someone who makes their living trapping furs is considerable money, more so for the sole provider of a family. But his sled came in heavy and it was empty outside the motel a block away and he'd already bought supplies and had a backup twenty in his pocket for emergencies. His eyes met Peter's.

Peter said, "I haven't seen your old man in a while."

On his prior trips to town, Charles and Peter had played some hands together. No sizeable pots, nothing stand out. He recalled that Peter talked through every hand. He studied him now with a cold detachment that almost put actual distance between the two of them. Listened to not just what he was speaking but how he was speaking, for anything in his tone or pacing that might reveal a false strength or true weakness. Pocket jacks is a premium hand and of 169 possible starting hands it beats all but three. His opponent had money and liked to gamble. His opponent had been drinking. It was reasonable to try and build the pot, but their stacks were deep. A call is an acceptable play and that's what Charles did.

The pot at just under thirty-two dollars was already one of the biggest of the night, and this all before the flop. The night's soundtrack had its background voices dialled down. The only person who spoke was Bruce. "Here you go boys." He dealt the top card face down and dealt the flop one at a time. He called them as he laid them.

"Seven of spades. Jack of clubs. Four of diamonds." A rainbow flop.

Charles had been watching Peter and Peter had been watching him back. Neither looked to the flop yet. Their fate laid bare before them and yet neither having a glance at that naked future. Peter smiled at that.

Bruce motioned with an open hand towards the big blind, who is first to act.

Peter with his tongue and teeth moved the unlit cigar from one side of his mouth to the other. "Yes. Potential for a sizable pot." Finally he looked to the flop. He paired a melodramatic sigh with the raising and lowering of his shoulders and made a clicking noise with his mouth and said with about as much emotion as one might order deli meat, "Oh, too bad. I thought we might've had something here. I check to you, sir." His hole cards lying on the table before him he tapped them once with a heavy finger, then drew the rest between them out uncomfortably long, before he tapped them again.

Charles now looked at the flop. He loved cards. His old man loved cards, his boy was taking to them too and had even pulled off a bluff against him once before. The whole family, they'd all play No-Limit Texas Hold 'Em some nights. Every year he started looking forward to this same rare trip to town at about the time he was leaving from the last one. Right now he was looking down at three of a kind. Not just any three of a kind—*top set*. Not just top set—he had the stone-cold nut hand, and the man giving him action had an ego to rival any of those belonging to the politicians printed on the bills that lay between them.

When Charles made a weak hand on the flop, he would take a little drink. And when Charles made a good hand on the flop, he would take a little drink. He set the glass tumbler down. He lifted from before him a twenty-dollar bill and as he was raising it from his stack it came with a sound of a teapot whistling. A rising sound. Whistling that came from the big blind who then said quickly and before that bill was put down, "Think carefully here son that's a lot of beavers." He said *son* to a grown man with a family. One of the spectators made some kind of audible exhale and another who was not between them leaned back anyways.

Charles paused with the twenty in his hand above the table. Then he actually did retract that paper.

"See, Yuri." Peter looking at Yuri nodded sideways at Charles. "A man with some prudence."

Charles returned the twenty back to his stack. He picked up the small pack of Camel cigarettes. Brought the pack to his mouth and withdrew it one lighter. He took the matchbook with one hand and while looking at Peter he opened its paper flap and bent from the comb a single stick that he folded to the back of the matchbook, pinching it between the opened flap and the striker, then he snapped the matchbook between his fingers and the bartender looked up thinking someone had ordered a drink. The match lit, still attached to its comb. He brought the flame to his cigarette. Blew out a thin cloud above the table while still watching Peter, then he wafted out the match.

Peter subtly nodded and said quietly, "Yes." Like praise, or someone appreciating something made worthy by its rarity, something most people even if looking at it couldn't see. Finally here was a game. For some the game was hardly worth playing—didn't even start at all—until taken into its folds were the people behind the sums. In this little bit of theatrics came the chance for more than mere dollars to be put at stake.

"You see that, Yuri?" He wasn't looking at Yuri.

Yuri was smiling and respecting the etiquette of conversation best being kept between those with skin in the game.

Peter took out a Zippo lighter and flipped open its metal top and thumbed its flint wheel. Closed its lid with a metallic snap. The stream of smoke he blew above the table was thick and dark. "I played with your old man before. Several times. You know that? But if I'm being honest with myself, and this being an honest game among friends, so why wouldn't I be, I'd rather not even know just how much I've lost to him. A lucky man. And there are easier men to bluff than one with a wolf laying at his feet." He looked over at Yuri. "I think that's an old Ukrainian saying, eh, Yuri." He looked back. "What was that wolf's name again?"

Somebody who had earlier coughed out a laugh said, "Seven."

Peter turned to him. "Hey. Shut. Up."

Charles picked out a five-dollar bill from his stack and laid that on the earlier twenty and pressed his thumb into its top while supporting the underside of the lower bill such that the bills developed a rigid under-spine along their length. He pushed the bid of twenty-five to the pot while saying Seven. "Dog's name was Seven."

A round of drinks was brought over and Charles lifted a pair of dollar bills from his pile and outstretched it and that payment was declined as someone had already covered his.

"*Was.*" Peter had returned the cigar to a corner of his mouth. "That's a shame. You tell him a rematch is a standing invite." Unlikely Peter had forgotten his cards, but he picked them up right off the table. Raised his eyebrows very high, then at once lowered them and the cards back down. Then he lifted his whole stack of bills save one and pushed that big note out from under them. "I raise to one hundred dollars."

The trapper's father watched him coolly.

"I believe that's one hundred and fifty-six dollars and fifty cents in the pot," said Bruce.

Charles unhurriedly and silently counted his stack. He slightly splayed the bills to verify their denominations and his hand holding the cigarette moved above them in a motion of tally. In the bar's still air, the cigarette smoke traced a rather artistic silver calligraphy. As if held just above the table by some unseen agent of chance was a contract of misfortune denoting the impermanent riches of gamblers, and a signature was being signed in disappearing ink above an invisible line. The smoke slowly rising from the bar's tabletop into its raftered heights. In his accounting he pointed to a wristwatch slumped against his money pile and said to Peter, "Call it fifteen?" and Peter nodded. About four hundred and fifty dollars including the watch, not including the twenty in his pocket.

He drew on his cigarette and it was quiet enough you could hear the paper burn. He drew the smoke into his lungs and he drew the range of his opponent's hole cards into his mind. The weak overpairs and weaker made hands, the draws. He weighted that range with a non-zero chance that the man was making a loose and weak gamble. His eyes squinted in thought while he gauged the strength of his opponent. Could be Peter was feeling loose because it was Saturday night and the big man has been tipping the drinks back. He has money and maybe he feels like throwing some of it around. Charles tried to put himself inside Peter's head. Inside his skin. What is this hand to him? he asked himself. Some people never bluff, some bluff every other hand. How does he believe others see him. How does he see me. How was he seeing the game, the stakes. The world, even. He ashed his cigarette to a tray.

That someone likes to gamble and drink does not make them a fool, and the trapper's father did not believe Peter to be one. Unlikely all this posturing is from a pure bluff, he thought. So it's either a made hand, or if he's drawing, it's probably a decent one, and the man hamming it up here is only partially acting. He might have a hard time folding that draw. He could hold queens through aces and was making the mistake of believing that their value preflop was still good here. Every game is specific to its particular locale of play: if it's common for players here at this bar to not let go of weak made hands, to overvalue single pairs and chase draws, could be Peter thinks any decent hand is worth putting money behind in a loose and alcoholic game. He could hold two pair but my jacks act as blockers. The only question: call this raise to one hundred and then get the money in on the turn regardless of what card comes because holding top set while playing heads up is worth going bust over. Or, if it wouldn't scare him away, get the money in good now while I have him crushed.

Charles' face did not hint at the excitement from his great advantage. The cigarette glowed.

He said while exhaling the smoke of his conviction, "All in." He put two hands behind his whole pile and didn't push it far, as the gesture itself was sufficient to make it official. He watched his opponent, the big man with the gold, and took a sweet drink of chilled Coke and Crown Royal.

The pot now surpassed any previous that night and was one of the year's biggest. Like theatre patrons gripped by the rise to a climax, nobody in the game's audience spoke and nobody looked away.

Peter's stack was smaller and he had what looked like between two- and three-hundred dollars there. He could call that bet with what he had and Bruce would return the excess to the button. Then they'd reveal their cards and put it to chance. He could do that.

He wouldn't do that.

The small crowd waited for Peter to call or fold.

Peter said, "This pot has grown quite large for a family man..." Peter himself had a family, "in the fur-trade business." His hand holding his cigar rested above the table and the long grey ash looked like it would fall. "Would you even call that a business? How many beavers we got swimming in this pot? Is there even much market for those things anymore?" He looked around the table. "All I'm seeing is wool, fleece. Yuri here, the crazy bastard, is wearing jean. Mine is goose down." A sleeve of his jacket lay on his arm rest and he flicked it. He shrugged. "In fact does anybody here have fur on something other than their nut sack?"

The spectator behind the small blind who had named the wolf-dog had a jacket with a hood sporting a fur rim, fox or mink. It was draped over his chair. He was going to advise Peter of that fact but he'd already been admonished for speaking out and though he didn't know what the word *rhetorical* meant he still understood the concept well enough to keep his tongue, marinated in Budweiser, from expressing his thoughts. His thoughts being, Got me a fox hood here, Peter. It's real warm. Instead, the man just crossed those words off a mental list of things worth speaking and crossed his arms.

"Could be time for your family to consider alternate means of employment, a new line of work. I'm not saying that to be rude, son." He brought his hand up in front of his chest and made a stopping gesture as if to preclude a retort, whether verbal or physical. "I'm offering advice from a business man." He turned and flattened that same hand as one might offer an animal a treat. "You guys could consider joining the twentieth century. Think about your future. Your family's. So here's what I'm going to do. A proposition. And whether you decline or accept you ought to think about it carefully." He half-turned around and called out to the bar —"Ivan!"—and when Ivan came over Peter made a writing motion and Ivan went back and returned with a pen and a blank slip of receipt paper. Peter started writing.

What was to follow wouldn't be allowed in some casinos, but this being an unregulated cash game—and so minorly illegal from the get-go—the rules were up to the players. The stacks on the table did not necessarily have to represent the total depths of available pockets. Sometimes side bets were made. Side bets bigger than the pot itself.

Peter transferred the cigar from fingers to molars, surely that precarious ash would now fall. He held the receipt in place on the table and the scribbling on the thin paper sounded like a rodent trying to scratch its way through the wood. When he was done he handed the pen to the man sitting behind the small blind and said, "Hey idjit, sign this." The man took the pen from his employer and witnessed the paper. Peter dropped the paper and it fell like a leaf to the pile. The hundred-dollar bill shrank in size as the chit approximating its dimensions but lacking its gravity settled beside it.

"This is a legally binding deed to my business." He called it a hotel but really it was a small motel. "Dated, signed, and signed by a witness in the company of witnesses." The only eyes not now watching Peter were Peter's own. "Decline this proposition and I'm going to fold and the pot is yours. You win the hundred-dollar bill plus whatever little change. But if you accept that paper into the game—if you call my raise—we run it for *deeds*. Don't answer yet. Over the course of our lives we may be lucky enough to be presented with one outstanding opportunity. Some don't even get one. Whether or not you'll see another, this is yours. And pardon me for saying it, but given where you live, *how* you live, this is likely the only significant financial opportunity you'll be presented with in your entire life." Peter shook his head as if the opportunity here was staggering even to himself. "Take a minute. If you don't at least entertain the idea, you're going to regret it when you get back to business. Back to lifting the next frozen rodent from your trap. Then when you pass that trade on to your kids. Like your old man did for you. Or. This is a very big *or*." Peter spread his arms wide like he could barely hold the big *Or*. "There is an opportunity in front of you to be a land and business owner in a growing town. Up to you. Put your title beside mine. Our fates together in the pot. In just the turn of a couple cards here, things could change drastically for the better. Entire futures stand to benefit here." Whether or not Peter knew that their family had started a fledgling hunting outfit he didn't mention it. "Or maybe this isn't even your decision to make hey and I'm wasting everyone's time. Who's running the show up there nowadays anyways. You or Dad? Take a moment. How do you feel about the cards you've been dealt?" He lowered his cigar to the tray and finally tapped that long ash to lie in one length, a cremated caterpillar.

During that rant a couple people had leaned back and by the end a couple more. Last year when this man who had just been insulted came to trade furs, some of them had watched a violent altercation arise from out of far less provocation. This man now sitting on the button who most figured just had his buttons pressed.

Charles neither frowning nor smiling. Just smoking. For those who thought they had him figured out—*you poke the bear and the bear bites back*—they were mistaken. He had a temper but it was more like when it rose it was simply an available option. Even when emotionally charged he wasn't impulsive and retained the faculty of decision. Most people don't. His was just a question of whether to indulge in an internal invitation to a primal violent urge. Some people enjoy fighting. The physicalizing of strategy. The feeling of knuckles on head meat and the sound of a dull smack. A softer sound, but with results no less immobilizing, of landing a low hook to a liver and hearing air expelled and watching a man bend in half. The fighter having bent the opponent to his will. Life feels most keen when stakes are highest: the potential for broken bones, cut skin, bled blood—and it's up to you to make sure it's the other guy. He wasn't enraged by Peter's words. To lash out would be acting as if Peter held a string across the table tied to his pugilist puppet-wrists. No, the trapper's father simply smoked coolly and listened to what information came, as he had all night. And to hold as invalid anything one's antagonist said simply because the listener dislikes the speaker is flawed logic. Two plus two is still four regardless of what nonsense surrounds it. He didn't buy into Peter's bullshit but neither was he beyond sifting it for clues.

And had he been a man whose penchant for violence sometimes got the better of his restraint, my God it's easy to keep your
composure when you're holding the nut hand against a jackass.
In fact, it's a rare pleasure. It's a moment worth savouring. He
wanted to bust the man's ego, his wallet rather than his nose.
It occurred to him that Peter might even be trying to induce a
physical outburst in order to get the pot cancelled. Everything
here was information and he was draping himself in Peter's skin.

Earlier he thought Peter could be holding a good draw, not
now. Unless you're a falling-down drunk or an idiot or a degen-
erate, you don't back up a bet like that with such sizable wealth
when lacking a made hand. And you don't arrive and remain at
Peter's position being one of those types of people. Peter had a
made hand, he thought, and he was wagering from a position
of strength. Charles processed. It's no overpair—even in a loose
game, that's too loose. Two pair would be overplaying the hand.
Then its truth just clicked. He had *set over setted* Peter: his own
three jacks reigning over Peter's inferior three of a kind. Poker's
about using the cards to tell a plausible story and that story fit
like a missing link snapping into place. Sometimes even though
the proof is hidden, its veracity is tactile. The odds of Peter
holding a set were low, but the odds of Peter being beaten while
holding one *were even lower*. He knew Peter played enough to
know that. Likely he had seven-seven or four-four, and if he did
it would be reasonable for him to bet very large while holding it.
The same unlikelihood of Peter making three of a kind would

strengthen his conviction that now holding one, it was winning. Charles sipped his rye 'n Coke, the glass tumbler sweating on someone's behalf.

Late at night in the corner of a small-town bar under dim lighting, a poker table was enveloped in a smoky haze. Peter tilted his head a couple degrees, suggesting to his opponent it was time for a decision.

We don't always choose what words seep into us, those which soak our core. We don't even have to be listening to be affected. But Charles had been listening to Peter. He had sifted for truth in that rant and some truth there was. Having property and a business in town were valuable things. The town was growing, he was right, there. In savouring this moment of advantage he allowed himself a minute to consider owning one of the town's main businesses. He allowed himself to imagine being back home sitting with coffee in the morning with the old man, just pouring him his coffee at the table and then casually slipping him the title to the hotel. You remember Peter? Smiling while saying it, pouring Dad's coffee. We just doubled our holdings. And Mom and Dad were getting older. Get them their own room in town at the top of the hotel. How about that. How about that. The ice clinked in his glass. Pass down a hotel to the boy one day. You do make it big by getting in early with prime real estate in a growing town, that wasn't bullshit, Peter was only echoing something everyone knew.

The trapper's father reached out and covered his hole cards and pried their corners again. One red jack. And the other. Looked at the flop. *Seven of spades. Jack of clubs. Four of diamonds.* Asked himself what angle he might be missing. Went over all his former deductions and once more calculated the probabilities. He replayed all his opponent had spoken, trying to shake out information like a boy holding the trunk of a fruit tree. Weighed what he knew about the heavy-set man. After revisiting it all he felt even more sure than prior to his recalculation. *Peter had a weaker set; he had Peter crushed.* And now came the idea that perhaps not taking this wager might itself be irresponsible. This was hardly even gambling anymore—you'd be a fool not to accept, was his conclusion. And it was true, you only get one or two of these in your life. Here comes trotting up a gift horse, here fallen from the sky is a golden goose. What do you do with that? he asked himself. Hell. You make good on it is what you do. Someone had bought him another round. Might just name the hotel after my boy. Shit. His cigarette had burned to the filter and a flake of ash lay on the felt and he nubbed his smoke out in the tray.

"Let's see that." Charles nodded at the paper.

Bruce looked hesitant and he took more than a second to satisfy the button's request. Then he dutifully picked from the pot that paper of misfortune. Set it down by Charles' chip stack.

He read it over. Simply written, and whether its words were legally binding, that it was pledged in front of this crowd made it so. They'd see to its enforcement more effectively than any magistrate. He didn't need to check his hole cards again, but he did. Didn't need to look at the flop again, but he looked. Scanned slowly around the table and to the players, to the crowd, to even the mute saviour hanging around Peter's neck. Held it all in his head.

He sought out from all those eyes watching him the furthest pair away. Nodded to Ivan behind the bar. Ivan's footsteps on the wood floor didn't creak, they tolled. One after the other. Paces. Of. Reckoning. Two years ago Charles' father, Norman, transferred the land's title to him. Charles now signed his full name to the bottom and pushed it to his right and Yuri said are you sure and Yuri watched him nod and Yuri signed as witness.

Bruce counted out the big blind's stack and it came to three hundred and forty-five dollars. He then counted out the equivalent from the button's stack. He reached outwards over the table and swept each pile towards the other to marry those sums, while the minimal air currents were enough to collapse that ashen caterpillar. He placed the two fateful chits side by side. What a species are humans that the thinnest lines of ink on a weightless piece of paper can build lives and break them; form and dissolve countries; detail recipes for nuclear arms; declare bankruptcies, wars and treaties; swear oaths and love. There are few combinations more reactive than ink on paper. Two men had made their mark and something larger than wealth was put on the line.

Half the spectators were now standing and half were on their way up. Some looks of concern. As if cars had crashed head-on and a body was twisting in the air, yet to settle.

"Okay fellas. Let's turn 'em over."

By the rules of the game Peter had to show first. He turned a card: *Eight of spades.* He turned Charles' face, which never showed much emotion in general, nevermind when seated at a card game, into one marked with confusion. He turned the second card: *Nine of spades.*

His stomach dropped. *A draw. The hell.* He hadn't expected a draw. Why would he risk so much on a draw? he thought. It wasn't even a flush draw, just a gut-shot straight draw with a backdoor. *Reckless.* Jesus that's reckless. That's fool's work.

The small motel needed a new roof more than it needed new carpets, and those were the type of carpets you'd be glad they couldn't talk. Peter had other priorities. What looked like a steep wager to one man was of less value to another. And for some the gamble itself has value. The pleasure not totally from the win but as well from the risk. The potential of those dice rolling across the table before they come to rest, or in that moment of hope while a dealer's hand slowly turns the last card. When the trapper's father had tried to drape himself in Peter's skin, he hadn't assigned enough gamble to the man's bones, or perhaps he was unable to look through the eyes of a man playing for something not visible on the table.

He lowered his internal temperature by reminding himself of the cold math: *run this hand one hundred times I win eighty-two of them*. He was still a large favourite. He still had the nut hand against a draw. He raised and drank that tumbler dry. He turned his cards over.

The small crowd sounded like revellers at a beauty pageant where the future queen had just taken to the catwalk.

Peter spoke above the blanket of their marvel. "I'm not surprised. Looks like you've got your daddy's luck." He didn't sound so dismal.

Bruce holding the deck, "Here comes your turn-card boys." He burned the deck's top card to the discard pile and turned the next. The sound of the spectators was unruly.

"Jack of spades!" Bruce no longer hiding his favouritism.

Most players won't ever see a royal flush in person and straight flushes are very rare and Charles had never made one and this was only the second time he held quads. He loved cards and anyone that does remembers these hands. He had gone from holding the best hand you could possibly make on the flop to holding the best hand you could possibly make on the turn. They're simply nice to look at and lying there appear surreal, like seeing a movie star at the grocery store. And quads beats a straight and quads beats a flush. His mind ran the numbers. Deal this river one hundred times, I'm winning ninety-eight of them. He reached for his drink, forgetting he'd emptied it, yet didn't care and didn't bother to order another because in a few seconds he'd be buying the whole bar a round, and then about a half dozen more.

Peter sat with his severed odds. He smiled. "Yes. Looks like you do have his luck." He was either taking it well or hadn't put as much on the line as people thought. Or his bluffs extended outside the game.

Charles hung a smoke loosely in his lips and took the matchbook from his pocket.

Bruce was patient in delivering the final card, waiting for the background chatter to settle before turning the river, hardly more than a formality at this point given Charles' impending win. Finally he said, "And now your river." He burned one and then dealt a man his destruction.

The room sounding like they'd watched that body hanging in the air get wrapped around a telephone pole. Some reeled back, others groaned. Bruce who had flipped the card didn't name it when he laid it down, like his complicity in being the vehicle of that misfortune silenced him. The fifth card was the *Ten of Spades.* Spades like it had buried something alive. On the turn, thirty-six cards still remained in the deck, only one mattered. It came.

Peter looked at his straight flush. It wasn't the first he'd made.

The groaning subsided. People walked away as if pushed back by Peter's widening smile.

Peter looked at his opponent. "Looks like you don't."

The trapper's father had an unlit smoke in his mouth. His hands that held the matchbook had stopped en route to their destination, the matchbook hanging absently in front of him. Illustrate this scene but swap out the matchbook for one of those miniature bibles and maybe he could find some comfort there. His eyes were set on that *Ten of Spades*. In his personal dilation of time, Peter's words were echoing in his head. Their meaning wasn't clear. He looked to their source.

Peter must have sensed his confusion. "His luck. Looks like you don't have it." More factually stated than salting a wound.

Bruce didn't push the bounty to Peter, he just gestured from it to the winner. Then he got up and left.

Peter didn't reach for the pot. He drew deeply on his cigar whose cherry was centred in his mouth. He smiled, exhaling smoke around it, the cherry fading in the cloud. He reached out his arms as in a fond embrace, like a man might put them around the back of a woman. He pulled her in close. Didn't look at the trapper's father.

That man's shock not yet turned to violence.

WOODS

THE FACE REFLECTED BACK in his handheld mirror almost
made him drop it. Wild hair, dark sags under his eyes and the
one all bloodied. Cracked lips. That's you, he thought. He
turned to assess the ear and saw its outer rim, though cleanly
sliced, could use a stitch or two. But he thought that should
have been done yesterday when it was first cut. Maybe too late
now. Looked like pressing it against the pillow all night had
clotted it. His temple was cut laterally towards his eye and it
was surprisingly shallow for all it had bled. Taken as a whole,
the right eye looked like it'd been chewed on by a dog. Eyebrow
and eyelid with parallel cuts. He figured from two of the three
broadhead blades. A few cut eyelashes. He was curious if they
would grow back. It's not like eyelashes ever need trimming, he
reflected. Didn't care either way, just curious. His upper lid was
sliced deep enough that the underlying main protractor muscle,
the orbicularis oculi, had been cut, resulting in an unresponsive
and drooping lid. With index and thumb he pinched and lifted

that sagging lid. He rolled his eyeball around to assess its health, the evasive eye as if under an examination too personal. In the mirror, the eye was red and veiny and kinda wild looking, but the arrow hadn't cut all the way through that skin shield and so hadn't nicked the eyeball's membrane. No slit on the surface leaking its jelly. He let that lid back down covering its wild peep. Everything on the right side of his face looking worse for all the blood caked around the cuts.

Maybe it truly, truly was the boy's ghost, he considered it might have been. Nearly every culture as far back as recorded time has stories or explicit beliefs of the supernatural. On a shelf somewhere nearby was a book on the history of the paranormal across various geographies—if that particular book hadn't fallen or been thrown in his recent destructive night. Seems foolish to quickly dismiss the paranormal as an invalid concept. Ghosts. Maybe, he thought. Or maybe if you fight wolves with wolves, you ward off looming insanity with insanity, and what he'd just experienced was all his warped mind's reasonable doings. Maybe a part of himself when he wasn't looking had crawled out of his head and played the role of boy in a hallucinogenic performance of self-preservation to convince himself he'd said goodbye and could now, with the boy's blessing, move on. He looked around the cabin, even his good eye unsteady.

From the fire he had started, the cabin was beginning to warm. He righted a chair and picked up some books from the floor and put them on the table and set the handheld mirror against them with its handle vertical but upside down. Dipped a clean rag into the water that had warmed on the stove and first pressed it to the cuts to soften the blood before he gently wiped at them. Got lucky not losing the eye, he thought. He applied more pressure to wipe the blood in the channels and it stung. Got unlucky being shot in the head with an arrow, he countered. He removed the cap from the iodine bottle and dipped a cotton swab and then floated that little wet pillow stick towards the gashes. He pressed its chemical-soaked tip into the wound channel and inhaled deeply the pain of iodine sting.

To the cleaned and pinkened skin of his ear, he applied surgical tape; laid Band-Aids vertically over the temple; cut a custom bandage to fit around the side of his right eye. He surveyed his handiwork then tipped the looking glass face down on the table's dark wood.

This survivor taking in the quiet ruins. His maimed head corroborating the story of a bombed world, while somehow he only suffered their shrapnel. The disarray of personal belongings: his own, the boys, hers, strewn memorabilia of older family. On the floor and surrounding his chair was a circle of guttered candles and he now sat where his captive once sat, where overhead a rope had hung, where a neck strained in that rope. Now it was him centred in the crude altar he'd made. He looked down to the coil by his feet. A spot on the floorboards minorly darker than the surrounding wood was a dried puddle of scared piss he'd frightened out of a man. He continued surveying the chaos. Dented stove pipe. Scattered logs. Shattered glass of varying thicknesses and colours. Guns on the wall.

Where formerly in those rifles he saw an elegance to their blued steel and dark walnut stocks, a certain romance in their heritage because they'd belonged to Granddad, a charm to their glinting triggers like the eyes of a pretty girl waiting for someone to ask her hand, now in their shine he saw another kind of temptress. One who offered a dance for a lifetime and then some and he could take her hand and they'd dance and just never stop. He knew the curved butt of their stocks fit his shoulder like a heel fits a shoe, and bet his toe would feel right at home resting on one of their crescent triggers looking right now like a small scythe. He wasn't much for music but considered taking one of them down, and like an oboe, placing his lips to its mouthpiece and pressing its single polished key. He wondered if before the impact he'd hear that solitary note. He had played that note many times before, played it for many animals. He was curious how it would sound playing it for himself. It might pleasantly contrast all these new silences.

Stop! Just stop. Some voice. *You're in a new world. Former alliances are no longer to be trusted. Certain allegiances are broken. Leave the guns on the wall. They're no friend of ours.*

He continued his survey. Fallen books with broken spines. An arrow sticking into the wall. Empty stairs. He paused. He wasn't sure what a *right-mind* was, but figured from the phantom he'd seen, from the way his skull throbbed now, his probably wasn't that. Between the pounding he tried to recall the steps of his list, if there were any he could mentally strike through. *Coffee. Was that one? It is now.* He got up and stepped over some things carefully and others he booted and yet others when he glimpsed he looked away.

Percolator. Coffee grounds. Water. The glass bulb started to bubble brown and the percolator sounded like a train complete with steam. The cabin should have been warmer given how much he'd stoked the stove and he now saw why. Where the morning had swathed the windows golden, he saw whole panes and one with a jagged hole. He poured the hot black coffee into a white porcelain mug. Held it a minute. Smelled it. Smelled it more. Smelled it again.

Before he went to the shed for one of the larger panes that he'd score with a handheld cutting tool and set that cut-line against the edge of the workbench to snap it cleanly, he prepped the exterior-facing side of the window by removing the thin wooden retaining strips and pieces of glass. The new pane seated well and he carefully tapped the nails of the wood strips to their original holes then set a steel nail punch to their tiny heads and sunk them home. To seal it off from the wind and moisture, it should be caulked and he knew that but didn't have any caulking. Balsam pitch or even wet mud could work, he thought. It would dry in place and provide protection. Even smearing on thick bear grease would stop the drafts and waterproof it. Not so sure I want to wake up to some critter licking at the windows though. He settled on strips of duct tape until his next trip to town. To town. *Town.* He was unsure if his vocabulary contained a more revolting word. The woods lacked their former charms that's for certain, but people were worse. Problem was *people* included his own self and he didn't care much for that company either. Looking outside in, from where he'd finished framing the window, he saw that row of triggers hadn't stopped winking.

Back inside he stepped on a thin piece of bulb that under his boot's hard rubber gave a muffled shatter. He looked above at the hanging socket and spiky remains of a lightbulb he'd days ago swiped at with an angry paw. A bulb that smashed like a broken idea. He figured that even though the filament was cut, the circuit running off the battery trickle-charged from the creek was live. That thin cut wire looking pretty, too. *Wonder if it's enough to cook a man.* His thoughts darker than an unlit bulb. But he figured it would most likely just annoyingly zap him. He pulled the chain-switch, breaking its circuit. He didn't need to go to the cellar, there were a few meals worth of potatoes in the kitchen and he halved a spud then pressed it into the protruding glass. Unscrewed the broken bulb with the vegetable, then screwed in a new one. He shelved books and rehung pots and pans and felt like shit and stacked the wood he had earlier scattered.

If he could have cleaned the room blindfolded he would have, 'cause every other item was charged with the past, some just tingling, some nearly pulsing and radioactive with it. He began to believe that not just dead things haunt. Some items lightly pulled at him, while others nearly bent him in half like they'd kicked him in the gut. When he picked up one of her books, its weight was heavy, though not quite as heavy as it had once been in the months following her death. When he stooped for items belonging to the kid, their gravity seemed to warp space, him falling into their centre. He had to stop cleaning a few times and breathe.

He picked up a single red mitt. That Gran had knitted, he thought. He held the mitt up so long in two hands you would think his arms must be getting sore. Like he'd seized in place, like the poor Tin Man, lacking a heart and now short on oil.

Some part of him, maybe the one that spoke up before or maybe a novel voice, tried to unstick him. *Just do simple things for now.* Encouraging words tenderly spoken. *You're doing good. Make it clear with simple steps. Look: pick things up, then put them down.* The character of that voice in his head was miming the action. *That's it. That's all we're doing here. You can do that. Take your time, this is extra, you did the list already. That was really good.* A praising voice. *All this is bonus.*

The red mitt was knitted from yarn so light it was a peculiar thing to hold with two hands. But black holes, small as they are, are very heavy for their size. He started searching for the other while carrying this one no more sanely. Eventually he did see a bit of red fabric on the other side of the room, half-hidden under a quartered log. He went to pick the log up but wasn't sure if he should set down the mitt and grab the wood, or pick up the wood with the first mitt still in his hands at the risk of getting bark in its sacred fabric. He kinda started at one method then switched to the other. Then he stopped and started over. He was breathing heavier and his stomach was turning. The opposing forces of defecation and vomit were things for fate to decide—or if these bodily urges, like everything else, were just the playing out of cosmic pool balls having been predetermined long ago in that fateful dawn when the big bang put things into play, whether and which one of his orifices were destined to purge in this moment was yet to be revealed.

But he neither shat nor puked, and instead he settled on leaving the first mitt on the floor and lifting the log with one hand. Then he wasn't exactly sure why he had left that other hand empty in the process. He felt as confused as he looked. He walked to the other side of the cabin and tripped and almost fell and then put the log in its bin because that's where it belonged. "That's where you belong." He said that. Completing that most minor of tasks actually came with a small bit of satisfaction and he was well enough only to realize that was a ridiculous sentiment for the very pathetic action he had just accomplished. That satisfaction itself only seemed a further indicator of his mind's degradation.

In his travels to the log bin on the other side of the cabin, he had been thinking about the mitts. He didn't feel good about his decision to leave them there on the floor, and so after he'd dispensed of the firewood he hurried back. He balled up their cuffs like socks. *Remember when you threw a pair of balled up socks at the boy's back when he'd come back with wet feet on his first solo hunt? Oh man. Remember that? Oh man.* The very sweetness of that memory nearly rotting him from the inside out. The trapper was caught. *I told him to put them on and he smiled at that.* The trapper turned and looked towards the door where it had all happened. *Right there, right there.* He looked at the scene like it wasn't over. Like time, or whoever bagged up the past, had forgotten to collect it because he could see his boy there where the socks softly hit him in the back, after he turned, as he smiled, before he left on his first hunt. The trapper wasn't looking at a ghost like earlier, but it was more substantive than a common memory. Somewhere in between. The man here was smiling watching scenes from a projector playing in his mind.

From a small and dark hole inside the trapper's skull came a burp. That sweet memory had fed the little trapper's soul, nourishment enough to sustain him forever. The little trapper lovingly sighed, and the vast tangle of ignition wires he'd twisted around the trapper's neuron terminals, sagged softly.

In actual fact, the day the man threw the socks at the boy, he was not heading off on his first solo hunt. Already the truth of former days was distorting—this his first involuntary yet inevitable infidelity to the past. The snake-oil salesmanship of memory had already begun. Since his wife had passed, his subconscious had mostly picked the glossed cherries of her memories and she'd become polished to legend. Time would tell what warped shape the boy, never so far from his thoughts and floating inside him, would take.

The tin man holding both mitts while gazing affectionately at the empty space in front of the door.

Just balled up socks like balled up socks. It's okay. You're okay. Put them down.

Where?

Keep it simple: put things where they belong.

Where do they belong? On the shelf by the door was their place. There?

For now, anywhere. This voice speaking was pretending to be strong, but really when the man wasn't looking it was crying too, from a loft inside the man's mind, it cried too. When it had to speak it just took in a big breath and tried to sound convincing and strong. But it was not strong.

Or put everything of his on his bed? Does that make sense? All in one place in case he comes back again?

The voice didn't respond. It had its small hands across its small mouth to hold back a large scream.

Or maybe in a box then take them to the shed?

He considered laying them in the open grave outside the door, but in the interval between covering them with soil and the ground freezing over, which would prevent his digging them back up in an all-but-certain moment of weakness, he didn't trust his resolve to leave the past buried. The man was sweating and pale, as if this cabin hadn't been conventionally bombed it had been atomic bombed, and everything around him including these plutonium mitts were radioactive. *It's all poison. Don't even drink the water.*

He said looking at the door talking to no one, "Little boy, are your hands cold? Look, they're white." He said, "Put them in my armpits." The trapper was laughing now so he must have been able to feel the boy's frigid little digits in his own hairy pits. That meant this was beyond memory beyond dream beyond past beyond ghost. Maybe they're all built from the same unbelievable stuff. Him laughing in the cabin now. On the wall the scythe-shaped triggers were winking and the noose on the floor was a mouth gaping and the curve of every blade smiled. "Here, let's put the mitts on you." He unballed their cuffs. In the middle of the cabin he held an open mitt to the empty room.

To those who don't hear the music, dancing will always look crazy. Those words printed in a book on his shelf. On another shelf, a different book by a different author: *We are sane to the degree that our actions are humane.* If the second is true, that would make the first author crazy: a cruel and misogynistic man, a proponent of slavery and genocide who employed pretty words to argue for terrible ends. But the second statement also seems dubious because sometimes crazy is just crazy. The trapper here was going nuts. This man here unmoving for so long he was becoming a huge mushroom rooted through the cabin planks that piss and blood and bile and dead memories had begun to rot. He was turning sickly grey right there in the cabin, feeding on the enormous decay of the past, and when some woodland explorer opens the cabin door in a year, or ten, or in a century when it's all fallen down, there beside the rusted stove, would remain this exhibit of the standing dead.

Suddenly a large bang came from one of the windows. Like a snowball, or a single knock from an unexpected visitor. The sonic intrusion momentarily broke him free from the spell of the mitts, disrupting his standing mental breakdown.

From within, some voice whose throat was being throttled by the grip of the past had found air enough to cough out hoarsely a few choice words: *Put down the fucking mitts!*

Where?

Anywhere! Fucking anywhere! Do it now! Make a decision. Doesn't matter where just do something. Go! It implored, ordered, pleaded like those mitts could strangle and not let go.

The trapper, forgetting the window bang, set the mitts on the table. Then he stepped back and ineptly stared at them. In his past he had once fought a bear and liked it, liked even the feeling of pain because that felt raw and raw felt good, and maybe he was just built a little differently because that time and other times he had never winced, never wilted.

He was wilting. He thought he was stronger than all this and had you asked him beforehand he'd know that he was.

Forget all that—who knows about anything before you're in it. And now you're in it. Now you know pain. Real pain. In one way or another and whether you acknowledged it or not it was always coming and now it's here. And if you survive it, one day there will be more. This voice all rock, all granite, all shield. *That should be page one in the manual of life. That should be bedtime stories. If you had left the world before him, you'd have hurt him just as much. At least this way it's you that bears that burden, not him. So bear it. Move forward.*

He was still looking at the mitts. What was clear was that he had picked one of the very worst places for them. In fact, it was the worst place he could have put them—*central*. Everywhere he might move in the cabin they'd be in sight, their weight bending his world.

You did something. You made a decision when that was hard to do and even if it wasn't the best one—even if it was the worst one—you tried and you did it and you'll try the next thing. You soldier on if you have to. A step at a time and you won't get it all right. To hell with getting it right and to hell with the past. It doesn't need you and you don't need it.

Maybe this voice knew what it was talking about, or maybe it was just trying to save the man by any available means, willing to perjure itself to save the greater whole barely balanced at the brink of insanity.

The little trapper inside him was frothing at the mouth and raging to those words, one thumb on the red detonation button ready to blow it all up and burn it all down at this staggering disloyalty to his nation, The Past.

Just care and try, then try again. That's it. Do that till the day you die and it's a decent biography of a life well lived, even if it didn't work out. Small things. Each at a time. Maybe you can take things back slowly. Not all at once but maybe you do that you reclaim your hand.

A hand that once held the boy's, he said to himself.

I know. Maybe you do that you reclaim your arms.

Arms that once carried the boy.

I know. Fact is, you're up. Right now you have a breath and you may get one more. You could be lying on the floor right now and you're not. Maybe you will later and that's okay too, that's okay, but right now you're not. Just put more of them together and see what happens. Maybe it's two steps forward and one step back.

Like I told the boy.

Yeah. Like we told the boy. But let's just stop saying 'the boy' with everything.

The trapper needed a break from drowning. Though his movements were laboured, he managed to put on his jacket.

The frosted wood of the porch creaked under his steps. He tried to ignore the gaping earth, the open grave he dug for his captive. The outside air was clean and cold. He instinctively scanned off to the forest edge. As instinctively as a father asks if his son is cold, as instinctively as a timber wolf surveys his land for prey. His eyes searching the edge of the trees for movement, the snow for tracks. His ears alert. Some old habits don't die hard 'cause they don't die at all.

It hadn't peeped or flapped but beside him he noticed a whisky jack on the porch below one of the windows. The window wasn't broken so he assumed its head was. It was upright, though kinda squat and sitting on its thin legs. Its eyes were open but those eyes weren't moving. Looking at it there he thought it might have died then froze. He stepped once towards it and his looming presence did not rouse the bird. He stepped closer and this time it did blink. It lamely waddled a half step away in some abbreviated attempt to flee. When he arrived beside the bird it tilted its head upwards, and then it fell over.

"Hey."

It lay there. Its eye facing upwards was open.

"If you'd have knocked I'd have just let you in."

The humourless, possibly dying bird, blinked.

He knelt and carefully gathered it up in one hand clutching his fingers around the soft feathers of its closed wings. It protested weakly and he thought that was a good sign. He righted the bird on its little claws. It swayed to one side like this whisky jack was whiskey drunk and actually lifted one foot off the porch hilariously, then pulled itself back to centre. It overcompensated and tipped over to the other side. Out of embarrassment or anger or shame or distress or perhaps some emotion particular only to birds or this bird, it peeped. Once.

He gathered it up again holding it in his hand curved like a big ladle and supporting its tiny head with the meat of his thumb.

"Hey. You're okay. You just rest up."

He walked the bird to the far corner of the porch and cleared the railing of snow with the back of his hand and set the bird down carefully. He left it like that and went into the cabin. He returned and set the concussed jack into its new dishtowel nest. Bunched up the towel so its folds would keep the bird sitting properly.

Above its head he rubbed his flattened hands together vigorously, appearing to be performing some shamanic healing ritual. Between his milling hands a crust turned to flour: tiny crumbs sifted down around the bird's spinning head.

The air was clean and cold and the sun was bright and yellow. He lifted by its back a simple wooden chair that stayed out on the porch and set it into the sun. At the edge of the cabin clearing grew evergreens with the undersides of their bows green and the branches bowing under the weight of the snow. Birds chittered. His coffee smoked. Between the cabin and the forest edge were a few spaced out trees: aspen, alder. Closer to the porch was a maple of moderate size. He was looking at one of the few remaining leaves that had not let go. It was yellow. It turned a bit. The boy after out hunting alone had told him some story about a magical leaf, then had taken from out of his backpack the folded and crumpled proof, traced his finger along a rib of the big leaf, told him how it was a secret map and where it had led him.

The man looked away from the leaf and lowered his head and stared at the snowy porch because the unscrupulous past was beyond the pale and it was now holding hostage every innocent thing it could wrap its claws around. He should have expected it would come for the leaves and the birds too. He didn't dare look at the clouds for fear of what the indecent past might do to their shapes. His eyes on the snowy porch. He heard a couple birds land in the maple—mourning dove, whisky jack, stellar jay—he couldn't say because he didn't look up because what's the point when everything is something else.

The sun, as if denying him his averted gaze, projected the birds' antics to the porch. It reminded him of a morning out hiking with the boy when the boy had pretended to flitter up and give a turn with the birds. That made the sun here an accessory to the crime of impersonating the past. Nothing was sacred and sorrow had infiltrated everything: from the sun to its shadows. He would have closed his eyes off from the birds' shadow-play, but the images of his inner world were no lighter.

His coffee almost done, what remained had cooled. He swirled it. Sat there on the morning porch in the winter forest in a heavy landscape of loss.

He sat under a sun, unsure if he could trust its shine, though he couldn't doubt that its rays were still warm. And he hadn't asked them to be. Among trees he hadn't asked to be green, and among the birds he hadn't cued to sing, in air so undeniably pure it was like he was in the very medium of truth. Maybe right then he would have preferred the world to align itself with his sentiments. Maybe right then he would have preferred the world coloured grey, grey and hurting, where the sounds of trees moving in the wind were just their moans from sore trunks and aching bark. Then they could all hurt together. Less lonely that way, 'cause as it was, he did not feel connected to these sunny woods at all. But you don't get to tell the world when and what part of it is allowed to be sad, kind or colourful, and neither does the rain ask your permission to fall, and maybe even within the palette of one's discontent, though you would have preferred it otherwise, some pretty colours are never gone entirely. Maybe you don't feel like you deserve those nice things. But if those nice things bring with them a bit of guilt because green should be grey and yellow should be broken and birds should just shut the hell up for a time, then so be it. So be it. What's a little more self-loathing from the guilt of a silver lining—you can take that if you're still kicking after all the rest. And you are still kicking. And you will still kick. The world with its colour and song did not conform to his own sad perspective, and the warmth of the sun was insulated from his own cold heart. The trapper swirled the cold coffee in his mug. He drank it and though cooled it was still rich. Still rich. And so be it: have the strength to take the light as well as the darkness. He wasn't even sure if he was listening or speaking. Still broken, still so very broken. But he just resolved to clean the cabin.

· · · **·** · **·** · · · ·

The trapper organized and swept. From where he'd ritualistically placed the candles on the floor two days ago, he saved the ones with some wick yet to burn then took a flat metal scraper to all the hardened wax globs pooled on the boards. He swept up the waxy curls and chips as well the various sizes of broken glass, which clinked in the dust pan. All the while he was in some awkward and unacknowledged dance manoeuvre of the wilfully blind, stepping around and sometimes over the bear cloak on the floor where Jacob had left it.

Then he did acknowledge its existence. This time before he went to pick up the cloak he decided where he'd put it so as not to get hamstrung with indecision again. When he lifted it he saw it had been covering thin and shaky letters etched into a floorboard: *REVENGE*. Even staring at that irrefutable evidence—the word essentially his signature on a passport for his recent trip to the colder reaches of humanity—his recollection of carving it was hazier than a dream. Even with the corroborating evidence of his wrist still wrapped to heal the vein he'd pricked that same day. He put the bear cloak away. He coiled up the snake of rope and untied its boa-constrictor head. He started sanding out that word and while he was at work on the *V* he heard a plane.

The yellow fuselage chased its preceding bass drone over the trees.

The sandpaper still in the trapper's hand while it cruised above, as though he might reach to the sky to try to buff out this image so similar to a past invasion. The plane disappeared over the trees, its engine throttling down. When in about half an hour he heard it overhead again, he didn't even go to the porch and look, as he knew, most likely knew, those boys who took his son were now gone. He just kept sanding out the *E*.

By midafternoon he had the cabin pretty well cleaned up. He knew that the guns on the wall were a threat to him. On a trip to the shed, passing the open grave, he considered laying them in the ground. But that'd just be false comfort. He didn't need a gun. A knife, a rope, a bottle of bleach, the tip of a broadhead, even a humble piece of glass; the generous world offered innumerable ways to remove oneself from it. He filled in the hole with soil.

To those items on the table glowing with the past—mitts, portrait—he'd added a few more. Having them all in one place seemed like a reasonable idea, it'd let him make a decision where to ultimately put them without being caught off guard by a charged relic waiting to entrance him. But concentrating their weights was like stacking supernovas, their gravitational fields bending the current reality around him into former worlds.

He carried a few items to the shed. On the farthest wall hanging by nails were dozens of animal traps, rust-free in their lightweight protective oil. He took down a steel conibear trap. *Eventually you'll need money.* Just him alone now meant his base supplies would last a bit longer: grains, sugar, salt. Clothes and boots and arrows and ammunition were fine, batteries he could go without. But by next year he'd need some things. The animals' coats would be thick now and he could start trapping anytime, even this afternoon if he wanted. *You could head out in the morning. Lay some cold steel down to end life. Take some life and put it in your wallet.* He walked over and took down a set of heavy jaws engineered to withstand harsh weather while patiently waiting to snap bones. *Could head out there first thing in the morning.* He had been a hunting guide for several years but had been a trapper longer. So had his dad and his dad's dad. Holding the trap like he was holding a part of his own self, like he was holding a heritage. Its cold weight. *Maybe get a few things done around here first. Maybe a couple days getting things in order then be all ready to go and get back out there and get on with it and hit it hard.* The trap in his hand all polished and shiny. Like something a salesperson would tell you you just couldn't do without. *This mechanism will put food on your table. Money in your pocket. You'd be a fool to pass this up.*

He saw the dark shape hanging from the rafter. The shed cold enough he couldn't smell any rot. He walked over to the hanging hindquarter of the black bear his boy, like some legend, had killed. The outer meat all dark and leathery. There wasn't much left of it after he and the boy had worked their way through it. He hadn't turned on the shed's hanging bulb. Grainy light was coming in through the shed's dirty windows and that paltry light fell on the quarter. It looked like a shrivelled and partially mutilated nut sack of some slain woodland giant. He had smoked and wrapped most of the meat from the other quarters and backstrap and stored it away in the cellar and he could eat that now, but preferred to save it for the middle of winter, as you never know how hard the coming days could get in the North. He grabbed the hock by one hand. They'd eaten the shanks. The rump had a deep strip gouged out of it and that cavity was only of a slightly lighter black than the rest. He considered a dinner of root vegetables and pickled things. With his knife he poked the black outer layer and it was straight leather. There's a reason ancient cultures the world over once wore it in battle. The knife did not impale. He let go and gave the quarter a light punch and though it swayed slightly, the meat did not indent. But he knew it looked worse than it actually was and under that tough skin if he cut deep enough the meat would be okay.

He'd been raised to not waste meat and to be grateful for an animal whose passing he had inflicted. Especially grateful when that animal had tried to pass you first. In his shook world at least some core values remained.

He unhooked the dismal ham and set it on the workbench and sliced into it. First cut showed a blushing grey that reddened as he deepened. He trimmed it to the salvageable core. A couple meals worth anyways. When he was done he had one last look around in the shed. The tools and instruments for carpentry and general home repair, archery and gunsmithing, food preserving. Empty mason jars. Some old jackets. One all white and that was Granddad's and once the boy had asked if he could wear it and was told a hard no. The trapper took his bear ham and the bones for soup and the scraps that he'd throw away back into the woods and closed the door on the shed that felt like one big trigger pan baited with memories.

He cubed the meat for stew, seasoned it, seasoned it some more, seared it in the deep Dutch oven's hot oil and added onion and garlic, then flour and a mason jar of preserved tomatoes. Filled the pot about a third full with water and added carrots and potatoes and a bay leaf to make a stew. When the hottest part of the stove had it roiling he pushed it off to a cooler portion to simmer.

He sat by the stove with his back turned to the table and caught glimpse of an arrow stuck into the cabin wall. While spooning up hot stew he debated carving it out or snapping it off. *Maybe try to unscrew it and leave the broadhead buried but save the shaft?* The cabin was so quiet he could almost hear the echo of his own thoughts, so he tried to give them a rest. Listened to the fire, which was okay. Heard his spoon in the bowl and his own sounds of chewing and swallowing, which was not so okay.

Just listen to the fire and eat your stew. It occurred to him that given how his boy had killed this bear, it was kinda like this meal was one of the last prepared by his son. He wasn't sure if that was good or bad. *Just try to eat a bit. Just be warm. That's it. Read if you can read. Maybe pick a simple task, sharpen or clean. Then go to bed. You survived a hard day. Maybe the hardest. That's bigger than it seems. That's huge.*

He spooned up more steaming stew but hesitated on its delivery. His hand began to tremble. The spoon lost half its contents. He returned the spoon and put the bowl down and rested his elbows on his knees, wove his fingers into threaded fists and set his chin on them in hopes steadying his head would steady his thoughts.

Look, plan a couple things for tomorrow. Focus on that. What's priority? He looked around the cabin. The place was now clean and orderly. *Could store more food. Cut more wood. Kill a bunch of small animals. That's the plan, right? I'm going to store more food and cut more wood and kill some things. Right? That's me, right?*

No answer.

The contents of the cabin loomed about him but he was more nervous for what the night might bring. His heart rate was up. He looked around. The edge of the dark loft. Then he looked at what had been watching him: the nearly animate items on the table. His stomach churned, not from the stew.

Bed, just go to bed.

You mean the bed where her and I used to lay curved up and curled together spooned warm against the night. That bed?

Yeah, that one. Just go to bed and turn your mind off. If the past wants you it'll know where to find you.

He had the childish thought of locking his bedroom door, but none of those doors had locks up there and certainly not the ones to the past. He set his half-eaten stew in the kitchen sink and blew out the candles. When he passed those heavy items on the table, that pile of gravities almost tipped his teetering mind over an edge, almost had him falling to their weighted centre, like a marble on a cotton sheet with a cannon ball for company. The boy liked marbles, he thought.

· · · ● · ● · ● · · ·

In the night a demon at the foot of his bed shrinks itself into a tiny beetle and crawls over the hills and valleys of the bedsheets. When it scurries above the man's chest its eight legs clutch the sheet as his pounding heart almost trampolines that crawling mite. It scurries delicately up the man's neck—not delicately enough that he doesn't scratch at his crawling skin. It climbs up his chin, over a cheek, enters the cave of one nostril, then buries deep into the meatloaf of the sleeping man's mind.

It sees film reels of memories strewn about, unplugged projectors. The beetle crawls past the feet of some worn-out formerly-manic film operator asleep in a chair. So many rooms and corridors and attics and basements to explore, the options are wondrous. It chooses the closed door ahead, slips through the crack underneath. Finds itself in one of the many storehouses of the man's mind. Artifacts like discarded stage props—knives, books, clothing, etc.—some rather shiny, others with dust layers of varying thickness. In one corner stands some tall mummified relic so entombed with silt the beetle cannot decipher it, so it reaches out a thin black leg and swipes a dust-free streak. The aluminum hull of an old family canoe lost long ago. The beetle turns in place, using all its many legs at once, and even to its own ears, the clicking on the plank flooring sounds creepy. It looks down. The floor appears to be well kept—so either frequently trafficked or routinely buffed—and the beetle wonders if perhaps the floor is also something stored, and given that the best place to store a floor would be on the floor, that's simply where it had been put.

A large drum catches its attention. It scurries, clicking over to it. The drum on a stand and the drum walls with cut-out moons and stars. The beetle looking up at the big instrument. The insect shifts shape back to demon form: lower half of its body equine; donkey or horse, some cloven beast. Top half more evil. The skin of the drum all dusty and a mallet laid atop it. It wraps its skinny claws around the long handle, hefts the mallet to gauge its top-heavy weight. Looks around first, not immune to persecution. Sees to its right two red lights. At first it thought they were the taillights of a parked cop car and it almost trotted scared out of the man's head. It leans towards them. They glow brighter. It squints. They narrow. *Oh.* It smiles. Its demon face reflecting back in a handheld mirror hung from a nail hammered at an imperfect angle into the meat-wall of the man's mind. It winks an eye at itself.

The creature returns its glowing gaze to the dusty drum. It draws that hammer high overhead. In the dark room it looks like the shadow of a villainous Thor. It brings that swing down hard enough it must have been intent on busting through the drum's stretched skin. Huge cloud of dust. Huge resonant boom.

He's up. Our man wakes up. Holy shit is he ever up. His one good eye in the middle of the night snaps wide open. Into the midnight pond of his mind a dropped boulder erupts the calm surface and the wave rolls out until even the trapper's fingers and toes tremor. Wakes up scared from a nightmare that he's not sure is a nightmare. A grown man scared and curled up alone in bed. Who knows something's lurking.

Woken from some fantastical dreamscape where horrors *do* roam and where he *is* hunted, his mind still hazy, like swept dust in his head yet to settle, his eyes search the dark. Aware of something—no *might,* no *maybe.* Something's not right. Him lying hazily alert in bed.

"Who's there," he says. But immediately regrets it for fear of being answered.

The demon leaves the mental storage room and takes up a chair in the theatre of the man's mind. A red pair of eyes blink back at him. Another. Many.

The trapper listening to a deep quiet like buried silence. A night absent of wolf howl geese honk crow caw, no nothing. No winter winds.

Maybe you choked out the winds like you hanged that man. Now it's you caught in the snare, little rabbit.

Feet on the bare floor. He takes a step and falls in a crevasse of the past and falls and falls and falls. That startles him awake for real this time. He doesn't pinch himself to verify he's awake because the acuteness of his pains seem quite trustworthy. Feet this time on the bear-fur floor. Long johns, no shirt. Cold immediately. Can't see a thing.

He steps on the floorboards and is doubly sure he's really awake because he believes dream-boards don't creak. Reaching the doorframe he leans against it. Still confused by the doom he sensed, its mysterious presence. The fog of sleep begins to clear and soon he starts operating out of the faculties of his right mind. *Just go back to bed.* Curious though—he did sense something. He looks to the window, but the night so dark it scared off the moon. Spends a minute at the doorframe waiting for his eyes to adjust to pitch black and they do not. He wonders how long that would take.

No glow from the stove to orient his navigation, but that path is hardwired anyways. He steps once. Stops. Listens. Nothing. Twice. Stops.

There's nobody here, of course there's nobody here. It's okay. Just relax. It's okay. Only nightmares.

He makes it to the stove and sets the palms of his hands on its top. Hardly warmth, forgot to stoke it before he went to bed. Listens for its smoulder but the fire within is dead or dying. Kneels to it and sets both hands on its thick steel wall, but finding little comfort, each hand parts ways and feels around its sides in search of warmth. And now this picture is kinda sad, him embracing the cold stove like that.

From within, a message is reaffirmed: *There's nobody here.* And he does relax. The cabin so quiet.

But then he gets it. Then he's back to nightmare. It's not what he sensed—it's what he didn't. It's not who's here—it's who isn't. *There's nobody here,* that voice says again.

Town

"Who benefits from me confessing?" Jacob had been saying variations of that to Dave since they started their walk back from the trapper's cabin to the lodge the day before. They had just arrived by Beaver plane back to town, and at the floatplane base were sitting in Jacob's pickup truck, its windows frosted. They were about to discover a dead battery. "It was an accident. If I get sentenced, if I go to jail, who benefits? Me in jail doesn't prevent someone from making that same mistake. And I don't deserve that for an accident. *I don't deserve to go to jail because someone else was an idiot!* It looked like a bear. Who dresses it up in a bear cloak? Next to a fucking hunting lodge? Christ sake. *He* should go to jail for negligence. Not me."

"You keep saying *it*."

Jacob looked at him. Then looked away. "Look. Dave. It was a mistake. Of course I wish it didn't happen. But there is a bigger point here. Me going to jail doesn't help anything."

"You might not even get sentenced. Accidental manslaughter or whatever. You're right. He bears some of the fault here."

Jacob with traces of disgust looked at him at that unintended pun.

"Sorry."

"Some? *All* the fault here."

"Don't you think word will get out sooner or later? He and his boy come into town every year for supplies. Even if he doesn't report it, people will be curious. If you go talk to the police now, that has to look better."

Jacob stuck the key in the ignition. "But he might not even report it. Then I put myself at risk of going to jail for nothing." He put his hands on the wheel, though it wasn't yet started. "What about this. I volunteer every week and I give my money to charity. I mean that. I'll do it. If I were to go to jail, the world would be worse off. So we keep it between us. If he reports it, he reports it. That's up to him. I could say I never actually knew what happened."

"How do you mean?"

"If one day he reports it, we say we never even knew it wasn't a bear. We got our story. The hill we shot from. The river. The storm. That's it. Then we went back to the lodge. Came home when the storm lifted 'cause you hurt your ankle. Never found the body. The bear body."

"He'll say we were at his cabin."

"Maybe, maybe not. Then he has to confess to kidnapping and attempted murder."

"You did find the bow on the hill. And where was the boy the whole time up there?"

"I don't fucking know! I'm not his biographer. That's not my problem." Jacob's white-knuckled hands gripping the wheel. "You know what? Actually. Actually—you know what? Maybe I don't even believe him. Maybe I don't believe him and it was just a bear the whole time. To hell with him and his bushed-out mind and redneck life and his stories. How do I know it wasn't just a bear. He says one thing. I saw another. I don't know anything at all about that asshole and I never saw a boy, that's fact, and that hillbilly can claim whatever he wants. They can hook me up to a polygraph. I'd fuckin' pass. I'd pass. So we just see if he wants to confess and even if he does we see how this unfolds."

Dave didn't say anything.

Jacob wishing that Dave's silence now was him practising to be silent later.

"Dave you are under no obligation to report what he claims happened. We never saw a body. And it's all between him and me anyways. And for real, if you do report me, because I promise to donate my money to charity, it's actually *you* that's making the world worse off. Really though, it would be, if you think about it. If he calls it in, okay, that's one thing. But don't you do it. It's not on you Dave."

Dave looked at Jacob. "Things would start to get complicated."

"You're my best friend." Jacob lowered his voice. "I was ready to *kill* him to save you. I sent that arrow to save you. I did that I'd do that again. Fuckin' heartbeat I would. This is not your battle or your responsibility. Leave it alone. I tracked that asshole down and sent that arrow to save you in a noose. *You were in a fucking noose.* Hey? What the hell. Don't forget that. The guy's an absolute nut case. Now you owe me this."

Dave began picking at the skin around one of his nails. "So what, we live with that secret forever?"

"There's no good option here. There's just bad and less bad. He screwed up from the start with the bear coat. Then he kidnapped you. Strung you up from a rafter." Jacob shook his head and squinted looking at that ludicrous scene. "You don't owe him anything. The only reason we have laws are for justice. Justice means a better world. So think big picture. What world is better off? Me potentially behind bars? Or me making donations and volunteering at charities. For something I never did. Bad and less bad."

Dave shook his head and stared at the glass and picked his finger. "Tell me again what happens if he reports it."

"Then it's his word against mine. I shot a bear while I, a licensed hunter on my private land, was legally permitted to. River—*can't cross*. Storm—*snowed in*. Plane—*we left*. Simple story. Story ends there."

"And if they dig up the body?"

"That's what I mean. I just say I didn't know and never found the bear and my god I'm sorry now. If only I'd known."

"It's not just you. They'll question me too."

"Yeah. They will. So it's his word against ours. It's loyalty to your longest friend who saved your life, or siding with your attempted murderer. We never went to his cabin. What cabin?" Jacob looked at him intently. "What cabin?"

"That gets messy. Maybe there's DNA or something. Not reporting it is one thing. Lying and lying to the police is another. And what do I say about this?" Dave pulled down his jacket collar and pointed to his throat. He looked like a ring-necked parakeet.

"Turtleneck."

"Turtleneck. Yeah right. What do I say to Sarah?"

"Seriously though, I'm not even joking. Just wear a scarf outside and a collar inside. It'll fade away in a few days. And if she does see it, say you were too embarrassed to mention it and were trying to hide it and make up some story involving alcohol." Jacob nodded. "She knows me. Say we were snowed in and trying to pass the time and we made up a drinking game of lassoing shit in the cabin like cowboys for drinks. You were heading for a piss and I thought it'd be funny and tried to rope you but it landed high and got your neck and you fell and hurt your ankle. Jesus, that's got a bow on it basically. Say: Jacob feels really badly."

Dave was looking at the opaque windshield. He squinted, as if in the ornate details of that cold and florid scene he could see new characters appearing in the frost. "What about the other owners?" Dave referencing the two other co-owners of the lodge who lived in another city.

"Ah shit. I actually didn't think about that. I'll talk to them."

"What will you say?"

Jacob reached for the keys in the ignition. "I'll think of something." He looked at Dave. "Just don't say anything to the police. You owe me that." They were looking eye to eye. Jacob turned the keys.

WOODS

TIRED OF BED AND impatient of dawn, the trapper rolled his body over the mattress and got up dutifully with the rote mechanics of a hollow machine. He went to the stove and grabbed the handle. Then stopped. He found a towel and covered the hinge and carefully turned the handle upwards and pulled the stove door open silently and didn't look at the loft. The previous night's logs now skinny and charred and eaten away at their centres. A small bed of quaking coals had survived, though, and began glimmering into life as reds and oranges scurried among them, like fire ants excited from under an upturned rock. He laid thin kindling and blew on the coals. The fire ants came back and he blew heavier on them and they lengthened to fire centipedes, then their backs stretched up into flames.

The light cast by the stove's moving flames flickered over those cumbersome items on the table as if to showcase them.

The trapper filled the percolator and set it on the stove. Ticks slowly turned into low rumble of coffee bubbling in the predawn morning. Its aroma spread throughout the cabin like a flowering dracaena fragrans in the night. Trance-like he watched the fire, enveloped in the sound and the smell of coffee. The rumble and the fragrance. His body was still damp with nightmare sweat, but gradually the fire dried him, and the dawn dissolved the remaining terror of night. When the sun fully crested and lit the forest, he would head to the woods for medicine.

· · · • · • • · · ·

In these November days, the big lake next to the lodge would have ice at its edges, soon to be skimmed over by a thin frozen skin. The small pond closer to his cabin was already covered in snow and a set of deer tracks were printed down the middle. He went to the pond with an old board under one arm and an axe in the other. He tapped the butt of the wooden handle to the pond's frozen edge. He tapped further ahead and that too didn't crack. Then he reached the handle out as far as he could and tested the ice before cautiously placing his first step. He followed in the small deer tracks.

A few dozen paces and he was at the centre of the pond where the water below wasn't much deeper than his height. He laid the board down flat on the ice and perpendicular to his body and put his knees on it to spread his weight. He thought there might be medicine in the water.

Not even swinging, he chipped lightly at the ice, while at the moments of impact he closed his one working eyelid to the flying shards. If he'd come one month later he would have been at his task for much longer, but after only a few minutes, the axe-head punched through with a controlled splash.

When the hole was about large enough to pull a perch through, he kept chipping. When the hole was about big enough that he'd have no problem pulling a decent trout or northern pike through, he kept at it. There weren't fish in this particular pond and likely that was because on the coldest winters it froze straight to the bottom. When the hole was just larger than shoulder width, his shoulders' width, he set the axe down.

Time for your medicine.

The hole was coloured an uninviting midnight blue. Small ice bits floated its surface. He picked the axe back up and using it like a paddle he flicked those bergs. He stood up slowly, reluctantly. His weight over the board so as not to crack the surface.

He wasn't superstitious but still he looked around for some anomalous event in nature that he would eagerly interpret as a sign not to do this. He hated cold water. Just looking at it had his Raynaud's hands already anticipatory white. *Just show me anything. Doesn't have to be a wolf howl, not even asking for a crow caw here. I'd take a common bird chirp, a tree popping off in the distance even. One single bark of a squirrel would do as a sign to head back to that warm and moderately haunted cabin.*

Silence. Both within the audible distance of the surrounding forest, as well as in that skull-sized little wilderness between his ears. No intervening voices telling him to turn back. But to be thorough, he gave it a minute while staring at electroshock therapy of the North—patient: *you*. He hated cold water. *Not the boy though. Like that day when we were hiking and he wanted to swim, after he'd kicked the arrow onto the bow. That day I got so mad at him he cried. Why would I do that? I always did that. He was just playing. He didn't do it on purpose and felt bad enough about it anyways he didn't need me adding to that. That day I yelled at him like other days I yelled at him.*

The past was like some hideous golem out there sleeping in the woods, one he'd just woken. At this hour, normally not a concern because, no doubt, night was its country. It must have heard his anguish it was hungry for. It crept up on him—remarkably quiet for the size of it, its huge footpads spreading its weight over the ice—and reached its big arms to take the trapper by the hair and drown his head in the hole he himself had chopped to the water, as if accommodating the monster's plan. The beast gripped his head and he did not resist.

There—there's your reason to take your medicine. Not everything should remind you of something else. The bird was a bird. You know that rescuing that bird won't bring the boy back. Hey. You know that, right? Some part of himself accusing himself of ulterior motives for a previous kindness. *A bird, not a boy. Cold is cold, water is water. This water doesn't have to be another water. Now take your medicine.*

He shivered from the cold air and the monster lost its grip. The trapper started unbuttoning his flannel one slow button at a time while begrudging the prescription of his better nature. That golem behind him, now lowering its arms, now standing there awkwardly, now shrinking in the courageous light coming from a person willing to do an uncomfortable thing.

A pile of clothes over his boots, him naked and shivering. Spread across his chest were ten boar-claw indentations that had shallowly impaled him when it tried to stamp out his life. Connect the dots to draw up two big bear paws, like he carried the imprint of a constellation. He looked down at them and wondered whether it was possible to sand out the past tattooed across his chest like he'd buffed out the profanity in the floorboard. His mind answered his procrastinating query: *Fuck off. Time to swim.* That voice all rock.

He looked up. *Have a plane fly over now. You thought you saw crazy before.* He looked back down to that murky hole and if he dawdled much longer he'd have to chop it again. He had his white hands clasped together, not very reverent-looking because he held them covering his dried fig of a nut sack recently absent its cowardly balls gone off in search of warmer places.

Submerge for truth and let's see if pain can purify. One last dreadful minute as that dreadful cold air was far better than what awaited him below. *Medicine—ah, hell.* He lowered into a push-up form with his hands beside the hole and his chest overtop, allowing his shrunken lower appendage to dangle just above the surface so as not to freeze the tip of his cock to the ice and have him planking there until spring thaw. He breathed a few quick hyperventilating and motivating breaths. He visualized one swift motion, then quickly brought his knees up under him while his arms supported his weight like a gymnast on a pommel horse—and during that flash-second he did wonder if his arms would just punch through the ice—then he cleanly dropped in. A great *sploosh*. Head under.

For the couple seconds that he could stand it, that northern land got a touch more sane to about the same proportion as the submerged absence of a peculiar animal willing to inflict on itself a type of significant misery for uncertain gains. For those couple seconds all other problems in his world shut off, while the doctor administered her medicine with ten thousand angry needles.

His steaming head re-emerged from that murky hole, like some queer winter polyp. His smoking head, already starting to frost, yelled into the cold winter air with tremendous zeal a great string of short and abrasive words. He was panting ar-rhythmically and kinda moaning while he stayed in up to his chin for a few more seconds. Then he kicked his legs and put his hands on the long board and squirmed himself back onto the surface with both the grace and colour of a harp seal. He lay: tingling, panting. He coughed several times, all of them misting.

He scrambled up to his feet before he froze to the ice like an idiot and grabbed his boots in one hand and pinched all his clothes under his other arm and ran for the sauna he'd set to bake before he left for the pond. He had the belief that like a coal-walker impervious to a footpad burn, if he was quick over the snow he'd not freeze his paws.

When he got about halfway off the pond, he realized he forgot the axe and the board. *Fuck it*, sang a choir of his fractured selves all harmoniously agreeing. He didn't stop and in the distance he saw the sauna's smoke in a narrow grey line, not blown by the winds as there was none, just angled a bit by some suggestive current. He saw the sauna with the smoke, and the sight of it didn't warm him, but there was something akin to that. Like a single one or two of his feathers got a bit of uplift.

Deer tracks like he'd seen on the pond reappeared below him, though even in the blur of his jog he could tell they weren't the same. *Keep watching the ground like this and I'll run into a tree. Moose? Nope. One moose print has a cloven hoof splayed far apart and this one here has them rounded together. They look nearly moose in size though.* Realizing that this was not a bull but a buck, buck naked he skidded to a stop. *Couldn't be that big, the deer must of slid a bit when it stepped.* But all the edges around the tracks were clearly defined and sharp; they hadn't been elongated or widened by the animal making a skid or slip. He like some puzzled eunuch looking for what he'd lost in the snow, car keys or contact lens or sanity.

He set a white hand sideways to measure the hindfoot of this Zeus buck. *What I'd give to pursue this animal with Granddad.* The trapper would say his left nut, but that was no longer available for barter; his genitalia had turtled themselves nearly out of existence. His teeth between his blue lips had begun to chatter. He thought to interrogate that reference to Granddad and the past, whether it was permitted, and even while going numb with cold he was curious as to which memories were allowable and could be trusted. Should he castigate himself after every reference to former times? But that type of deliberation required a skull with more blood circulating than he presently had, so he just ran that thought to the sauna.

· · · · ● · ● · · · ·

Outside the square steaming cedar shack, he let the clothes fall from where he'd pinched them under his wing and let his boots drop from his hand. Exchanged them for two scoops of snow.

Hot, dark, wooden. The little potbelly stove hissed then steamed. Hissed then steamed again. He clapped once and the clinging snow exploded from his hands and the stove sizzled. Daylight through the small window lightened a square patch on the wood floor. He sat on one of the two wooden benches permanently fixed to the walls. His lungs felt clean from running hard in the cold air and his muscles felt good and tight from the

120

jog. The incredible transition from extreme cold to hot had his blood racing, his skin all flush, his mind electric.

The immersive electroshock-therapy-of-the-North had given him some relief from dread and weariness, and even his brief preoccupation with the buck tracks helped set his mind to a new task. He wanted to try to leverage this positive feeling for future gains. *When you're up, try to set yourself to stay up.* He wasn't sure if someone had told him that or if he'd read it or if it was just some piece of common wisdom not so innovative but still helpful. He started formulating another prescription.

Cold, heat, exercise, try to get good sleep, good food, give effort and do hard things. Take your medicine seven days a week. Take it even when it tastes bad going down. Take it even when it feels like it's not working because you'll never know how low you'd be without it. And before you call one thing another thing, before you try to fit something into a prior shape, try to know it for what it is. Let's get high resolution on this. Where are you folded? Because there you are a lie. He'd read that before. *Right now, dig up the demons so they don't slowly eat their way through you.*

It wasn't that he thought he could put such extreme loss so quickly behind him and move on from significant trauma in only a matter of days. Maybe no passage of time is sufficient to heal a wound that had cut right through him; he was pretty sure the blade of loss had been travelling so fast that its friction generated enough heat to cauterize where he'd been cloven in two so he could never fuse back together. It wasn't that he thought he could just heal up and get past it all—no, this was pure survival. Painful and unprocessed memories embedded in the body's jelly puts whoever preserves those memories at peril. Like a cyanide capsule not carried under the tongue but stored in a fat reserve of the body. His nights so dark and the threats during his day only too real: if he didn't try to lift some weight off his soul it'd pull him down permanently. He was sure about that because he'd felt his hands itch for the blade, eager to chamber the round, string the rope. And though it'd be his hands that would bleed him, shoot him, hang him, the mastermind of his end would be the past. *So confront it. Then put some distance between you and it.* This broken man just tryin' to keep on by any means necessary.

He didn't have the luxury of professional counsel. He read profusely and nearly an entire wall of his cabin was books, from the early Greeks to modern works. But none of them were self-help; there was a real chance this was the exact opposite of what he should do.

Go ahead, sum it, he said to himself.

You're going to need money soon enough. You only have one trade and you don't seem so enthused about it.

And it's a dying trade anyways, he added.

You're middle-aged and alone. The first of those will only change for the worse. And the second, well, look around. That is very unlikely to change.

He didn't need to look around. He nodded in agreement to himself. Keep going, he said. I can take it. What else?

There's a real chance you could go crazy out here alone.

Who said that?

None of him laughed.

What else. Brutal honesty. Let's go.

...

What?

You failed them.

What?

Your wife and boy. You failed them. They're dead.

He was silent. Seemed like that accusation was something that could have been arrived at more gently, after a bit more time, and delivered up with a lighter touch.

Your wife and boy. You failed them. They're dead.

Whether or not the voice had actually said it again or if it was a truth so hard it simply echoed off his skull. The sauna air suddenly got so hot his deep inhale felt like it was singeing his lungs.

Yes. I did. Yes, they are. He faced it. The burn lingered after his exhale.

Say it again.

I failed my wife and my boy. Now they're dead.

Again.

No.

Again.

They're dead.

If you need proof, the bodies are buried just outside.

I don't. I buried them. His mental voice was weaker. He felt that at least with that admission, he and this voice could move on.

That is your fault. You were a husband and now you are not. You were a father and you're no longer that privileged thing. If their love nourished you, that means you are now starving. The voice was harsh. *If their company strengthened you, that means you are now weak. If the purpose of family gave you structure, that means you are now without form. The things you loved the most you ended up caring for very poorly. That's fact. That's truth.*

He felt like that voice in his head was pointing a finger. His head had been low, but now it hung lower.

Feel that. How does that sit?

He didn't respond to himself. That was all overstepping. He had started this exercise in good faith and it had quickly gone too far. He should have tried this over a few sessions or with some sort of safety word.

Sorry could be my safety word, he thought.

Sorry's not good enough.

Perhaps this interrogative part of himself had been wanting to call him out for a long time and get something off its chest—maybe before the boy even. Maybe he had invoked his demons, the darker parts of himself with a penchant for cruelty and proclivity for harm, even if its target was himself.

The trapper was short on breath, and that asphyxiation worsened by the sauna's intense heat.

Don't turn away, it said.

Then again, could be some part of him was trying to toughen him up at its own expense, and this wasn't cruelty it was galvanization. Push him to the controlled brink but not over the ledge. And if he wouldn't speak to that part of himself afterwards, so be it, teach himself hard lessons at his own expense until he forged steel that could cut stone, if he had to. Maybe this voice was trying to walk a thin line. Overly cruel and it'd leave him as an unsalvageable mass huddled in a corner. Too gentle, even in this time of severe loss, and the man would be left raw and unprotected from an abrasive world ready to wear him away.

Whatever the internal intentions, where both malice and kindness could manifest similarly—the mother cleaning a wound may be loathed by the child—the man was reeling inside. The acid he just drank swirling in his belly like a beaker. Where normally after this quantity of time in the sauna he'd be glistening only, already the sweat dripping from his body was tapping on the floor, sounding like the beads of an abacus, one by one each bead tallying up his ledger of ruin.

I need a break. That thought arid, like his mental throat was dry.

So now they're dead. Dead! The boy and the woman. Remember them? Remember them! Don't turn away. Your little family.

All the love. All gone. This voice possessed. *Feel that gaping hollow pit. That's you. Remember carrying your little noodle-boy somehow gone limp in every muscle up to bed?*

Oh god. That was beyond apostasy, beyond treason. A crime against his own humanity. In this dark self-exploration the trapper had slit some internal cyst of self-loathing and a vile pus of accusatory words began to ooze.

You don't get to do that anymore. Remember how you once watched your wife and your boy. That was a statement not a question. *You said it was like a fruit pit fitting with the hollow core. Tiny fingers and toes that couldn't even be real at all, you said. You let that fruit rot. Then you buried those fingers. They're in the dirt and they're never coming back. Not ever.*

No doubt this part of him had been inspired by what it read from a book on his shelf detailing the interrogation of prisoners in Russian gulags. The trapper choked and felt lightheaded and heavyhearted and he felt like his head had been snakebit. He considered letting the poison out by swinging his throbbing head against the cedar walls intolerant of abuse. If all that was the truth, he wanted nothing to do with truth.

He whispered in mental words as quiet as someone fatally shot might speak their last: That'll do for now. "I think that's good for now," that one he whispered out loud trying to get through to his psychotic self.

His spiritual wounds were now so fresh he would not have been surprised to hear a vulture perch on the sauna, where it would wait for him to limp out the door. No species more talented at detecting fatality. The ugly bird would first peck out his crying eyes to further disorient him, then stab its beak through his chest and pull out from between his ribs each little piece of his broken heart.

He had pretty much dialled things up to stress-test levels here and something was about to break. It felt like something was actually breaking within him. The bolts in his mind starting to rattle loose, the beams and girders and cables now reaching their tensile capacity and they might snap leaving him tipping over dead having ruptured some vital blood vessel, or maybe he'd just fall into some steep-walled well of permanent psychosis inside his own mind. Why would he have thought that only days after most severe loss and while body-sick with bereavement all alone in the woods and still pulsing from the extremes of ice-cold to oven-hot, he should then dwell on his life's colossal failures?

His anxiety-ridden heart knowing what awaited it outside kicked at a rib wall trying to break it down so it could jump from his chest and take its life in a big red puddle on the sauna floor.

Be with those thoughts! said the fucking witch-doctor inside him.

Those thoughts were all cement blocks tied to his ankles and he was back in the lake. Head under. Sinking. The bottom close, thank God the bottom was close.

Tell me about pain. Whether it was the same voice or another. *If your pain throbs what's between the pulses? What shape is it?*

What sound and colour is it? Stop telling yourself a pain story, and feel it clearly. Breathe and pay attention.

He closed his responsive eyelid. This rush of loss like a rogue wave standing up behind him and his body wet not from sweat but from those first tsunami drips before the rest of its heavy water crashes—yet to be seen if its spectacular volume would drown him or snap his neck.

Breathe.

He took slow air. He drew a laboured quarter-breath.

Tell me about pain.

What? he asked weakly.

Tell me about pain.

It's very dark here, he whispered in his head.

Good. Be with it. You should be so lucky. Deep heartache is not possible without having first profoundly loved. Existence is rare, life is short; pain is proof of the privilege of life. The problem of how to bear it will one day resolve itself. Until then, what colour is the dark?

He was going to instinctively say black, but he looked at the back of his closed eyelid and among the black he saw red spots and lines, orange, even a yellow tinge.

What do fear and anxiety smell like?

He expected smells of rot and decay. He inhaled slowly through his nose to find fear's fragrance, but only found a clean fire smell, and sweat, and cedar.

What sound is sorrow?

He listened for cries and wails. He considered making his own to sound his internal grief. He only heard the tempo of tiny pats from saltwater drips. Its humble rhythm the most basic musical beat. The quiet burn from the little stove beside him. His own breaths. All of it like some unnamed melody.

That's what sorrow sounds like. Watch your mind.

Tingling and hollow and heat and heavy. He watched his mind and it was an interplay of disparate things. Awareness of a general bodily ache and mental agony; urges to exit the sauna; for a moment he saw the boy fishing; there were even brief interjections of trivial thoughts, inconsequential ideas like what he would make for dinner and whether he needed to bring in more firewood; things that didn't actually concern him nor did he desire their presence but that still bubbled up to the surface of his mind; then back to nausea, the sensations of heat. All of it seemingly random and emergent and transitory. He had an awareness of being aware: that while he was waiting for the next mental phenomenon to arrive, he existed as the space between thoughts.

That's pain. Listen to its story. Not just the words, the letters. The space between the words, between the letters.

He wrung his short beard into his hand. He doused the stove with the sweat of his concerns.

The sharp hiss like a provocation.

The decrescendo.

The quiet sauna, its saltwater drips tapping, tapping, tapping.

TOWN

Dave and Sarah had a long-standing pact of full disclosure. They called it, "The Long-Standing Pact of Full Disclosure." When that pact was made they pinky swore it official. It originated before they'd been married, before high school even, back when they'd met in grade eight, junior high. She'd heard such jargon from her father, a notary public. The pact even had a weird little clause. If a third party told one of them a secret, they could inform that third party *said* secret would still be a secret and not shared with anyone else, because with regard to the realm of their bond (which included their sharing of secrets), they considered themselves one entity: a *pod* was what they called it. Thus making them two peas within the aforementioned pod. Therefore, they could ethically promise those external to that pod—everyone else—that any secret shared to one of them would not go any further. When they were twenty-two years old and legally husband and wife, they engraved their creed on the inside of their wedding rings. *Two peas in a pod.*

When Dave got home to Sarah they sat on the couch and he started with, "Jacob and I were out hiking and I left my own rifle in the cabin that day." He was telling the story how he himself had experienced its turns. When he got to the part of shooting the bear, he called it that: a bear. When he got to the part where he tackled Jacob on that snowed-in night at the cabin, she didn't show it but her insides gave a quiet little *fuck yeah*, just a little one. He told her of the dead rabbit and the blood in his hair that morning. She was revolted, expressing concern for her husband's safety as if he was not now sitting in front of her. He told her all of it, and besides not recalling just how he had found himself roped to a sleigh being pulled deeper into the woods by some freakish apparition in a jackrabbit suit, nor recalling how he came to be tied to a chair in the middle of a crude altar, his memory had no gaps.

"But the bear wasn't a bear," he said.

Sarah looked confused.

"The bear was a boy."

Sarah looked confused.

Dave just nodded gravely.

Sarah said, breathlessly, "No." Then she said nothing further, she just covered her mouth. They both didn't say anything: she in hopes he would overturn his account, he wishing he knew how to. Her eyes were large and wet, then wetter. She lowered her hand to her chest and covered her heart, like how a mother covers her child's ears to protect that child from corruption, from stories so dark they threaten a child's innocence.

At the part of the story when the trapper pulled the rope and stood Dave up to his toes and kicked out the chair, and how the man's breath was smoking at dawn when most of the candles had snuffed out and those eyes were hellish eyes, and how he was yelling at Dave his deranged philosophies and Dave knew he was going to die and was already choking in the noose, his one foot off the ground with his hands tied together and losing sight, there on the couch Dave involuntarily started picking at the skin around his fingernails. Sarah listening, fully present but nearly in shock. After so many years together the word *empathy* doesn't suffice. It does not suffice. It was her anguish. She was in the rope. She didn't break from Dave's gaze and didn't say anything while he told it, she just took in her hand his fingers that were picking at the skin around his nails. She might not even have known she'd done that.

Eventually, after consoling and questions, "What happens now?"

"I don't know."

She hadn't attacked Jacob or said anything negative at all, in fact she'd exclaimed at one point, "Poor Jacob." Dave had given a defence of Jacob, who wasn't suffering Sarah's nonexistent attack. He championed Jacob's valour in making the rescue.

She ran her fingers over his noose-bruised neck.

"Jacob asked me to keep it all under wraps for now. To not say anything to the police." He omitted the part about Jacob suggesting he tell Sarah his bruises came from lasso tosses for whiskey shots. "He said I owed him keeping it a secret."

"He said that to you?" she said incredulously and leaned away. But she was not so incredulous. Sarah had met Jacob around the time she met Dave. She was about as big a fan of him as she was of the small town, as she was of fishing and beer and six months of snow and twelve months of gossip.

WOODS

HE HEARD IT CHIRP before he saw it. The bird that had tried to smash through his window. He'd forgotten about it. It hadn't moved from where he'd placed it among the folds of the towel. The crumbs were gone. He kinda doubted the bird in its state had eaten them all. He looked around to see if the bird had invited a friend to help out with lunch. No droppings lay on the towel, no squirrel tracks printed the snow. He felt badly for leaving it there overnight and was surprised it was alive and thankful a fox or a hawk hadn't come, and he hadn't thought of that until now. He was about to pet Jack's head—short for Jacqueline or Jackson, he wasn't sure, as his vast bushcraft stopped short of sexing a whisky jack. He outstretched a finger but then figured that little head under its feathers was probably grape-skin bruised if not cranium cracked. "Probably your world is still spinning, little bud."

The bird was oscillating its head looking around. Maybe for its kind or an escape, or maybe its movements mimicked its dizzy mind. Given that the man had not retracted the finger it could have been deliberating whether to try and perch on it or evade its poke, or was getting all flustered at the finger's accusatory insinuation. Could be the bird was just bashful; the man's clothes were under his arm and his naked skin all pink from the sauna.

He returned to the porch clothed and with a toque over his wet hair and he set down a tiny thimble of water beside the bird. He left to get old Mother.

The cellar looked like the charming home of a hobbit. The thick wooden door was hinged to a frame that was set into a large mound of earth, a rise hardly big enough to call a hill. The inside of the mound had been hollowed out and a timber framework built inside. He opened the heavy and creaking door and inside it smelled of musty earth, punky and damp, cool but not frozen. It was a great smell, all earthy. The cellar like a tomb inside.

He found the old lady on the shelf, the quart mason jar of bacterial life. It was something of a standing joke between him and Mom, him and Gran, him and the boy, to call the jar, *Mother*. The ambient lighting of the midmorning sun brightened the vault enough he could see the still bubbles in the levain. Resting microbial life underneath a thin skin of gunmetal-grey mould. He grabbed the jar and a bag of rye berries and a bag of Red Fife wheat berries. Both were lighter than he had hoped and a trip to town lingered unenthusiastically on his mind. The contents of his shelves were not so sparse. Mason jars of preserved blueberries, strawberries, raspberries; brined walleye and pike. Smoked bear. He turned and saw a big tin of ground coffee. If he was out of coffee the decision would have decided itself and he'd have started that five-day trip to town that afternoon. Bread he could consider going without.

In the kitchen he used a knife to scrape the dried mould off the surface then to stir the old lady up. A bouquet of fermentation: sourness and sweetness and alcohol. He thought that probably described many grandmothers. Permanently mounted to the long kitchen counter was a hand-powered mill to grind wheat and oats, coffee for the times they returned with whole beans. He poured from the first bag the rye berries into the mill's wide hopper, then started turning its arm. The auger fed grains to the flat burrs. Flour sifted down between the circular burrs into a wide porcelain bowl. He brought his fingers under the falling flour to test the coarseness and it was very fine. He didn't grind much rye as its low gluten content didn't make for a dough that trapped the gas expelled by the feeding organisms. But even adding a bit of rye increased the complexities of the loaf's flavour. He ground up the Red Fife and then into another bowl he scooped most of the sourdough starter from her mason jar. Added water and stirred. Added to that paste the flours and salt. The gluten bonds start forming on their own and he let it sit a few minutes before he kneaded it, that way less dough would stick to his hands and the counter. He fattened up Mother with freshly ground rye flour and creek water and returned her to her contemplative and quiet life in cellartude. He only thought of that joke now and to his List of Regrets he added not being able to share it with Gran.

He tipped the bowl and coaxed the shaggy dough onto the long counter and the dough was formless and ragged. He set his hands under the sides of the dough and lifted, but not so high, and it sagged and some of it stuck to the wood. He plopped it back down and folded the closest side halfway back onto itself. He quarter-turned his hands and scooped underneath it again. Lifted it gently and brought it down and folded it over on itself. Quarter-turned his hands, repeated. His thoughts on the craft. Already the surface of the dough was showing signs of elasticity from the gluten bonding during the agitation of kneading. Transforming from less ragged to more smooth, from a mass without form to a dough with shape. The repetitive motions and the sounds were rhythmic: scooping, lifting, slapping, folding. As the dough grew stronger he lifted higher, slapped it down harder, and it made a loud smacking noise and he picked up his tempo with the cutting board pounding. Now when he lifted the smooth dough none of it stuck to the wood and the wood looked shiny and his hands were clean.

He cupped both his hands behind the far side of the dough and gently scooped and shuffled it towards himself while also turning his hands to shape the dough into a rounded mound. When he took his hands away it did not relax its shape. He scooped it and eased it into a bowl where it would bulk ferment for a couple hours. He covered the bowl with a tea towel.

While the mother's billions of children fed on sugars and passed gases that began slowly rising the dough, the trapper cleaned up and then over by the shed split wood and brought in armloads. When he passed Jack he told him or her a late lunch would be served soon enough. His route to stack the split wood by the stove had him walking back and forth past the table of supernovas and blackholes.

TOWN

Outside the door to the bar it was very cold in the wintry night. A man who had lost a lot was leaning on the railing looking out at the street. His jacket was open. The trapper's father only smoked when he was drinking, gambling, or after he did something bad. He was standing on the cement sidewalk leaning against the cold metal railing under the fluorescent green sign buzzing high overhead. A small group was off to his right, likely having a final bullshit before dispersing homewards. Another man whose "Hey" he didn't acknowledge was off to his left. The trapper's father stood alone.

The same cigarette that a few minutes ago had dangled unlit from his lips was now half-smoked. How to tell the bad news, how to phrase it. Looking at the empty street in front of him, he shook his head like he disagreed with who or what travelled it. His anger at the fool who risks so much on a draw: the man who risks what he has, to gain what he doesn't need. That fool.

Standing there in the cold of the night it dawned on him whose motel he had earlier checked in at.

Off to his right some few dozen paces away someone from a group of three leaked out three words louder than the rest, "No self control." Prior to those comments, any voices he had heard were mostly murmurs, or broken pieces of stray sentences about poker in general, though earlier he thought he heard his name, "Charles." He tried to ignore them. Whether or not they were even talking about him, whether or not they even knew it was him over here. People tend to think others are thinking or talking about them more than they actually are. Mostly people are just thinking and talking about themselves. Though that comment caught his attention, he kept his ruinous gaze on the desolate street, where around the corner lay his sled outside another man's hotel. Motel. He gave a weak little booting motion to the snow at his feet. He'd already dismissed those three words and didn't care to hear any more.

But having been raised in the woods, ears like a predator, his hearing was very good.

"Maybe 'cause of his Indian blood. Drink got to his head most likely. You know they mixed blood a ways back. I heard that."

Well now. Charles pulled on his cigarette whose grim glow reddened his face, and not like a blush. Like another red. Now he didn't have to guess. Now it didn't matter. He didn't turn to them, he just dragged long and slow and the paper burned and the red got brighter and the smoke churned in his hollow belly. If right then someone were to walk down that street and see his face it might not look so displeased. Like one at a sweet shop considering an indulgence. He dragged on the smoke and the burning core consumed paper and tobacco and the other shit they put in those cancer sticks romantically marketed by corporate lizards packaging addiction and decay in pictures of cowboys and models. Held that smoke curling within him a second. He straightened. He flicked from two fingers the unfinished cigarette away and it cartwheeled through the air, tracing a red burning circle, like the first small performance at a carnival to stoke the crowd while letting them know greater acts are to follow. It hit the snowy street in a splash of sparks.

He started walking in that group's direction, exhaled straight ahead, then walked through his own smoke like emerging from some brief confusion. Halfway to them, ten paces or so, he took off his heavy winter jacket and didn't look at the railing just laid it over its top rung. Two hundred thousand years as modern humans and millions more as some primate version highly attuned to even subtle social cues of the other monkeys—body language displaying interest, invitation or threat—and the group of three casual bullshitters picked up on the hint of aggression no slower than a band of baboons.

The least sober of them set down his bottle in order to free up his hands. The most sober of them tipped his up, draining it, then gripped the empty bottle by its neck. The third man, either a pacifist or a coward, or holding a pocketed knife, kept his hands in his jacket.

Charles' father, Norman, was a good storyteller and he probably would have come up with something clever to say in approaching those men. This man here was quieter, the type to let his fists articulate his inner feelings. Faulty as his reasoning at the poker table turned out to be, he applied a similar process here. Figured the eyes of the hands-pocketed man were the least narrowed and thus showed the least threat, and the man who'd set the bottle down was a step behind the foremost, and so whatever his intentions his greater relative distance made him for the moment less of a concern. Charles' focus was on the foremost man who wielded a weapon when it was three against one.

In the span of half a second he considered coming in and delivering a side kick to that man's knee or lunging for a superman punch to his head. Both of those could work, but as underdog he figured he'd need the most surprise possible, and surprise is aided by speed. Fewer than ten paces away, he stepped into a dead run.

The closest man half-raised the bottle but didn't have time to get it any higher before Charles landed his shoulder hard into his chest. He stumbled backwards then tripped on the drunk behind him and dropped the bottle and both those men fell. The third did withdraw his hands from his pockets and they held no knife—that man looked shocked and unthreatening, and to confirm it Charles threw a heavy right to the man's open jaw and that man was asleep before he lay down and Charles did not care and did not watch what happened to his head hitting the pavement only thinly covered in trodden snow.

The drunk in back lay with the other man on top of him and both were trying to get up. The top man scrambled halfway to standing and Charles kicked him hard in the stomach and he groaned and fell back again towards the drunk but not directly this time. The drunk managed to roll to the side, out of the way, then used the outside wall of the pub to help right himself, and before even fully standing he landed an off-angle punch directly on Charles' chest. It had little effect. The drunk felt fingers scrabbling on his scalp and then his gripped head bounced off the brick wall, hard enough to knock him out, probably not so hard to crack open that skull. He dropped like a sack and didn't move.

While Charles had seen to the drunk, the man now no longer with a bottle, had gotten to one knee. From that low and braced position he threw and landed an uppercut to his groin. The pain arrived higher than where he'd been hit; his stomach quickly felt hollow-sick. He wheezed and bent partways over and coughed more than once and that man got to standing and sent a left hook just back of Charles' temple. That rattled him. His vision blackened. It almost faded out entirely. He managed to straighten up in time to see the man swinging a right hook. He dodged that hook not by moving away but by moving even closer to his opponent—the same counterintuitive evasion his son would one day use to confound a swiping bear—and in dodging the punch with a forward motion he used its momentum to deliver home a nasty headbutt. Just brutal. Barred even in modern cage fighting. Where his cropped hairline met his forehead, right at the aptly named widow's peak, he landed with devastating impact a headbutt to the man's nose.

The man's nose broke horizontally along its bridge and from that particular fracture little blood came, while from his nostrils it flowed profusely like some gothic fountain. His eyes watered up heavily as they tend to do from a struck nose, and though still standing he was effectively incapacitated. He was breathing heavily through his gaping mouth where blood over his upper lip thickly poured. His heavy exhales sprayed little blood drops into the air. To that ugly and gaping mouth, the trapper's father landed a straight right. Two top teeth broke away from their gum and flew as if possessed to the back of the man's mouth. He choked, both from the force of the blow and also out of a reactionary spasm to not swallow his incisors. He dropped to one knee. Then the other.

In his kneeled and dizzy state he was fully at the will of a man whose violence was of the worst kind: you might neutralize an aggressor whose actions arise from an urge to steal or defend—just give him what he wants or leave him alone. Harder to restrain a man who fights for the love of the fight.

The kneeling man was too absorbed with the fatness of his mouth to feel the cold concrete against his knees. He tongued his cratered gums. He had enough faculty to consider whether he should spit out the teeth, or squirrel them to a cheek for safekeeping and reassembly. He should have applied that faculty to wiping his bleary eyes and throwing up his arms in protest or protection from the heavy boot coming towards his head.

Whether this man by saying those dirty and racist words was deserving of this other man's boot; and whether this man would have broken that beer bottle on the other man's head and then tried to slit his throat; and whether this man was just a by-product of his environment and history; and whether this man was just an unfair target for misplaced rage by another drunk who had recently lost so very much and failed himself as well his family—his head looked like a football that though it had burst its stitching was still waiting to be kicked. The buzzing fluorescent sign overhead hued this man's face weeping blood in a tinge of green. To the man indulging his anger: *Green for go.* He might just punt that broken head now choking on its own teeth clear off its stump.

Charles deliberately took two steps back so as to deliver the kick with his more adept right foot. Such a subtle consideration in the intensity of this moment is only for those who are not short-circuited by impulse. His violence was thoughtful.

The injured man slightly leaned forward, more likely from pain than prayer. But if he was in fact praying, his devout pose only gave the kicker a better angle.

Like a placekicker Charles pointed the fingers of his lead left hand at the man's head. Then something in his head told him not to. Then something in his head told him to. He listened to that one. He took the first step towards the bowed man while lagging his loaded kicking leg and his eyes are narrow for violent acts and he sights them on the leaking skull and closer now his left hand raises a bit to fully jack that boot swing and he sweeps that strong and loaded leg just above the concrete towards its cranial target and he puts all his effort into the kick now halfway delivered and building speed and then feels two strong and arresting arms around his chest. He hears a word too short to hold much of its speaker's accent: "No!"

The arms under the jean jacket of that logger had a thing or two in common with the trees they felled. "No." A thick Ukrainian spoke that word again with not such a thick accent. "He's not worth it."

It was cold outside. So cold. Cold enough to freeze this frame. The green lighting could almost hue these men as not so different trees in some peculiar wilderness.

WOODS

He lifted the towel covering the bowl and the fragrance was sweet. The dough had risen higher at its centre, tiny bubbles pockmarking its skin. His Raynaud's hands often white were a baker's blessing, as less dough stuck to those cool digits. He handled the dough delicately; any undue pressure would deflate it and further limit its total rise. He tipped the bowl then eased out its pillowy contents. Stretched the far side of the dough outwards then folded that wing back over on itself, then same for the left and right sides. For the closest side to him, he stretched it and elongated it greater than the others and wrapped that dough sheet over the entire top of the dough ball, like a big bottom lip swallowing its head. He kept shaping that gaseous mound along the wood counter. It lightly stuck to the counter and that friction allowed him to draw the boule tighter and the dough to mound up taller. He dusted down more flour to its top, then deftly gathered it up and eased it to the proofing banneton basket. He set it closer to the warmth of the stove for its final proofing stage. With an iron poker he raked the coals flat and he put the heavy and empty cast iron Dutch oven directly on the coal bed.

A couple hours to kill. *Not to kill*, he corrected himself, *just a couple hours*. He took a book and sat by the window, just outside of the table's event horizon. The effort of pretending to ignore those items of keen attachment was approximating the effort it might take to face them. He'd made no progress on what to do with them and dreaded the confrontation and figured he'd already considered all available options and had ruled each one out.

Reflecting back on the sauna, he knew some of what he had been doing in there had roots in one of his guided hunts years ago. A client had challenged him to go a minute without a thought. He'd talked with that client about it during the following days, had talked about it years later with his wife, with his boy too: Just watch your mind. *Watch it?* Yeah, watch it, but tell me if you have a thought. *There, I had one. I think. Do pictures count?* Yeah, they count as thoughts. *Oh...then I had one, I saw a squirrel.* That boy.

· · · · ● · ● · · · ·

Wearing thick oven mitts he withdrew the Dutch oven from the stove then placed it on top. When he lifted its lid a small cloud of smoke rose. Wanting to not lose the heat he moved swiftly and shed the mitts and in his left hand picked up the basket now with a fully proofed and risen dough all rotund and pillowy, and he placed his right hand palm-side down stretched wide over the top of the dough. He tipped the basket upside down into his supporting right hand but very gently. He set down the banneton and got his other hand underneath that precarious pillow. The pot walls were deep and scorching hot and it was Gran who'd taught him these tricks and Gran who'd taught him how to carefully lower it and Gran who'd teasingly laughed at the boy when he singed his paws most times he tried. There are those with the pedagogical belief that positive reinforcement is a better teacher than negative punishment. But that boy still part of the trapper here could testify to the acute lesson of singed skin. He lowered with full concentration the dough into the iron pot, nearly as wide as that unbaked boule itself. The heat on his fingers and hands. His nails grazed the bottom and then he eased his fingers out from under the loaf and retreated them between the dough and the hot walls. He unclipped his knife without looking at it and thumbed the blade open and slashed the dough four times to score its top in a hash. Zorro got his start as a baker. Lid returned. Dutch oven laid to bake on the coals. Book in hand, back pretending to read.

· · · ● · ● · ● · · ·

Under the bottom of the hot loaf he played his fingers like piano keys. The tightening crust sang small snaps and cracks as it cooled. He listened to its tiny music. Its surface a Scandinavian pageant: mostly blondes, some brunettes, occasionally darker. Where he'd scored the top of the loaf, it had expanded in the slashes and that square island hash, one shade lighter than a char, had curled up at its edges. Thin and caramelized crust with aromas of tang and sweetness. The incredible fragrance of fresh bread. One of life's best smells. He could go to any corner of the cabin, even the porch, even the loft—though of course he would not—and he'd be in a cloud of this sacred aroma. He asked himself what else even compares. *Coffee. The smell of rain in the spring.* It's not pretentious to say the spring because fragrances trapped all winter in the soil are finally hydrated by the rain and released from the earth so it is in fact a spring rain which is more fragrant than a summer or fall one. *What else? Fall leaves,* he said. *Yes. Red and orange and yellow fallen leaves in the fall, that smells like fall. Fall is your world. What else?* A woman. *Yeah.* That woman. *Yes. The smell of her hair. Of her skin. Her skin. Turn back,* he told himself, *your world is all landmines.*

Nearly lost in a reverie like a corn maze where every cob was a face from the past, it was the loaf burning his fingers that returned him from his daze. He tapped at the bottom's centre. Had it sounded dense and flat he'd have returned it to bake, but that thump sounded hollow as a drum. He set the bread in the empty dishrack so its crumb would continue forming up and its flavours would further enhance. The smells were intoxicating and so he left the cabin as he knew he'd cave. On his way out he took the last nub of crust from the old loaf to the porch to feed the bird.

He stepped out onto the porch, leaving the cabin and its reveristic wormhole. He watched an icicle hanging from the roof sweat its existence. The rays warm on his hands. On his face. His face involuntarily melting of its frown. The rays stopped at his skin; their shine was not so penetrative as to thaw his soul's wintry discontent.

It was silly and maybe it was stupid and it was just a bird that he was anthropomorphizing. He could acknowledge that the part of himself which earlier had noted that his sympathy for the avian critter was masking an attempt to bring the boy back had sleuthed something. Some sort of conflation of kindness and an affection that coloured outside the lines of the shape of his son. But still. The opportunity for a mostly harmless distraction and a little selfless deed and tiny company of his new whisky pal was, to this broken man, rattled and spiritually shook, in this moment...it was not nothing. So why belittle life's unexpected simple pleasures? Lately, finding moments of relative levity and any pleasure in life at all made him feel guilty, pleasures that included the sight of the sun, and the smells of and appetite for fresh bread. *The boy loved bread*, a part of himself reminded. But he was convinced there was enough pain in the world already and he wanted less of that. So with strenuous fidelity to his value of kindness, he tried to be nice—even to himself. That was not so easy. *Stop framing it as whether you deserve it or not. Whether you're guilty or sorry enough. Whether bread should smell like bread or decay. Your skin's starting to look like scar tissue entirely, so just go easy on the self-inflicted wounds for a minute.* The broken man agreed to just accept any small pleasures if they came. One more prescription on his lengthening list of medicines. He walked the last nub of crust to the porch corner to feed the bird.

The bird was gone.

TOWN

Two young men sat at a table in the small town's only bar. It was the afternoon. They each ordered a beer. Three young men were sitting at another table nearby. Each of those three were drinking a beer.

A man at the table of two, whose camouflage hat sported a heavily curved brim, was talking to his buddy. "I was out with the .410 this morning and almost stepped on this grouse before it flapped up. I shouldered the shotgun and put the bead on it. Led it some. I was about to pull the trigger but a stand of alders blocked my line. Shit. Me and King Digger walked all morning and only heard one more. Never saw it though. Just out there beating his wings on his chest. Sounded pretty cool. Just me and the dog in the morning listening to that bird. Sounded like some sacred drum."

One of the young men from the table of three turned his chair partways out and it screeched on the floor. "Don't say that."

"What?"

"You know what."

The guy with the curved hat looked at his buddy, then back to the other table. "Actually, I don't."

"Sacred drum. Don't say that." He was skinny with a red bandana.

"Why not?"

"Fuck that. 'Cause it's not yours. Not unless you're from here. Are you local? You don't look like local."

"Lived here thirteen years."

"That's not local, bro."

"Alright. What's local?"

"Local is born, bro. It's blood." He pointed to the two others at his table who were staring and quiet. He pointed to his cheeks. "It looks like this." He pulled up a sleeve of the sports jersey he was wearing and slapped his bare skin. "It's bones and buried bones. Local looks like me," he pointed to himself. "Not you," he pointed to both of them at the other table. He kept his eyes on the young man with the curved hat and raised his beer and his fingers were tattooed. He drank and set it down. "So you from here? 'Cause it don't look like it. And if you're not from here you're trespassing."

The curved brim watched him then looked at the guy's buddies then back to him. "So you speak for everyone at your table?"

"Fuck yeah I do."

The other two neither nodded nor shook their head.

"You speak for everyone in your family?"

"Fuckin' rights."

"And your people?"

He nodded up and down. "For *my* people."

"We see that differently. Nobody speaks for someone else. There's only people: early and later ones, dead ones and alive ones. Too many differences *within* groups for there to *be* groups. Too many similarities *between* groups for there to *be* groups. Someone took something from someone else. Yeah. And before that, someone else took it from someone else. Same thing before that. Early and later. Early enough we're all the same monkeys. It's just land and water and then more land and more water. And what if someone is told they belong to one group but disagree with their group's beliefs? Then what? They don't get a voice? Someone speaks for them? Nah. How do you know who I am? How do you know what's in my bones, that my family didn't have an old drum they played at births and funerals and rights of passage? How many cultures do that? Only yours? What does it matter if it's only yours anyways? One group invents a lightbulb, another can't use that? Makes a pizza, others can't eat it?"

Buddy of curved hat was watching his friend.

"What if I was adopted into something? What if I don't know my ancestors or who slept with who where? I need to get my blood taken so someone can tell me what I can say? What instrument I can play? Nah. It's just people. Nobody speaks for everyone. And hard as it may be for you to hear it, this land itself doesn't recognize your claims against it, and borders are just made up. Yeah I'm local. Local to rocks and trees and blood and skin and water and sky. Keep telling me who I am and what I'm allowed to say and who you are and how we differ. I say I'm a human being. Looking at a human being. Not some category. Bro, *I'm you*."

"Fuck you you're me." The red bandana got up and one of his buddies did too, and then the other also did. They walked over to the table of two. Those two stood up to meet them. All standing now.

The young man with the red bandana was in front of the two bigger guys who hadn't spoken. The young man with the curved hat squared up to face the skinny one. Everyone so close but only the two young men that had done the talking had veins throbbing at the side of their necks.

Red bandana said, "Say that shit when all your ancestors died from disease and your mom was raped in a Christian school and you got put onto a piece of land you don't get to own and you couldn't leave and people starved to death. You're ignorant as fuck. *Starved to death*. Are you even listening? And for all the talk and sorries you still can't drink the fucking water. Then tell me we're all just the same people. Bro. I'm not you. Not even fucking close." Red bandana took a step closer and there wasn't a full step to take.

Curved hat said, "Here's my category, my people, my blood, my fucking bones: Someone did something wrong, I'm on the side of righting it. Someone falls down, I help them up. Someone cuts a tree, I plant another." He said those words like an anthem stirring enough it didn't need music. He looked from the left one who was big to the right one who was bigger then to the skinny one in the centre with a red bandana. Neck veins bulging on the two young men staring at one another and at the top of their breaths their chest's touching. One of the big guys from behind just faintly looked to the other one.

Then one of the young men brought a hand up.

WOODS

THE TRAPPER IN HIS own way was trying to make peace with the past. Fire helped. This evening was very cold and tonight he'd lit eight of them. This one at his knees was still too small to even warm his hands by, and only made early fire sounds of cracking. The winter sun was just setting and the snow lightly falling and as the fire grew he listened to the occasional flake whispering its goodbye in the flames.

From where he stood in land cleared of forest he could see the other seven he'd lit that cold evening. Each separated by about fifty feet. The first no longer had flames and the flames of the second barely licked up above the footprint of snow they'd blackened. Each of the other fires with flames sized symmetrically larger to where he stood watching this one most recently lit. This one quite large now and its tattered flames flapped angrily where they reached into the winter sky. Sparks flying off into the night like burning little bees. Do not tell them that their futile race brightening their glow is only fueling their demise.

This fire was now bigger than him and its sounds increased from cracks to include loud pops and it had started to draw and draft the air making sounds of wind and its volume so loud it silenced the cries of dying snowflakes.

The trapper stared at the core of the fire. If it could feed on hatred and loathing and doubt and scared and regret he figured he could keep it going long after it burned up all the wood. The list of what he didn't hate shorter than what he did, and of the hate-list, he himself topped it. But he knew that even for a fire of this size, his volume of black purge would be too great; if he let upwell all the darkness inside him he would look like he'd been struck in the mouth with a pickaxe by someone digging for oil, and his face would become a spigot spraying crude—crude thoughts, crude words. Yet if somehow the fire could take it all, the volume of that thick anguish would swell the burn so large it might just torch the sky, melt the stars to drip from the firmament like foundry slag. And if the fire couldn't consume all his unwell, the dark oil inside him made from dead things would drown those northern lands in a vast choking swamp and the hiss of the flames dying in the pool of spent black vomit would be so loud it would deafen any life it didn't drown.

Now he and all the area around him were illuminated in a wild orange lighting. Beside him, a bag of stars. As if a moment ago he had reached up and plucked from the sky those glowing points of reference no longer useful in navigation, sticking those obsolete celestial bodies in a bag. He looked at the bag. The bag glowed.

Had there been trees close to a fire of this ferocity, the heat itself, not even requiring a mischievous spark, would have ignited them where they stood. Huge trees, their bark never licked by a single flame, turning to lit matchsticks in an instant before one's eyes: *woof*. The fire's devilry would call forth those incendiary dogs of hell: *woof*, another tree enflamed. Like black magic in the night.

But there were no trees close by as they'd been cut down long ago to build the lodge and its seven cabins. *Scour his mind by scorching that earth*. Made some sense to him.

· · · ● · ● ● · · ·

Earlier that afternoon it was already one of the longest days of his life. A most recent night of little sleep, and the night's torments lingering in the day. Traumatic aftershock of severe loss, and carried on his shoulders was the weight of bereavement greater than the quantity of stones he'd piled to mark their graves. Side of his head in bandages and the wrist still wrapped from the vein he'd pricked with a broadhead four days ago. His body still smouldering on the inside from the sauna, not from its heat but from dredging up his life's worst failings and gross insecurities in some DIY therapy session gone awry. The coming night with its potential to reach new dimensions in anguish was not far off and if it was going to be anything like the night before, he did fear it. After baking the bread, he had returned from filling the jug with creek water, passing the birdless porch, and sat down in the cabin beside a chair without a child. That table of talismans loomed large. He closed his responsive eye to open up to the anguish he felt so very total. He only heard the stove. That slow burn. The burn of the fire. He opened his eye.

He hiked for three hours and arrived at the lodge and its cabins. The evening was very cold and he lit seven fires and not because the evening was cold. He opened the door of the biggest cabin, what they once called the lodge. He could smell the past and he wanted to walk in and he almost did.

He wedged a thick roll of birch bark under the cabin's open door then he pulled a match from his pants pocket. Before he changed his mind by heeding to a part of it strongly advising against this, he set the phosphorus tip to the doorsill and drew the match along the threshold. Looked like he was drawing a line. The match sparkled. He touched the flame to an inner curl of the bark. The flames grew inside the curl and then the whole papery roll was burning. The flames at first timid with youth tentatively explored the base of the door, as if unbelieving they were actually allowed to play.

He felt many emotions but all of them variations of distress and all from distinct psychic afflictions. The trapper breathed in deeply, then he blew out measuredly from his belly. Trying to exhale shame and sadness and regret and scared and lonely and broken and fear. He made a long wordless apology to many people. The fire seemed eager to receive it.

He stepped back to the snow beside his backpack. He considered just shouldering it up and taking his bag of stars and returning to his cabin. The open doorway to the lodge was dark and the flames burned around its border like some kind of flaming portal. He considered walking through it, seeing where it took him. No greater mystery. *Why wait for such exploration?*

The growing fire flapped its frayed red flannel cuffs and its tattered flames reached high into the dark sky. Sparks swarmed upwards from a torched hive like flaming bits of what was. The pine of the lodge so very old—dry as bones—and embedded in its woodgrain were dust and dead memories. His cut and bandaged eye shaping half his visible world narrow and burning.

He breathed slowly through his nose and paid very close attention to the fire. Felt it hot on his face. Listened to the burn, its volume increasing. At first it only made mild pops and cracks, like record player static. Now came wind sounds, drafts and draws of air. He'd sat beside a thousand fires and for the first time he heard, very clearly, sounds of rain patter coming from inside it. *Unmistakably, rain patter.* But if this fire had them then they all had them. The sounds of the fire now almost a baleful storm with churning winds and heavy rain and loud cracks.

He opened his eye and saw no record player and no rain and no storm. Everything flames. The fire had matured significantly, its breadth grown wide as its flames engulfed the tinderous lodge. A fire this size wasn't meant to warm or cook or light a path—only consume, to change one thing into another.

Again the heat became too much and he stepped backwards from this inferno while taking his pack with him. He loosened the bag's drawcord and its contents glowed so brightly all the sky's stars snuffed out and it faded out the firelight and he vaguely recalled an old vague dream. One where he walked and slipped, for his soles had no traction on ice the winter winds had polished smooth as temple marble. The opened bag was like a vacuum that stole the firestorm's thunder. His world for a spell gone silent.

Cremations are ceremonies of reverence. He kneeled.

This is a thing of love, he told himself. *Reverence and love. Put things where they belong.* Old stars and heavenly bodies laid to rest because navigating by their celestial light would only lead wayward this traveller who must set out on new journeys. If he buried them he'd only dig them back up. Their pull too strong to live beside. Their shine too bright to live beneath.

He removed the items one by one and placed them side by side on the snow between him and the fire.

He took up a wooden cooking spoon of Gran's. She had cooked with it almost daily and threatened his ass with it about the same. Small lines in the spoon's darker concave. The top of its long handle with an old chip. *If Gran was here she'd likely say it was from the last boy who'd spoken when he ought to have listened—which was always—so she'd thumped him one.* He kissed the back of the spoon, and would have laid it on the coals but the intense heat prevented that intimacy; his lob was gentle and affectionate. The fire took it within its folds.

His deliberate and slow gestures bordered on formality, giving the appearance this offering was a tradition long practised, a Japanese tea ceremony of peace-making with the past.

Blue bandana. Both Granddad and his wolfdog used to take turns wearing it. Granddad sometimes wearing it around his head or neck, sometimes tying it around Seven's neck. The trapper had it wrapped around his fist now and actually wished he himself had worn it once in a while and wasn't sure why he never did. Even liked the faded colour. He unwrapped it. He smelled it. Just smelled of the cabin. He kissed it. To send it to the fire he'd have to scrunch it up and he didn't feel right doing that so he folded it into a square like a flag for the burial of a fallen soldier and he got up and took two steps and thought his eyebrows might alight and held his arm in front of his face and spun the square to the flames.

He took out the deck of Bicycle-brand playing cards worn at their edges from years of shuffling, their spines pliant as a yogi from years of bridges. He removed the doubled-up elastic band. Then he cut the deck, why not. Didn't look right away. *What card would be most fitting? Queen of hearts if this night could be more cruel. King of hearts for irony. Joker for reality.* He turned the card and looked. It was just some middling card of clubs.

Then he thought perhaps that was most fitting. He wholed the deck to his right hand and held it by its narrower ends, arching it loaded, that yogi bending his belly outwards. Then fifty-four cards flew firewards and the fire's draft so strong it actually lifted some cards upwards where they lit before they landed. The thought of kissing the cards didn't occur to him. A few cards didn't make it all the way and they now looked like little paving stones laid between him and the fire. Like steps of the common path for ruined gamblers. The final card or two of that path themselves burning. It looked like only minutes ago one could have been witness to some damned game of chance, the players now departed. Maybe souls had been gambled. Heard He walks among us. Heard He doesn't lose often. Heard He's yet to lose.

His mother was a selfless woman. She enjoyed working in the garden and she was fond of a few poetry books, but for the trapper, any of those items just didn't seem charged with her aura. And he was less inclined to burn a book anyways. She loved her family most of all, but save for one, that was all gone anyways and he'd already considered walking into the fire but had for right now ruled that out. So he just brought his lips to his fingers and blew that kiss to the fire now grown too large to heed his wishes.

Two remaining items between him and the big flames and he wondered if they would even ignite because they were both made of lead. He picked up in his hands a black-and-white, sun-worn picture in its metal frame. The glass was missing. He saw her in that faded photo crystal clear. He saw in its monochrome his wife in full colour. Full colour. Tell him otherwise. Shoulders defined as if drawn with the finest pencil sharpened by a surgeon's scalpel. Individual strands of hair, even. He watched a few of them move like caught in a wind. Could have been heat warp. The sun had long ago taken her neck's freckle, but his mind of that dot was not spotless at all. Bleach his soul, burn his eyes, sandpaper his memory—he'd know her or he'd know nothing at all. He was convinced she would always be free from time's twist and erasure. Living eyes. Living smile. Smile that when he saw it for the first time he saw she was smiling soft enough to crack stone. His heart now cracked, crumbled. Always the same. Never easier. He kept holding the picture. He looked to the fire. This seemed some terrible betrayal and part of him knew for certain it was. He had vowed *always*. He hadn't said till death—he had vowed *forever*. Doesn't matter if it was the false promise from a young man whose ignorant self-assurance had him believing his love was too strong for even time to bind. He had said it and meant it.

The little trapper inside his head was shaking in rage and nearly convulsing with threats and hardly making sense and each of his thumbs were set precariously on the red trigger and he says, *I dare you. I fucking dare you.* The big man all torn up and had he not already broken the frame's glass during one night's rampage he might have been convinced to shatter it on his knee and unwrap his tied wrist and take a shard and finish the job proper.

Teared-up eyes and torn insides he crawled forward under the heat, not entirely sure what he'd do when he got there. But most of him understood he wasn't putting her to the flames, he was returning her for safekeeping to the place where they'd first met. He withdrew his hand, now empty. On his knuckles all the little hairs curled then melted away and the fabric covering his wrist was on fire. He moved backwards retracing his crawl and with his hands in the snow he inadvertently extinguished the flame.

The little trapper inside him had seen enough and knew the greater whole could not be salvaged, so with kamikaze conviction he bowed his head then pressed the red detonation button.

Nothing happened.

Inside the trapper another fraction had been quietly sobbing, kneeling beside an empty bed in the loft of his mind. Her falling tears had soaked the explosives and shorted the detonation circuits.

He took some time to regroup but he didn't regroup so he just carried on.

Last item. The boy's red mitts that Gran had knitted that he himself had worn as a boy. One time the trapper came in from the sauna and the boy was sitting in a chair wearing the red mitts and reading a book. He asked him why he was naked, and the boy said 'cause I got hot. He asked him why he was wearing just the mitts then, and the boy looked at him like that was

the most stupid question he'd ever heard. "Because I got cold."
That boy. Those mitts. This kid killed him sometimes. If this
man were in some eternal recurrence, forced to go on cremating
the past every night again and again, probably nine out of ten
times those soft red mitts would be tearing through his chest
for his heart. But that tender little memory that had arrived
unwilled on its own just kinda swelled him up with stupid love,
and yeah he was crying and yeah he held each one in a hand with
their cuffs facing outwards so it looked like there was someone
wearing those mitts right then, but kinda looked not so much
like someone pulling him, as someone holding him back from
the flames.

He placed the left mitt that Gran had knitted overtop the
right mitt that Gran had knitted then handed them to the fire.
The red of the flames and the red of the mitts. Like their ending
had been foretold in the colour of their fabric. Slow to take, or
just slow to show it.

They took. They were taken. They were gone. Mostly, in that
moment, so was he.

He stayed kneeling, looking like a penitent who was dissatis-
fied with the lashing he'd just taken and so was waiting for more,
and if he didn't receive more he'd taunt and blaspheme whatever
and whomever it took—call the mother of god a whore—until
sufficient brutality was administered to his prostrate back. He
closed his good eye from the fire to spend a moment with his
internal burning world.

He stood up and took off his jacket, dropped it to the snow. Unbuttoned his flannel shirt and dropped it also. Boots, pants, and the rest until his only remaining clothing was a charred strip of fabric tied around his left wrist. The fire hot on his belly and the snow cold on his feet. Watching that torrent of flames. From disbelief and anguish and anger, the man's mouth was slightly agape.

The fire moaned loudly, likely some heavy beam twisting in the flames, but his half-open mouth like he'd groaned it, or that they'd howled a single elegiac note together.

He loosened the fabric wrapped around his wrist revealing a dried little bead of a scab and he balled up the fabric and threw it to the top of the fire where it unravelled in the current then lit like a sacramental scarf. If he could have, he would have unzipped his skin and stepped out of that flesh pile then folded its limp sleeves and cremated it also. Then just be bones and blood and one-and-a-half eyes.

He turned. The fire so loud. The consuming flames made tempestuous sounds, rageful sounds, like it was fuelled by in-flammatory mistakes and incendiary regret of the combustible past. Like someone above had read the pages of his family's rather poorly fated history and cried tears of gasoline. That blazing backdrop so bright behind him like he'd lit his own dawn with hopes for a new day.

Into the northern woods his naked shadow led the way, like he was following a myth, some hopeful mirage of a newborn man.

TOWN

Someone plugged a coin in the jukebox. The singer's voice was just a medium for the muse and the muse was all the broken hearts singing of lost love. If someone thought their quarter was only buying them a pleasant tune, they were mistaken, 'cause really they were channelling so many lonely spirits.

A man in the bar heard his old lover's voice singing through that of another. He didn't mistake it. When he heard, "Will your restless heart come back to mine on a journey through the past?" he hung his head. Across the room, someone else only kept his head up by tipping back his glass.

The bar got stuffy at times and even during winter a window was often cracked for air. Tonight someone loosened a latch and parted the panes and that melody slipped out into the night. It curled through the air like a ribbon, and as the wind was from the south it blew north.

WOODS

Morning. He had a chunk of sourdough in his hand and was standing on the porch when he heard a faint drone. The buzzing coming from the general direction of the lodge—rather, the remnant smoking embers of the lodge and its cabins. He couldn't see the plane. Its sound had just the slightest perceptible oscillation. When eventually it finished its circling and flew southwards he saw a small Cessna on wheels. He hadn't heard it fly north and thought that meant it hadn't been specially chartered following a confession or the filing of a formal statement.

If one of those boys had gone to the police, the police would have wanted to touch down at the lodge, take a look. So this flight was probably from one of the smaller communities with gravel landing strips farther north. Maybe saw the big fire's residual smoke, turned for it. Something like that, he figured. The bread in his hand but he was chewing on how this would play out. *Probably something I should have given some pre-arson thought to.* He was sure there'd be another plane shortly. *This one tells that one.*

This one would report it to the police or the fire department. Or insurance company. Maybe another plane sighting or maybe I get a visitor. No helicopters in that small town. Not last visit anyways. Given I could stand on the small pond, the big lake has to be getting close to frozen over. Either they come now or they'll have to wait a while for it to be thick enough to land skis.

If those two boys didn't confess? He posed himself the question. *Then what? Do I report what happened? If they confessed then inevitably the police will show.*

Every inch of him wanted to just leave it all alone. *The only thing that comes out of telling that story to the police would be more pain. Nothing brings him back. Drag it all out and be mired in it. Barely breathing as it is. Probably they'd want to perform an autopsy even.* The thought revolted him. But the other option was no good either. *Suppose those boys hadn't told the police. When I go to town for supplies the first thing people will ask is, "Where's the boy?" He's sleeping. Sick. At home. Do that for the rest of my life, every year one more strand to the web. And what about the fire? If they point-blank ask about the fire. "Did you start it?" Would they even suspect me? If those boys confess, they'll suspect me. Then what?* He wondered too if he could be charged for abduction or attempted murder.

He rolled all that over and didn't come up with any clear answers. It mostly wasn't fear of reprimand that gave him concern. *Truth*—the seeking of it and living by it—was for him more than a personal value, it was a pathology. Honesty as bedrock and truth for bones. His ethics in that regard and perhaps many regards aligned with the birds and the trees and those other truth-tellers inhabiting the northern world he believed incapable of lies and deceit. He was raised to be like the shield that underlay this land where you always knew where you stood. But anyone to his or her own self can justify most things, and he floated an idea in his head just to hear how it sounded: the fire wasn't lit by a match it was lit by the muzzle flash from the gun that day, and the fire rightly burned the cabins in atonement for the murderers they'd housed, and the fire was an immolation to burn away the part of himself capable of lighting such fires. The fire as karmic rebound: returning a thrown stone.

You don't believe in karma. Some part of him was paying attention.

Those boys would have had a fire the morning they left, he was sure of that. *Newspaper left too close to the stove. A pail of fire-starter, diesel-soaked sawdust, caught a spark. Flames could've jumped from one cabin to the next and burned it all down. That's plausible. I might not even see a visitor and they might not even ask.* The Cessna disappeared southwards. He ate the bread.

· · • · • · · · ·

He was breathing heavy and his muscles were tight. He was planning on heading out for a hike, but first he had to take his

179

medicine. Each of his hands he placed on standing log rounds about two feet in length about two feet apart. His chest was suspended over the ground, raising and lowering with each push-up. It was cold enough for a heavy jacket yet he only wore an undershirt. When he had half his current age he could do fifty push-ups; that last one over the logs was only twenty five and it didn't come easy.

The winter woods looked good. White snow, brown trees. He had started following those big tracks he'd seen yesterday on the way back from the sauna, but he hadn't set out with the most militant intent for pursuit, maybe a stalk later if he was so inclined, or even just a hike. He said to himself he'd rather leave that mythically sized buck to be hunted by the ghost of Granddad. He mentally tipped his hat he wasn't wearing to his Granddad who wasn't there.

He snowshoed through the forest under the morning sun with clean air in his lungs, cheeks red. *Hunt therapy.* He told himself he was in hunt therapy. That didn't make him laugh, but if you put a gun to his head and demanded he confess to whether calling his trip out into the woods that morning 'hunt therapy' could be considered, even in the broadest sense, some type of light joke—like the tiniest of feathers plucked from a runt chickadee tickled for a half second on his smallest toe, kinda diminutive little humour—he'd be forced to say right then: *maybe.*

At times during the day different voices would motivate or reproach or instruct him. Some insights were not spoken, only felt, and the felt-truth of those insights—to the same degree as the voices—were of varying veridicality. Sometimes they got it wrong. And it likely wasn't from an internal dishonesty or cruel intentions. If inside him wasn't just one version on a moody spectrum but in fact distinct self-parts, it seemed like no part had total knowledge of all the others. Not some type of dissociative identity disorder, only an unconfident man staggering with grief, confused by biases and blinders and psychological scars and biological drivers and all the other obscure and convoluting workings of the mind. His only goal was to give the woods his full attention. That's it. Take it a step at a time. Bow in his hand, quiver of arrows: broadheads and bludgeon tips.

He hiked through woods and glades, over contours, up hills and down valleys. He wandered it as through a narrow tree line of eyebrows, a bramble of lashes, treaded carefully the iced ponds of glassy eyes, hiked the soft rise of a cheekbone. He passed a crevasse and stopped to look down into it and there came a draft like a sigh.

There's language to the woods and it's speaking to those capable of listening.

The trapper would at times swear he was hiking in a ventriloquial forest. The wind impersonated the water; the breeze blowing high up in the trees sounded like the big lake surging on the rocky shore. Then as if reciprocating the pretence, the water masqueraded as the wind; for a time he hiked near a riverbank whose flow and churn he mistook more than once for a swirling breeze. A type of odd foreignness imbued what he once knew most intimately. Some sounds arrived offbeat. Compared to former days, his vision of the forest seemed skewed. Once he even minorly rotated his head trying to correct what he perceived to be the slant of the trees. As if the fabric of his world had been pinched and then twisted a degree or two. But it was just his injured eye's impaired optics exacerbated by his lack of sleep and pounding head. He found himself off course. Not recognizing the area, he questioned whether he was exploring old lands with new eyes, or seeing new lands altogether.

A silver sky. A large tree off in the distance. He arrived beneath a leafless red maple. He thought he recognized it, and even naked of its colourful foliage it wasn't much less impressive now. Expansive trunk and widening branches like the arms of a zealot that exclaimed *Behold!* He stared at it. In former times he didn't wonder just what the tree was proselytizing. He did now. It looked like it had grown out of a dream and still had its roots there. His head was straight up and he gazed turning.

He gained some elevation coming up a gradual incline and found the sparsely treed plateau crisscrossed with deer tracks. Deer will often bed on hills and bluffs and use the rising thermals and advantageous view to be alerted of predators in the lower landscape. Wisdom he could never now quiz the boy on.

A poplar trunk in front of him as wide as his waist. He lowered his pack and took out old tree climbing equipment his dad and granddad had first used ages ago to clear the land while building the cabins. They'd since employed it to top a couple trees whose storm-damaged upper halves threatened a cabin. Sometimes he had used the climbing equipment to hunt. Fifty-year-old leather and steel properly kept doesn't degrade any. In fact it had improved, all supple and shaped to his own curves. He stepped into the harness and cinched its waist belt. Stepped each boot onto the climbing spurs' metal shanks that supported his instep and buckled each of their brace to the side of his legs. He tied a twenty-five-foot string from the waist harness to the riser of his bow. The lineman's belt was just a thick rope that connected to one side of his waist harness, and he looped it around the back of the tree, then connected it to the other side of his harness; he now with a loop around the trunk allowing him to rest his weight backwards while keeping secure to the tree. A sharp spur angled out from each boot like a fighting cock. He set one to the thin bark of the poplar and stepped his weight up into it. The spur sank into the tree and he was a foot off the ground—no clink of metal, no scratch of bark. He brought his left boot up and set that spur to the trunk then impaled it the same. The health of the tree could stand it and if he'd seen any signs of decay he'd not have asked it to bear his weight. When he leaned in towards the tree to slacken the lineman's rope, he made sure not to slap the rope against the bark when he raised it higher up its back. Without rushing he climbed quickly.

In two minutes he was twenty feet high. He buckled his backpack around the tree, allowing him access to clothing and water, then pulled up his hunting bow. That height wasn't a full bird's-eye view, but it changed his perspective dramatically. It did look like a new world. Expansive. He took a breath, took in the view. With his binos he started glassing the area methodically, looking for a resting buck beside a tree, looking for antler brown, nose black, eye blink.

Amongst the doe-sized deer tracks he saw many jackrabbit prints. He wondered if you typed "j-a-c-k" in Morse code how similar the dots and dashes would resemble these distinct snow prints: two long ones followed by two smaller ones. He also wondered why all the animals were named Jack and why he hadn't noticed that before.

He was scanning left to right over the North's telegraphy, when right to left he saw the messenger returning. Small hops, not big leaps. Little black nose twitching. Ears like elongated satellite dishes. A broadhead loosed at an animal that size would pin that animal to the ground, ruin the broadhead and maybe the shaft. He unclipped from the side quiver an arrow with a bludgeon tip made to deliver a blunt and lethal force. He drew back and anchored his knuckle below his ear like he'd done a thousand times before and looked through the peep sight tied into the string that captured in its circular vision the bow's single target pin. Floated the tiny green bead centre to the white rabbit's body.

It was the first time he'd drawn his bow since an arrow had nicked his eye and he was disappointed with himself in not having anticipated that of course his right-eye-dominant shooting vision would now be obscured. The bandages were still applied but it wasn't them hindering him it was his half-lowered lid at its new resting position. He tried to open that eye wider and his eyebrows raised but that lid didn't, and now his surprised-looking face befit his mind state. He tilted and turned his head trying to centre the window that connected his thinking world to his witnessed one. But his head's articulations altered his form and so too the precise alignment of eye–peep–pin–prey. Whether or not they look it, hunting bows are sensitive instruments.

The trapper had his eyebrows wiggling like earthworms and it's a good thing this massive great-horned owl swooping down had other interests. The only bird of prey known to have killed a human. Her brown talons curved like sickles. Her six-foot wingspan outstretched from a body longer than two feet, and she was cruising in right to left so he hadn't yet seen her like the rabbit hadn't yet seen her. She didn't flap, she coasted. A silent killer worthy of emulation. The grey and white of her huge wings broken up by black horizontal bars, as if she was flying on a frequency that the rabbit even with its dish satellites could not pick up. Her unblinking yellow eyes a hue that even the most haunting of moons could only aspire to colour itself, and she was gradually angling downwards silently coasting through the trees.

He had the bow up looking at the rabbit when all of a sudden his restricted sight window got entirely feathered. One of his eyes widened.

Close to the snow the owl flared her wings and lowered her talons and pierced the back of her aloof prey in eight places. In a flurry of feathers she swept her strong brown wings, brushing the snow below her, painting a pagan mural of her own legend. She lifted that doomed hare kicking its big pads, as if the rabbit itself was climbing up into the sky. She squeezed her sunk sickles and clipped the rabbit's spine. The limp and back-broken hare kicked no more as they flew low and away into the forest. The trapper still looking through the peep watching them go.

He descended. He hiked. He had fought off memories all day and now he was tired. Where he trekked now was where he had hiked only weeks ago with the boy. Where they had stopped about a few months—maybe a year ago—to eat pemmican. Where a lifetime ago he and his boy had been out hunting and he tried to have the kid observe his own mind. *Just watch it?* the boy asked. Yeah watch it. Once upon a time a millennium ago he had wondered if the very land they walked on could speak, if every other step it might cry. He didn't wonder that anymore.

Snow began falling. He trekked homewards and tried to keep focus, but often found himself hiking through the deep forest of his own memories, a woods of shadow and echo and doubt. He walked a narrow ridge where bedrock, in some Jurassic effort, had broken through the Earth's skin. He misplaced a boot on a thin patch of frosted moss and slipped but managed to keep his bow from slamming on the frozen rocks by taking the fall on his elbow. His nerves buzzed in pain then numbed his arm. He didn't swear, lying there, he just sighed most heavily.

As if the sky wasn't just coloured silver it was weighted with it, the man was slow to get up. Home was not so close but dusk and the night were.

He was descending a long sloping decline when he sensed something behind him. He was being stalked and he knew it. Not for the first time. This time he didn't turn to draw. He didn't run either as he knew that might trigger some instinctual pursuit in his stalker and he wasn't fast enough to outrun this peak predator and running would only make things worse. It was gaining on him. He did not turn to face it. The night was its country and he should keep on to the cabin. He didn't need to see its shadow or feel its footfalls to know this predator was growing in size, inflated by his present doubts that he hadn't succeeded in cremating the past. Snow fell heavier. Shadows stretched into the night's elastic fears. He now walked in a valley. The bow in his hand, unlike the staff of a prophet, provided little comfort for this man with no belief. Soon a darkness set in so total that he wished before the sun had set they had agreed on its return.

The trapper made it to his cabin and lay down in his cold bed. He did sleep but his body twitched the night through, as if his nerves were being plucked in a macabre performance by two dueling harpists. A finger and a toe would curl at once. His back would arch. He sweated the night whole.

A huge goblin shaped itself from out of the land. In two fingers it pinched the little cabin, plucked it from the ground like a vegetable that had lost its roots. It brought the cabin before one of its massive eyes, which were curious but unintelligent. Other monsters were evil but this one, having never been taught right from wrong, was not; the horrible acts it was capable of inflicting were carried out with a certain innocence stemming from its moral ignorance. It watched the twitching man sleep. Huge eye at the window. Had the man woken he might have just thought it was the low rise of some full moon. The beast placed the cabin in its open palm. Then covered that hand with its other—to warm? To protect? It squeezed like it was trying to crack a nut. Inside that crucible the crushed man short on breath turned sweating in his sleep. His dreams were worse.

TOWN

The pilot of the Cessna who had seen the scorched hunting camp must have mentioned it in town. At first the rumours were like small flames twisting in the currents of varying opinions. They would eventually transform from their kindled beginning into a wildfire of speculation.

There was the minority faction who believed it possible for an oil-soaked rag to spontaneously combust—hard to imagine those that proffered that hypothesis actually believed it themselves, more likely just trying to sound smart or appear as one with a mind capable of thinking outside proverbial boxes. Most people took the opinion that Jacob and Dave had started the fire. That theory was the lead contender because for certain that morning the men had started *a* fire to warm the cabin before they flew out, and someone said they had just seen Dave back in town.

But there the adherents to that root theory branched out.

"I bet they didn't close the stove door that morning. Spark hit the ground, spark hit some paper, spark found the kindling. Flames jumped from one cabin to the next. Sure as shit."

Another speculator. "Here's what happened. Most likely." The man began gesticulating with his toothpick. "I can speak to this. I almost burned my own home down last fall from a chimney all soot-choked. You're supposed to sweep it every year. I knew that. I hadn't in four." He shrugged. "Shame on me. Neighbour called—like, not phone-called, Ivanna yelled over—tells me there's flames in the smoke coming outta my chimney! Holy Christ. Didn't know I could still move that fast. I closed the vents up and come out the house and got the garden hose angled up to it. Almost had to call the fire department. And, you know, for a volunteer fire fighter, that would have been embarrassing." He put the toothpick back in his mouth. "Anyways. I bet it caught fire after they left that morning. A spark can smoulder all day up in a chunk of soot then start up that night. Burned up the roof. Flames would be so hot from that old wood it wouldn't take much to start the next cabin even if the wind hadn't done it. I have the boy sweep the chimney twice a year now. Something you might wanna consider." He opened his mouth wide and with his tongue flipped the tooth-pick vertically end over end.

Rumours began spreading around the town with the speed of a flu virus, and similarly mutating into various strains were its theories. A certain unpopular theory was mentioned, not from *thinkers-outside-of-boxes* but *stirrers-of-pots.*

"*He'd* done it," someone said at the gas station while nodding northwards. "I know it, he'd done it. Just watch." Some speculator just happening to be right. Closer to a broken clock telling its perfect truth twice a day—though this clock telling its truth more often than that. He hadn't made some perfectly reasoned deduction, this was more like that long-bearded monkey who from out of that fabled band finally types the complete works of Shakespeare while not understanding a single word.

"Who?" someone asked at the grocery store.

"The trapper," that man grinned at the post office.

"Nah. Not him," someone said at the bar. "Why now?"

"That hunting operation was vacant for a while. Now it's running. Now it burned. His family used to own it. Coincidence? Nope. No way."

"I heard it wasn't running. Just Jacob and Dave were up there. No clients yet. And the trapper worked for prior owners beforehand—right after his family lost it. Why burn it now? It doesn't fit. Just stop your gossiping."

Other theories made more sense and few people really entertained the idea the trapper had started it. Those that brought it up just liked to talk, mostly just unsubstantiated fodder useful for little more than something to chew on while tipping up a Bud—that is, before the coming day when news of the boy's passing would arrive. When that would hit town, a fringe theory could get real popular.

Woods

Sweet rumble. The percolator at dawn. Coffee was on his side—of everything and everyone else he was less certain. Its aroma civilizing the dark. He held that warm mug and sipped that rich elixir like he was drinking his religion. Here was a clandestine little shoal in his world's heavy seas. Maybe he'd be swept off again soon and maybe this morning's early peace wouldn't last. But when nothing really lasts that's hardly a reproach. The horror of night still bled a little into this grey dawn, but there was comfort in the warm orange flames crackling in the stove, the mug warm in his hands, the smell of coffee and fire and his insides warming. The forest at times seemed unfamiliar and the birds were history birds and the sun an accessory to crimes, and when considering the track record of his reckless decisions as well his conflicted impulses, he had low trust in his self. But somehow coffee and the fire had held their ground. He didn't understand why. He didn't dare question why. He just for a little while longer held the white porcelain reef like a ship to its buried anchor.

When enough light from the window had him no longer keeping the dark company, he opened the book in his lap. Its pages held some of the most influential photos in the history of photography, up until its publication date of fifteen, maybe twenty years before. For about a half a cup he hadn't turned the pages. He had seen it before, but also he hadn't. Surrounded by spectators in the middle of a square, sat a man cross-legged. He was on fire. His eyes were closed. His face looked calm. People were watching him from across the square. The monk's face was calm.

· · · ● · ● · · · ·

Two mornings after a fire destroyed the hunting lodge and its cabins, one morning after he saw the small Cessna and wondered if he'd see another plane, he saw another plane: an amphibious Otter, a plane common in the North and ambidextrously designed to touch down on both liquid and land. Its small wheels were folded up above its floats. It flew directly over his cabin and it was heading in the direction of the big lake, the lodge—the former lodge.

Here we go, he thought. *If they came from hearing of the boy's passing they'd be heading to the lake beside the lodge. But if they heard of the burned-up lodge, they'd head there too. Police. Fire inspector. Insurance. Owners.* He considered who might be on the plane. *Likely not those boys. Whoever was in it, if they were going to make the trek from the lodge to the cabin, they'd be hours away. If they were even coming.*

He set two pairs of boots outside the front door. One his own, one the boy's. He dropped some snow onto their laces. Equally unsure of their plan as of his own, but he gave himself the option. A believable story lies in the small details.

····•·•····

The current from the river that fed into the lake beside the hunting outfit kept a long and narrow section of its surface from freezing until later in the winter. The pilot throttled down and lowered his flaps and with the water ahead, he grazed the floats over the ice. The surface changed from hard to fluid and he skimmed the water, reduced power, flared and touched down on a narrow and cold but liquid runway. When he killed the engine the putter petered out into a silence made enormous by its juxtaposition against the engine's roar. He stood at the forward end of the pilot-side pontoon. Of the two police, the younger was out on the other. All three looked at the charred remains, the wisps of smoke, the open land where before stood eight cabins. The two men on the floats each had a wooden paddle in their hands. They began chopping at the ice and stroking through the water. The thin ice separating the plane from the

195

shore broke up in plates that submerged just enough to have their light snow washed clean, re-emerging to the surface as glass sheets. They paddled the Otter to shore.

· · · ● · ● · ● · · · ·

Putting an arrow exactly where he wanted was something that for a long time the trapper had taken for granted. It was grounding to do one thing very well. He had other interests—cooking, gardening, books—but archery was something of a base he could touch back to and being an archer was part of his identity; blinding bullseyes brought a self-assurance. In front of the cabin, he set the bag-target, an old pillowcase stuffed with stained and cut or threadbare towels, shirts and sheets, leaning against a tree.

He walked back twenty yards and nocked an arrow tipped not with a broadhead or bludgeon tip but an intentionally dulled field point. Raised the bow and drew it like a brush stroke over an artist's canvas and lightly anchored his knuckle behind his jaw bone, below his earlobe, and sighted on the obscured bullseye. As if a string were tied to his elbow that pulled his arm smoothly backwards, he squeezed the trigger release and loosed an arrow. The bow pivoted forward in his tensionless grip and the arrow struck the bag: dead centre on the vertical plane, four inches right on the horizontal. That painted dot perfectly unpierced, and so an imaginary deer, depending on which imaginary direction it faced, now hobbling around wounded with an arrow in its gut or leg. He lowered the bow.

He had touched back to his base and his base was gone.

Unquestionably the worst shot he'd made in years. Worse even than he'd seen the boy make over the whole of that last year. He stood there in disbelief. He casually looked around like he was asking if anyone else saw that. *Probably best the boy hadn't seen it, I'd never hear the end of it.* Though the man's wrists were so far free from nickel-plated cuffs, the rest of his body was still shackled to memory. It was time for his medicine.

A skiff of snow lay over the frozen pond. His earlier tracks were covered. He had to grope under the snow to find the abandoned axe before using it to tap on his door to therapy. His toes white on the board. All the rest frigid also. Scrotum under his clasped white hands like he held some prized Turkish date.

The first ice dip had been an attempt at a deep wash: immerse himself in northern serum, snap himself out of his despondent state and zap some life into his zombie mind. This was also that, but also something else. An exercise in self-imposed discomfort. Given misery's constant lurk, it seemed worthwhile to try and evolve his relationship with suffering. Seek out discomfort instead of fearing it. He was curious if he could use the intense cold as training for hardship, prescribe himself regular ice baths as continual reminders of the harshness of life, at once increase his endurance and toughen his skin. He was staring down at that ice hole, him naked and crazy-looking as ever, about to will up some pain to beat life, his tormentor, to the punch.

The calm face on a body lit with flames. The trapper was so cold standing there that his shivering almost caused the photo in his head of the burning monk to shake along with him. He didn't think he'd ever seen anything that impressed him more or that he understood less. He didn't idolize the monk, but that man's actions were truly remarkable. A human set himself on fire then sat without flinching while being eaten away by flames in a charring pile of skin. The trapper, even in this present discomfort, knew that in this icy task he neither was nor would be anywhere near the vicinity of that monk's pain, and yet his clenched jaw had already tightened in anticipation of coming torments.

He told himself this practice will be a recurring reminder of how soft skin is. *Don't forget how quickly you can be made to bleed. Keep death close. And regardless if one day you find some peace, or if even your yesterday just wasn't so bad, a day comes where once again life will be hard or cold or over.* He had realized the folly in expecting constancy in this world of change. There are always icebergs coming no matter how titanic your resolve. He flicked out a floating ice chunk with the axe head.

He stood there a minute longer and wondered how that spiritual savant had done it. *Had he put himself inside some trance-like mental fortress where every repetition of his mantra was one more stacked brick walling him off from the burn? Is that possible? Or was his method the opposite? Maybe by being aware of the minute details of the intense experience he had dissolved it, like bringing your face so close to a picture it becomes meaningless dots on a page. Or did he focus on something very meaningful to him? Some mental image that transported his mind away?*

He didn't unclasp his hands and he didn't lower down. He didn't listen for the world to offer a signal of intervention. He just reluctantly drew in the half of a sigh you don't exhale and went to get some questions answered. He stepped into liquid then sunk into pain.

. . . • . • . . . .

After the horrible polar-bear dip and another sauna session of self-exploration, that like the first, spiralled into deep trauma, he didn't rebandage the cuts at the side of his head. It seemed like the scabs might hold.

He had the compound hunting bow clamped in the vice mounted to the workbench. Allen keys set to hex bolts and the sight, arrow rest, and stabilizer removed. He wanted to start over from a naked bow then build the weapon back up to fit his altered face. He transferred the bow to a homemade press and tightened the chain, which took the tension off the limbs, causing the string and cables to sag. He poked out the peep sight woven into the string. Unhooked the string from the limb posts and unwound all its turns and inspected the full length.

He pulled the string between his fingers to feel for any knicks or frays hidden from his eyes. He twisted it back up, counting the forty-five turns out loud.

He began relaxing the bow press, returning the draw weight to the limbs, the string and cables slowly becoming taught and horizontal. He put the bow back in the vice and clipped a small string-level and trued the bow. Most serious archers shoot a more complicated type of arrow rest, one that drops away when the shot is fired. But he liked the dependability of the simple bristle rest: no moving parts, nothing to fail. He favoured simplicity over a slight increase in performance because reliability was its own increase in performance. He aligned the centre of the whisker-biscuit rest with the bow handle's Berger button then zeroed to its middle hashmark the single-pin sight in his hand, remounted it to the bow and levelled it along its three axes. He was thinking about the bow.

The bow now reset to factory specs but lacking a peep sight. He raised and drew. He positioned his head to allow his hampered eye maximum vision of the bag's red dot. That would be his new shooting form. He pressed the bow, sagged the string, set and repositioned the peep to its new location, then wiped it all down and applied a thin smear of beeswax along the length of the string and massaged the wax to smooth any strayed fibres. He drew the bow again. He'd need some time to break his muscle memory reverting him to old ways. But the new eye–peep–pin–prey alignment looked good and the bow felt good. He actually smiled at that. His lips, not used to that shape, might have cracked if he hadn't already smeared them with the remaining string-wax.

· · · ● · ● · · · ·

The trapper had worked out and ice-dipped and sauna baked, then cleaned up the kitchen and himself. Nobody had shown up yet but he hadn't heard the plane leave, either. He sat on the porch with a book. He had read this book before because he'd read them all before. Words that, though they were written by an Austrian psychiatrist who claimed they were first written by a Russian novelist, sounded in his head like the voice of an old lady. He set the book down but not the last sentence. He couldn't set that down so easily, was unsure if he'd ever read more human triumph in so few letters. A sentence so simple and humble it could get lost on a page. *The only thing I fear is to not be worthy of my suffering*. Similar to the standard that Gran had charged him with when he was a boy. He once complained about his hands blistered from splitting wood and then reached for the bread basket. Gran slapped his paw, not hard but not light, making it sore on both sides. "If you find yourself suffering, now you have a chance to bear it well." Whether she had read the same book or if the same has been said in many books or if she had come to that philosophy on her own after decades of caring for her family, at times, no doubt, while bearing stoically her own discomfort. Not base endurance, not just surviving hardship, but finding something good there. The valour of a person as told by how she faces her darkest moments. He sat with that. With her. His breath rose in the midday air like the smoke of a thinking man's cigar.

Beside him a pair of his boots and a pair of his little ghost's boots. *If the plane held police and they were coming here they'd have to show up soon to make the trek back and fly home before dark. If they know of the boy, they likely wouldn't mention the fire—not right away at least—too trivial compared to the death of a son. If they make small talk, they likely don't know of the boy. Right?* he asked himself. *If they say anything other than 'sorry,' they likely don't know. If they came about the fire, then for sure they'll ask, 'Where's the boy?' Likely first thing. Then what? I laid him down. That's the truth. 'He's sleeping?' they'll ask. Resting, I'll say. In peace, I'll think. 'What happened to your eye?' Archery accident. 'So the little guy's not feeling so good, hey?' I'll say he's felt better. 'Can we see him?' I said he's been laid down, let's just let him rest. 'We'd really like to see him.' No. Sorry. Now fuck off.*

· · · · ● · ● · · · ·

As if his uncertain but growing anticipation manifested his concerns, in the early afternoon he watched two officers appear at the forest edge. Snowshoes, backpacks, winter jackets, toques. Even from the hundred-yard distance he could see their silver badges and belted pistols. Both of them looking his way and the lead officer putting away his GPS. He didn't recognize the younger officer.

Bill was the sergeant of the town's police force. A thin man of small stature, and the strong arm of the law was a rather modest-looking figure. People liked that about him. He was reasonable and he used people's names, even those belligerently drunk, and he always first exhausted the options to defuse an escalation with words, even when physical force would be justified and likely would have been used in another jurisdiction not under his watch. People liked that about him. He was nearing seventy. Through his eyeglasses he was watching a man on the porch. Watched him stand up. Dark hair almost to his shoulders. Longer than Bill had last seen it, much, much longer than Bill had first seen it. It looked combed, like he'd never seen it.

If the trapper watching them trek the final distance to the cabin was concerned about their presence, his face didn't show it. The game of poker modelled life and not the other way around.

He waited for one of them to speak first.

Bill was standing just beyond the porch.

Bill said, "Hello, Ethan."

WOODS

Midday at the cabin and two police officers in snowshoes stood in front of the porch. It was Steve's first year out of the academy and right now he looked even younger, almost like a boy might look while staring at some statue he'd only read of in a textbook. The porch, being two steps higher than the ground, had him looking up at the man he'd only known through rumours. "Hi." Even though that was the second-shortest word in the English language, Steve tripped on it. A second before he said that he almost called him *Trapper*, as if it were a proper noun.

Bill was smiling. "Hello Ethan. Been a few years. We came over to tell you that the lodge and its cabin burned dow— What happened to your eye, son?"

He didn't even know how long it had been since he'd heard his name. It kinda caught him off guard. It sounded like a call from the past. He was wrong about that.

Bill patiently waited for a response. He knew others who lived in the woods and he'd found that it sometimes just helps to pace your demeanour to the often slower behaviours of those living a little isolated. Steve was staring and Bill was looking around. Saw the two sets of boots by the door. He'd met the boy once before at his mother's hospital stay where three arrived and two left. Bill asked still smiling, "Where's your boy, Ethan?"

Standing on his porch, the trapper took a moment. This man just looking at the police. He finally said, "Come inside." Ethan said that.

The cabin was warm and clean. The officers took seats at the living room table and Ethan made fresh coffee. Neither noticed that a section of the stovepipe had been tapped from the inside back out to its original cylindrical form as it only showed the faintest ruffling in the metal where it had once been caved in from punches. If they noticed a small patch of floorboards curiously brightened, they didn't mention it. The stick jutting out from the far wall at about head height, off of which a toque hung, didn't look all that strange—just some redneck hat-hanger. Steve's eye caught a glint from under the stove and he got up and walked over and knelt and picked up a broken arrow tipped with a broadhead, about the only thing out of place in the tidy cabin. He remarked when seeing the dried blood on its edges, "Hunting must be good."

Ethan started the story from his version of the beginning. "My son's dead."

During his account from his best recollection, he described some details as fuzzy, and he acknowledged there were some gaps in the story. It was obvious to the officers that while some particulars were unclear, others were sharper than the speaker would have preferred. When he told of the boy being hit by the bullet, he said the impact came with no sound, just a puff of feathers swirling out of the boy's chest. "Feathers mixed with snowflakes," he said. As if he'd seen it the first time and this time too in slow motion. "His blood in the air like mist." Ethan made a hand gesture. "I watched him drop to his knees." Like the axe chops that earlier in the day broke thin ice, the spiritual blows from that memory watered the surface of Ethan's eyes. He continued and his voice cracked too. He stopped talking. He hadn't noticed he'd balled his fists and neither had Steve. When he was able to continue speaking he did so a bit quicker, as men do when they feel the speed of the telling may keep them from breaking up. His pace matched the part of the story he now told about hurrying to carry the limp boy home.

Ethan went to the loft and came down with the bear cape. He hadn't cremated it and he wasn't sure why. Showed them the hole, not the one he'd stitched up after the boy sent a broadhead through it, the one punched through the hide from a black-magic bullet, that piece of lead that had altered time and changed worlds, even ended them. He told where the boy was laid and nodded to the window and the grave's general direction. He described what he'd wrapped him in, including its colours, and after he said, "that Gran had knitted," he felt silly and childish for being a grown man using words like that. They just came up involuntarily. He said he didn't recall digging the grave nor refilling the soil, only patting the earth smooth. He made those movements over the table. Bill just watched Ethan. Steve and Ethan both watched Ethan's hands. They saw different things. Only one saw those many hand-shaped depressions being slowly filled by snowflakes. He was silent a minute. They all were.

His visitors, like sympathetic listeners, or like good detectives, encouraged the speaker by not interrupting his silence.

"That night I went to their cabin."

Though Ethan had not yet said anything that might require a formal reading of his rights, Bill interjected and advised him of the benefits of legal counsel. Bill then said, "So far, from what you've told us, there'll likely be a charge of murder. Likely involuntary manslaughter."

Ethan shook his head. "It's over. Nothing brings him back. I'm not pressing charges."

"Well. I can understand that. I can. But that's not exactly how these things work. Not when someone is—not in these circumstances."

Bill asked if Ethan could please start the story again and depending how this all played out in town, he may not even have to come into the station or the courts. Bill looked at Steve and pressed his thumb into the air and Steve took out a digital recorder. Ethan started over and told it again with no more, though no less clarity. When he got to the part Bill had interrupted, he continued on and told about the abduction of one of those men from the lodge. Arriving at a certain detail of the story he looked above them and pointed to the rafter beam.

The day before when the Cessna pilot called the police to report the burned cabins, Steve had taken the call. He searched a database for the owners. When he called the first name listed, a number with a non-local area code, that co-owner told Steve that as far as he knew, Jacob and Dave were still up there, scouting the area and fixing things up and making plans to run the hunting outfit in full next year. Steve told the co-owner he'd contact him again when he had more information about the fire or Dave and Jacob. Reading down the list, Steve recognized *Bauer, Jacob*, but not the next name listed as a co-owner, *Miller, Brian*. The last one, *Mosley, Dave*, he did. The first owner saying that Jacob and Dave were still up north corroborated with Steve not seeing those boys around town, and neither he nor Bill saw any reason to make any calls inquiring about them as that would only start people worrying and the town talking. Flying up, though, Bill told Steve they were going to see either two stranded and cold boys, or two burned-up bodies.

Bill asked Ethan if he knew whether it was Dave or Jacob he'd taken that day from the lodge. He said *taken*, not *kidnapped*, not *abducted*. Ethan said he never did know their names. Then

he said, "No. Wait. Dave." He told how Dave had sorta intro-
duced himself as he was leaving. It was him he'd strung up.

Ethan was getting used to his right eye's halved sight, but it
looked mangled enough that Bill, who never got an answer to
his earlier question, brought it up again. Ethan got up and lifted
the toque off the arrow stuck in the wall—the one Jacob sent
that nearly killed him—and Bill just shook his head and Steve
said, "Christ."

He told how it ended with those two walking back to the
lodge that morning, then hearing their plane. Bill asked some
follow-up questions making sure he had all the details clear.
Finally he closed his notebook and the recorder was recording
silence. Ethan was looking out the window. Bill nodded to Steve
without the thumb-button gesture this time and he turned it
off. As he did so, Steve accidentally bumped his mostly empty
coffee mug with his elbow; it fell to the floor and landed loudly
just as Ethan who had been looking more *at* than *out* the window said, "I started the fire."

Steve said, "Shit, sorry," as he bent for the mug.

Only one officer heard words he'd already guessed after having taken in the sight of the smouldering ruins that morning.
When he heard this man tell how he'd been shot in the head with
an arrow by the man who killed his son—a man who owned
some cabins nearby, now only their charred remains, which the
trapper's family had owned on land his family had lost—a small
suspicion had grown to near certainty. Bill had not forgotten

in what manner the lodge's ownership had been lost years ago and he could well recall the picture of that rage. A man only one branch lower on the family tree, where it looked like that family member had torn off that particular branch from that family tree—and it must have been six feet of solid oak—and used it to beat nearly to death another man. Samuel Reed came into the station one morning to file a charge against Charles Edwards, Ethan's father. Reed could barely speak through his fat lips and he lisped from missing teeth and said he was submitting his whole head as evidence. Bill could smell the alcohol on his breath from the night prior. Reed named two others involved in the fight but said they were not filing charges. He and Reed were sitting in his office, the office door open. Yuri Kovalchuk entered the station. Bill told him to come in. Kovalchuk smiled at Reed, already knowing he was there. Said he witnessed a fight last night, said that while looking at Reed. He didn't sit down he said he just wanted to make some facts known. Facts like three against one and one of those three with a bottle as a weapon, he said that still looking at Reed. Bill that morning asked the complainant how he wanted to proceed.

Steve said from under the table, "I got it." His mug secured in his clumsy hand.

Bill looking at Ethan. What he saw was partly shaped by what he had seen when they'd first met. On that day he didn't yet know his name and that young stranger was crying very hard and he was very bloody. He was young, about twenty, maybe thirty seconds old. Ethan shared a birthday with Bill's daughter—a birth date, a birth hour, a birth minute. In that small-town hospital, they shared the same delivery room. The doctor hadn't even time to wash the maternal blood off his hands before he took a few lateral steps and delivered the next. He went from saying *push* to saying *push*. Someone had said, "It's a girl!" and that added some short-term confusion for the other mother who was squeezing out an angry son some people would later call the trapper. Two babies crying, two families smiling, two proud fathers with birth blood still wetting their hands when each man reached out and shook the other's. This nearly sacred moment sealed with a clasp bonded them in some kind of kinship. Could be that's why when Bill and Steve had looked at those black patches of burned cabins, Bill hadn't shared his thoughts on the singed playing cards. *Why would cards be outside the burned cabin?* The only people he posed that question to were himself and the royalty on the faces of those cards lying in the snow.

Steve righted himself and the coffee mug. His face was red from the blood rushing while hanging it low as well the minor embarrassment that comes more easily to a younger man in the presence of older men.

Ethan turned back from the window to see that he'd been heard. Met the senior officer's eyes. He waited for a response, follow-up questions, a formal charge of arson.

Bill nodded slowly, blinked his eyes. "Right. Like we were saying, the lodge has burned down. You might see the insurance company fly up."

Steve was looking at Bill. Then Ethan. There was a bit of an awkward pause.

Bill took off his glasses and cleaned them with his sleeve and said, "My wife sent me up here with muffins. I feel kinda stupid now bringing this up. Above all else, I'm just so terribly sorry about what happened to your boy, Ethan. There's no worse things and I'm truly, deeply sorry." He took a deep breath. "The thing is. If I got home and told Nancy I didn't leave the muffins with you, that she'd baked for you. Well. The world just doesn't need another crime scene and that woman can wield those knitting needles. They oughta come with a permit." He unzipped his backpack leaning against his chair. Placed a Christmas-coloured round tin on the table. He looked at Ethan with a look that might not have been entirely about muffins.

"Steve. Should we start heading back before that lake freezes up and we're stuck up here? Last floatplane trip of the year the pilot said. Maybe he's cooked us up a couple dogs over the lodge's coals."

They filed out of the cabin. The afternoon sky had clouded over. Wasn't snowing but its shade suggested it hadn't ruled it out. A floatplane doesn't land on a lighted runway and they had time for the hike back to the lake beside the lodge and its cabins, then the hour-long flight back to town, but few idle minutes to spare.

Bill pointed at the boy's boots. "You really oughta put those away. Seeing them there won't help you any." Bill said when they got back to town they'd go see Jacob and Dave, and it would be up to Dave to decide if he was pressing charges against Ethan. "As well, if Jacob doesn't confess, you may be required to come in and testify."

Steve asked Ethan if earlier he could see the smoke from the fire and Bill nodded sideways at Steve without looking at him and said first year on duty he thinks he's a detective. Steve looked like he dropped another coffee mug.

"Nothing you need we can have air-dropped?" asked Bill. "Batteries or sugar or whatever? A puppy on a parachute for company? A *Playboy*?" Not a great joke and he knew it, but he was just trying to lighten the atmosphere for what was coming.

"Last thing. And I've been putting off bringing it up." He turned to Ethan. "We need to see him."

Ethan didn't acknowledge the question.

Bill said, "It's not my preference either."

"I'd rather not." Ethan said that civilly.

"I know. I know, son. I'd rather not too. But there is a procedure for these things. Lesser crimes are one thing," he kinda squinted when he said that, "homicide is another. And better now than dragging this out and having to do it later." He nodded in the general direction of the cleared land in front of the cabin with its snow-covered garden. "Or if the ground freezes, us coming back in spring. That won't be any good."

Steve had noticed a shovel leaning against the shed and now walked over to it. Between the cabin and the shed, little wooden trusses for bush beans to climb in the summer had become frameworks catching snow. A few stalks of toppled sunflowers stood above the snow in one corner, plants that self-seeded, originally grown way back as feed for a small brood of chickens. Their big heads like ostriches buried in the snow. The full dimensions of that garden plot were concealed by winter but there was a narrow footpath trampled down the middle. It ended in front of two rock cairns. Those rock piles free of snow. They looked like what they were.

Steve walked from the shed to the rock piles. On the snow in front lay small bouquets of pine and cedar branches, twigs of mountain ash with tiny red berries, frozen and decorative. All their lower stem whittled clear of needles and leaves and bound with a pretty yellow string tied in a bow. A bit closer to Steve were parallel depressions in the snow, like might be made from a bereaved man kneeling. Steve was looking from one pyramidal pile to the other. *Fifty-fifty*, he thought.

Bill speaking to Ethan but looking at the garden said firmly, "Legally we need to."

Ethan said less civilly and more formally, like regurgitating a doctrine, "Better for what's past to stay buried."

"I'm sorry, Ethan. It is the law. We do it now or we do it later. But if we do it now, I may be able to work this out with no autopsy being required."

Of the two rock piles resembling prehistoric eggs, one was slightly smaller. That one had no moss between the stones. Steve noticed that detail, thought maybe this monument was sized accordingly to the smaller human it honoured. He stepped towards it. Didn't intentionally mean to stand overtop of the lying body buried there. He switched his grip on the shovel from single-handed to doubled.

Bill asked softly, "That one, Ethan?" He nodded towards it.

Ethan watched this sacrilege, watched a man standing on the chest of his son. His fractured self not often united was unanimous in correcting this dishonour. He shook his head slowly and he wasn't saying that's not the place, he was saying it was. The only eye he was at liberty to narrow joined the for-ever-squinting other. He sounded outright cold-blooded when he said, "Get the fuck off."

Steve looked to him.

"Leave him be." A voice like a bad man.

A lot of the academy's training is preparing officers to handle confrontations. Even still, Steve was caught off guard by the menace he heard letting him know things had just escalated. Fifty feet separating them and the new cop was beginning to feel on the verge of becoming one more story told in town. For a lawman strapped with a standard issue Glock, that boy's face looked unsure and uncomfortable, holding a shovel uncertain whether to dig it or drop it. His uncertainty only prolonging the offence and provoking the offended. Steve looked to Bill.

That senior officer just casually had his hands resting on his hips, just resting his hands there close to their assorted items—cuffs, pepper spray, collapsible baton, pistol—and likely after this many years he just sometimes rested them there instinctually.

For Ethan, this all came with zero forethought: no intentions, no premeditations. He had no plans to get physical and if later with a cooler head he were to be asked if the two steps he took from the porch towards that officer was a prudent move, he'd likely say of course not. But those steps came from a hundred-million-years' legacy of wild primate genes willing to defend kin that parts of him hadn't fully acknowledged was gone. Those steps were taken to defend blood he hadn't fully admitted had dried. Whether stupid or brave, reactionary or heroic, they were steps taken from one who had in no way fully let go of past duties: *safeguarder of stars*. The past pushed him from behind into two quick steps to prevent this present-day injustice. He'd remove by any means necessary the man who was standing on his boy's chest and that's all he was thinking and all he was sure about in that moment and he made to stride for a third—and maybe by the fourth or fifth he'd have reached for his blade—but all those steps were prevented by the hand that gripped his arm suddenly. He looked first to the veiny hand, then up the arm, then to Bill.

Bill raised his eyes to the afternoon's sky. Then back to Ethan. "Damn," he said. "Aw hell. There he is." Bill said that while looking directly at Ethan. "That's a sad sight and I'm sorry we had to do this. Policy and all. My deepest regrets. You can see the bullet hole. Lying there in his blanket." He spoke loudly and didn't look to Steve. "Steve. Would you call that a blanket?"

Steve hadn't swung the shovel. He seemed a little reluctant to put it down. A year hadn't passed since he'd sworn his oath and pinned his badge and that's not much time to distort that sound or tarnish that shine. This young man who wanted to be a good officer and who in this moment wasn't sure if that meant obeying the chain of command when its links seemed to be pulling you through some moral swampland.

Ethan still in the grasp of Bill turned his gaze to Steve. Steve who had better act now. That junior officer stuck between a pile of rocks at his feet and a couple hard things on the porch. He looked to the parallel depressions of snow in front of his feet. Then to the gravestone pile. Then not to his senior officer. He sighed and went from two hands on the handle to one. Stepped backwards. "I think you'd call it an afghan." He turned from where he stood and walked back on the narrow snow-trampled path to return the shovel. He said with his back turned away, "But it's kinda dirty."

On one side of the scale of justice is a pure and abstract ideal that doesn't suffer corrosion, and against its measure on the other side is set reality: actual dilemmas that entangle imperfect people trying to keep a real peace. Maybe Bill was looking at this man and couldn't help but see baby skin painted in newborn blood mixed with his own child's. Could be as long as the accused would later confess to the crime, digging up the dead boy wasn't really necessary, at this juncture anyways, and was more of an empty formality and it didn't help keep the peace any and he'd rather gamble on that than tell his wife and the town he cuffed this legend standing in the way of exhumation whose hands were still blistered from burying his son. Could be the afternoon was just getting so late. When they left they took the bear cape with them.

TOWN

THE POLICE HAD NOT yet returned from up north. Dave stayed close to home and Sarah, a nurse, was on her days off. A neighbour seeing him over in his backyard asked about his limp and he said he'd caught it on a stove leg and taken an unlucky fall. That was all true, he just left out the part about the cabin-fever-induced brawl with Jacob. Then smiled. Then hobbled back inside.

For three days Jacob hadn't left his apartment, hadn't called the police or the other co-owners. Those co-owners didn't live in town and believing Jacob and Dave were still up north at the lodge, and the police not informing them any differently, they had no reason to call. Jacob hadn't decided what he would do if they did call. Jacob was doing serious geometry trying to consider all the angles. All of them felt like they were trapping him in their corners. *Confess? To the story from a bushed-out hick and a body I never saw? But maybe that looks better. Or deny. Or ignore.* He questioned what to do with himself. Running the outfit was going to be his livelihood and lifestyle and in it all his money was invested. *Call the co-owners and tell them what?* The world was feeling suffocatingly small in his bachelor apartment and he left to try and stretch it out.

Act normal. Nobody knows anything. Figure this shit out.

He walked down the creaking steps of his apartment and turned for the grocery store. When he looked over his shoulder to see the presence he felt, he just saw an empty street. The gorilla-sized monkey hanging off his back must have ducked. In his ear was a light ringing. It had gotten louder on the flight home as if trying to be heard over the drone of the motor. It got even louder after the truck didn't start on that morning he and Dave discussed their plan. Both the cold and the night are good for sound and in the morning, the accusatory tinnitus hadn't diminished. Jacob walking now in town heard it the loudest it had been, as if he were an antenna and was close to the source of broadcast.

On the opposite sidewalk someone was walking his way. He rolled his shoulders inwards, head down.

The person neared. The sound increased.

The person passed. The sound diminished.

Towards him on the same side of the sidewalk came another. *Dammit,* he thought. His neighbour Irene. Jacob considered diverting, but to his left was the street and to his right a row of houses. He set his eyes to the shovelled sidewalk. Normally he shaved but for the past few days he hadn't. *Maybe that's enough.*

His back hunched, less so than an old man, more so than a healthy one. As their distance closed he had his head angled low and he wished he'd worn a hat. At least his frowning brows acted as twin brims over his eyes.

Murderer. Murderer. Murderer, sounded the heels of her boots.

His eyes on her black boots a few paces away now.

Boots stopped. *Fuck*. The left boot turned towards him. Its pointed toe looked like an accusation. To not provoke them, Jacob looked past the boots to the sidewalk where they'd just travelled to let them know he didn't want any trouble and didn't have any time. He kept his body moving to follow the aim of his deliberate and downcast eyes.

Shoulder to shoulder about to pass. She touched his arm. He swore in his head and almost out loud.

"Jacob! I'm sorry to hear what happened."

Jacob stopped. *Shit. What the hell?* He looked up at her.

She saw burden. She couldn't help asking anyways. "Do you know what started it?"

Jacob squinted at her. *Kind of obtuse-ass question is that? What started it.* He was never a big fan of Irene and less so now. *Who asks a question like that?* He wanted to yell at her *That jackass started it when he made the fucking bear cloak. That asshole.* But that line of thought got interrupted. *How the hell did she find out about the shot?*

Irene said, "I was so saddened to hear. Not one cabin left standing, imagine. I'm so sorry, Jacob." She still holding on sympathetically to the arm of his winter jacket. "I know you and Dave were excited about it."

Jacob feigned acceptance of her consolation, mumbling thanks and while gesturing with his body that he needed to go in the direction she'd interrupted.

He didn't go for groceries. He rerouted back to his apartment but not directly, both so that he'd not have to share the walk with Irene, and also to grab a bottle of Crown Royal, lubricate up the strategizing parts of his mind and make soggy those pulsing sounds. Jacob was nearing the steps to his apartment wondering how best to cross-check this fire rumour. *Burned down?*

"Jacob!" The guy across the street raised an arm. "Sorry to hear, man." He looked like he was going to cross but Jacob waved in acknowledgement and turned for the stairs.

Rumour confirmed. Jesus.

Jacob hadn't taken his jacket off. Dave answered the phone saying hey.

"You hear?"

"Hear what?"

"The fucking cabins burned down."

For a couple seconds the phone silence so stark, Dave heard the click of Jacob's fridge turning on.

"What? When?"

"I don't know anymore than that."

"Who told you?"

"The *town* told me. Stick your nose out it's going to tell you too. Did you close the fireplace door when we left?"

A pause. "Did you?"

"Ah for fuck's sake. Or it was him. I'll talk to you later."

Dave on the other end of the dead phone still held it a second.

WOODS

HE SET A FEW seeds on the porch railing while looking for morning life off in the trees. To his right at the forest's edge a thin alder branch started to slightly sway. Then it stopped. Then another branch swayed. That one stopped. The breeze just a rolling small puff of wind. Closer towards him down the tree line rested two birds unmoving, yet to be warmed by the timid dawn. Their silhouettes like replicas of life. Ethan saw their tail feathers tickle up as the breeze tousled them. One of them fluffed its feathers trying to shoo the wind away. Closer towards him some snow grains swirled up into the air as the approaching breeze chased its tail. Then a light blow cooled his already cold cheek and the breeze slipped into his ear.

This early in the morning Ethan was not with many thoughts and the wind blowing through the expanse of his prairie-like mind both found and intimated a barrenness. When Ethan exhaled to rid his head of its message, he shivered, and in that exhale he heard some type of rattle he thought came from his lungs. He put a hand on his chest. By his feet on the frosted porch a frozen leaf cartwheeled. He watched its lonely clatter. The wind continuing on its way swept some strands of his hair out in a small flourish like a matador's cape. A single lost swirl roaming the North. At the far end of the porch railing, some snow grains spun up and away.

The police had brought the prospect of legal closure, of potentially tying up loose ends for good. Being charged with abduction or attempted murder didn't seem so likely given how things were left between him and Dave. He had told Bill of the fire and that was enough to square it with his conscience. But the police visit did inflame a wound. Felt like a gash he'd been trying to close and had already told the doctor he'd gotten all the shrapnel out so just leave it alone, yet the doctor didn't believe him and jabbed and dug his finger all in it, prodding away and loosening up the sutures.

A squirrel climbed up a railing post just then and planted its legs where that little vortex had cleared the snow. Its black button eyes wide. Its body braced. Tiny nose twitching. It looked at the man, at the pile of seeds. It hopped once along the railing. Stopping and hopping. Inquisitive, hesitant, innocent, cute.

It's just a squirrel. Just a squirrel just a squirrel just a squirrel.

It hopped towards him.

You remind me of my boy.

He knew he wasn't supposed to think that and he believed he had been making some progress escaping the past and part of him admonished himself for this back step.

"You remind me of my boy." He said it again now out loud—genuinely to the squirrel, defiantly to himself.

The squirrel reached some invisible border of security. Its whiskered nose sniffing towards the seeds, and whatever it smelled in the man.

Some things are not constrained by form and two things can be the same thing and one thing can be many things. He believed that and had for some time. "Hey little guy." His words didn't seem to frighten the squirrel, just troubled a part of himself.

In a world of mimicry, where fire can sound like rainfall and the wind of rushing water, where pain can smell like cedar, where for him the sun occasionally evoked a certain feminine warmth, hard to fault him for at times seeing one thing in another. Innocence shared by a boy and a bird, a boy and a squirrel. That's not so crazy. A world of resemblance and mergence, where beauty and brilliance sometimes get coloured outside the lines.

But where does that stop? he asked himself. This voice sounded very similar to the one who had said 'cold is cold' and 'water is water' and Ethan believed them to be the same. *Where does that stop?* it asked again. *You take that line of reasoning, you might just end up loving the whole damn world.*

He outstretched his finger and pulled a seed from the pile and pushed it towards the squirrel.

TOWN

JACOB WAS PACING HIS apartment with a tennis ball in his hand. He bounced it off a wall and caught it in his right hand. In his left the ice clinked without spilling.

How does the town know that an isolated lodge and its cabins burned down? He bounced the ball, caught it. *Another plane? Or did the trapper somehow tell the fire department or the police? The guy doesn't seem the type to own a sat-phone. It's gotta be at least a three-day hike from his cabin to town and this would be the worst time to travel it with the lakes half-frozen. No way he made it to town already. Could the police have already gone up there and back? If the town knows, do the police know?* Jacob stayed on that question an extra beat. He checked his cell phone to see if anyone had called and it surprised him nobody had. He wasn't sure if he'd answer. He set it down. It rang. Call display read *Nick*, just a buddy. He didn't answer. Jacob threw the ball, caught it. Drank.

He called Dave and Dave picked it up first ring. Dave said their buddy Larry just called and that he was surprised when Dave picked up because he thought they were still up there. He was just checking in to see if Sarah had heard anything.

Jacob didn't even say goodbye, just hung up. The town was like a giant squid whose two-hundred-fifty residents were all tentacles and the first couple tentacles had begun to probe. Its other arms would soon be coming. The ringing in his ears got a decibel stronger.

Assume the police know about the fire because even if they don't they will soon. Would they go see that asshole if they found out? Jacob threw the ball harder. *Hard to say. Probably not. They might. If they did, what's he gonna do? If the cops go see him, they're going to ask about his kid. How could they not. Shit. So I call the police and tell them we were up at the lodge and now we're back and I say I've heard of the fire and we're going to go check it out. If they haven't already gone up there that keeps them from going. But then one day he does come down. Without the boy.*

He poured another thinking drink and opened the upper compartment of the fridge to its small freezer. Found he was out of ice. So just rye and tap water and the bottle half-drunk already and only buying a mickey was a mistake. He wasn't willing to go correct that mistake. He lay back on the used couch looking up at the ceiling dented from the spearing end of a hockey stick, those noisy assholes above him. Threw the ball up into the air directly above him and it grazed the ceiling and coming down, he missed the catch and took it centre forehead. Spilled his drink. Didn't even swear this time. He was thinking that things were getting away from him. He was wrong. They were already gone.

Woods

Hard to say how long this hatchet had been in their family or where it originated from as its iron wasn't stamped with a year or manufacturer. Before Granddad, for sure. Maybe even before Granddad's granddad. He wished he had asked him. Its current handle was birch and its handle before that was birch. The blade held its edge nicely. Ethan didn't keep it honed like a razor because an edge so thin, regardless of the quality of its iron, would only roll over from chopping. But it was about as sharp as an average chef knife found in a home in an average city. So about butter-knife sharp. The ease with which the metallic wedge slid through the straight grains of cedar and snapped off lengths of thin kindling brought him a satisfying feeling and sound. Aromas of trapped cedar released from the log. His tempo was quick and without hurry, the sounds rhythmic. On the ground beside the splitting block grew a large criss-crossed pile of kindling, tinder dry. He was reflecting on how some simple and common tasks come with an outsized pleasure. Instead of thinking about the next thing that needed to be done or other concerns, there was something worthwhile in this current thing. He got a small satisfaction in that realization, and it also surprised him that he even needed to identify that phenomenon to himself. But maybe epiphanies, both small and large, are easily missed because a person is so often lost in thought. Reflecting on the simple pleasure of paying attention meant he was paying less attention and he managed to bring the blade down on his left hand's index finger. His hand still held the log but it now did so with four and three-quarter fingers. He had chopped it at the base of the cuticle. No blood came yet, just a clean sever. The irony of it all was not lost on him, just his humour was, and he had so very little of that to begin with. He couldn't believe he had just done that. *Ah hell.* He looked about, the day was calm and the sky was clear.

He looked at the finger with its shortened and squared tip. He didn't curse from the pain, he cursed at his own stupidity. This was bad. Then he cursed the pain. The blood seeped into that shortened finger's cross-section, then dripped to the splitting block and wood-chipped snow. *Now what?* His right hand still holding the hatchet, he swung it angrily, sticking it into the heavy block. He didn't run he just walked for the cabin. If someone were to happen upon the scene outside the shed, it'd look for certain that he owned chickens and today was butcher Sunday. The missing tip lay among the cedar chips, some score for a critter to carry away.

He didn't have any paper towel so he grabbed a dish towel and wrapped the finger and sat down and it didn't take long for the blood to soak through. He opened the towel and had a look and said goddammit and moved the towel to a dry patch and applied pressure and it became saturated also. "Hell." He considered a small tourniquet. A sever can't be stitched closed and he wasn't going to try to sew on the tip and he had no satellite phone to call in a plane for the hospital. *Now what?* Sitting in the chair trying to stop the blood with his vision on the stove. "Ah hell."

The stove was slowly burning a whole log round and he fully ported the vent and opened the damper and then poked around at the coals to enliven the burn. Laid in a couple quartered logs. The heat came quickly and the metal of that stove got hot fast and he wouldn't have to wait long before the cabin would become uncomfortably warm. But he was sweating even before that.

Do it right on the stove and then every time I have a fire I'm going to smell cooked me. He did see some merit in that as it would remind him of the value of not being a distracted idiot. *Save the armchair philosophizing for the armchair. You idiot.* That idea too morbid, he elected to place on the stove a piece of metal whose post-sear odour he could take outside. He got up, still pressing the towel he'd transformed into the Japanese national flag, went to the shed and found a scrap plate of steel, small and square and about ten gauge. Laid that with a clang on the hottest section of the stove.

He figured it'd probably heat up enough in two minutes as it would in ten. He gave it about fifteen. He had read you could get drunk off water if you drank enough, and he thought of lying in the creek and pointing his open mouth up-current. The steel didn't smoke but looking at it, it sorta shimmered a little rainbow wave. He was momentarily curious about the physics behind that iridescence, such is the insatiable curiosity of some hungry minds. *This will be unpleasant*, he thought. He was thinking of his hypocrisy, of he and his boy out hiking. The kid in his excitement to go for a swim had kicked an arrow that rattled onto the bow. "Not everything has to be serious but some things are serious," he had told him. *Weapons are serious I told him. Now me daydreaming while swinging a hatchet. Nevermind parenting, now I can't even do simple things right.* He shook his head at himself. *What a joke. You're a joke.* He gave the metal another minute for the sole reason of not wanting to stick his finger on it—not yet, not ever.

Had he in this interval been sitting down with a psychoanalyst she might have asked him, "Do you see the significance of this?"

"What?"

"The finger. What finger is it?"

"Index."

"Yes. What does an index finger do?"

He'd stare back blankly.

"Index. Index is a pointer. It points. You see."

"I don't see."

"You've been blaming yourself for all you've been going through. No doubt your subconscious has been trying to get you to stop. Well, now in a violent expression to be heard, maybe it took things into its own hands. Or...into your finger, that is."

"I don't get it."

"You can't point blame without the finger that points! This is a message. So hear it."

He'd hold up to her his other hand with its working index and demonstrate his ongoing ability to point.

"You're more repressed than I originally thought," she'd reply.

Him staring at the metal's taunting iridescent heat wave.

In his last sauna bake he had been exploring an idea: that which is aware of something isn't entirely that thing. There is a bit of separation from consciousness and the mental object of which it is aware. Presently the finger throbbed horribly but in the trough of its pulses he wondered if when this intense pain came, he could experience it without being entirely defined and consumed by it. He had a chance right here to explore acute pain even more immersive than his ice-water baths. He grimaced and set to the task. "Alright. Let's do this. Quick sear, Chef. Keep it rare on the inside."

He planned to give his entire attention to his breath, then wondered if maybe there was something even more concentrative than respiration.

He wasn't much for music, but singing took more focus than just breathing and so perhaps brought with it greater mental separation from the pain. He didn't know many songs. A few children's rhymes sung to him by Mom and Gran. *Twinkle Twinkle Little Star* would not steel his nerves any. *Happy Birthday* was no better. Most of his catalogue was Christmas carols and *Silent Night* never armoured anyone prior to battle. The pain's dictatorship was restricting his thoughts, few ditties were coming to mind. Gran sometimes sang while working in the garden. When he tried to recall the first line of her old go-to, it came easy. He started humming *The Battle Hymn of the Republic*. His forehead was beaded up. That hot steel now had a grim red glow. He raised his hand and peeled away the towel, and the heat on his hand had the same unpleasantness as drinking a hot beverage after eating something too spicy. A drop of blood fell to the plate and he watched it sizzle and bubble then dry up leaving only a burnt circle. He didn't want to watch this but thought he had better just in case his whole finger lit up or whatever else. He stared at that little deceptive steel plate of heat and hurt and started singing.

"My eyes have seen the glory of the coming of the Lord," and the note for *Lord* was supposed to be lower but in his trepidation he went higher and it sounded bad to his ears *But fuck it just get it over with* and he brought his finger down to the steel plate like he was pushing the button to a bomb that unleashed hell, making him perpetrator and victim. The sound came before the pain. The metal hissed like an angry wolverine. "He is trampling out the vintage where the grapes of wrath are stored." He got the whole line out, his voice shaky, but it could be the case that no other singer in the history of that song ever rivalled his zeal. He was breathing through his mouth but could still smell broiled blood, fried flesh, all while singing in delirium a religious song whose words he disbelieved, alone in the North with his hand intentionally set to sear. If asked he would probably claim to be in his right mind, but if we are what we do, then those who believed him should have theirs questioned.

It took maybe a full second, maybe two, but the pain of his sautéing finger rose like magma. He tried to breathe into it and encourage his mind to only be aware of the experience, to keep his anticipation from forming it into a unified thing of torment. *Be aware of pain without being pain*, he told himself. *The monk.* And so he observed his mind and breathed and the shape it took was:

Pain. Consuming and total agony. He opened up to it and it was horrible and he understood he had no concentrative talents that enabled him to transport himself away. Again he looked in his consciousness to see if there was a place to observe this experience without being identified with it, and most clearly, distinctly, this he knew—*there was not.* The pain was stupid and total and worth avoiding. Most might suppose that was obvious, but this is what the poor philosopher must do: question the obvious. His conclusion: *Fuck the monk, this is horrendous.*

The song did not help it just made it all kinda perverse. Through clenched teeth he mumbled something discordant with the current verse and his rapid breathing had a fast tempo but no tune and he forgot the rest of the words and seethed at the stove, "Jesus fuck." The magma of pain arriving to his mouth in a volcanic eruption of expletives. "Fucking hell," he seethed gracelessly as he watched his finger smoke.

That Freudian shrink would now say that he's only undertaking this barbaric procedure as punishment for a huge internal guilt. Had he heard her and had his core value of decency been compromised from the pain, he might have just jabbed that smoking finger in her eye. But alone up north, she would have just been some figment of his imagination, and it would have been his own eye he was poking, and he didn't have a whole one of those to spare.

He figured that finger had been sufficiently cauterized, but this was a one-time show, so he leaned a touch more weight into it to be sure. The sound of sizzle sickened him and where he stood he felt woozy from the burn.

All this in the span of a few long seconds, and brutal as it was he'd say he knew worse, 'cause the charred remains of his heart were still smouldering before his finger had.

He lifted his blackened pointer away and had he wanted to scroll a smoky word in the air, he could have. But the world's not short of curse words, that's for damn certain; he refrained. A new entrant on his official List of Regrets rose near to the top: *Why didn't I set out a pail of water*. His dizzy mind didn't consider just heading outside and sticking that hot digit in a snowbank.

The jug's spout in the kitchen overhung from the counter and normally he'd hold a glass in one hand while turning the knob with the other. So now he set a bowl on the floor then turned the knob and water splashed down to the bowl, making a mess. He turned off the knob. He took a knee and dunked his smoking finger. He thought it would hiss but it didn't. His own breathing kinda did. A minute of that, taking a most curious, sorta oathful pose: he bent on one knee and pointing at the ground.

He cradled his wounded digit with a towel while being careful not to touch the tip. He sat in a chair and was about to close his eyes and sit with the pain, but saw the thinnest wisp of simmering blood rising from the steel plate. He raised a boot and kicked it off the stove clanging to the floor. Closed his eyes. His world all fireworks.

After some minutes he must have been coming out the other side of it because he had the lucidity to ask himself if he still wanted life. With all its misery and ugly and sometimes comical and stupid and senseless pain, if he still wanted it. And he said: *I do*. Said it like a vow. *Yes I do*. And he was nine-tenths pain, and one-tenth pain, and also some impossible fraction of hysterical love, 'cause for the smallest wild part of him, some piece at once defiant to and accepting of the misery and cruelty of life, and any circumstance or force that would impose on him great suffering which might break his will and then break the man—this felt raw and that felt good. See his resolve in a tiny smile.

Town

THE RETURNING AMPHIBIOUS OTTER floatplane lowered its wheels on approach, landing in a community shrouded in a fog of speculation. Where on that plane was a darker variety. The plane carried information like it might cargo. The cabin door opened. Clock the duration the details of the boy's death were kept under wraps, not in days but hours.

Sarah and Dave had eaten dinner and were sitting at the living room window when the cruiser pulled up. Their house was a half block from the small uncontrolled airstrip at the edge of town and maybe that's why the police showed first at Dave's. The car idled outside, its front headlights on, its rooftop flashers not. He could see the two men were looking through the window at him. He could see they were talking. One doing more talking than the other. He couldn't see the bear cape as that was on the back seat. The headlights turned off.

· · · ● · ● · · ·

A song being sung by the jukebox slipped out of the small-town bar and curled like a ribbon in the evening's southerly breeze. "Will your restless heart come back to mine on a journey through the past?" A man was having a cigarette outside the bar and his smoke, as if bewitched by the melody, followed its direction.

Music is capable of transcending culture and language and can affect a person centuries after it was first composed and so travel through time and over great distances to cause a heart in a far away place to fill, thump, swoon, ache.

But for all its magic, that tune didn't thread its way through the forest. Hardly made it very far at all. It got tangled up along the way like tinsel in a Christmas tree. Thank God for that. Suppose it arrived to a lonely man in the isolate woods and he, caught off guard, heard his lady singing of their lost love, asking him that question. Who knows what he'd be liable to do to convince her his answer is yes. That melody's ribbon curling in his ears might have wrapped around his throat and hanged him.

· · · · ● ● ● · · ·

Dusk fell. The police cruiser had left Dave's house and now travelled quiet roads the short distance to the other side of town.

Irene's living room window faced the street and she was already talking to her sister on the phone when the cruiser rolled up. Her sister said I knew it.

The police on his mind and an accusatory echo in his ears and the little bear in his eyes: Jacob. Jacob was not so well. Inside suite 202 was a hunting guide who kept guns and knives and ropes in a storage closet. A couple hours ago he had drunk up all his booze. Had called his one real friend more than once. Had called his ex-wife. He called her again and this time it didn't ring endlessly, it went straight to voicemail. About an hour before, he yelled belligerently at his ceiling after a neighbour above him asked that he stop throwing the tennis ball at it, so he stopped throwing the tennis ball and speared it several times with a hockey stick.

Irene was now discussing with her sister whether the cops were just there to take a report for the burned cabins or if there was some investigation. Insurance fraud, her sister said. "Why would they show up at night for a routine fire report?"

In his mind's maze he had tried taking as many paths as he could find. *Somewhere there is a way out,* he believed, yet encountered only dead ends or murky rabbit holes. His fright starting to feel fantastical by the stress and booze pressure-cooking inside his skull inside the small apartment inside the small town. As he began to lose his buzz, the whiskey-softened sounds rang louder.

Murderer, murderer, murderer.

He'd go back to the beginning and try for a path he hadn't walked, a fork he hadn't taken, a hole he hadn't stuck his head in.

Outside the front door, Bill ran a finger over the glass cover of the resident listing.

Jacob Bauer — suite 202.

The police climbed the old wooden stairs whose carpet, thin from wear, did little to muffle their steps. Those stairs kept their secrets as well as the thin wooden walls. Had Jacob not been so engrossed in climbing the walls of his inner maze he might have heard the heavy boots.

Woods

Ethan always used to cross off days on his calendar, but since the boy's passing he began feeling like he was only logging time since tragedy and that all the X's were some trail on a morbid map leading him back to his buried treasure. He stopped marking its little boxes and then burned the calendar. Nonetheless, days passed without his record keeping. He was careful with his short finger as it healed.

He could swear he was making progress. He mostly believed the steps he was taking were moving him away from the past. But then it was as if all it took was the wind to change and an evening might bring the predatory creep of self-doubt. The longing for family. The fear of not being able to start over. Seeing his life as a wasted affair. The doubt tarnishing things that only a few hours ago had shined enough he could see himself in them, see a humble future in them. Now buff as he might, the dark thoughts clouded that metal.

Not all knowledge is useful. There were certain books he wished he had never read. The pages of an innocuous biology book didn't just tell of certain phenomena, they showed it in pictures, and though it had been years since he'd looked at them, those images were only too clear in his head. Like how nails and hair continue to grow on the bodies of the deceased. He had the spine of that book facing the wall. Though he bathed regularly and combed his hair, he had not cut his own nails or trimmed his hair in some time.

Sometimes the doubt would at first arrive as a soft shape, like a downy little feather floating down on a windless day. A feather just like all other feathers that of course in no way whatsoever had ever caused anyone any pain in the history of feathers. They only came to insulate and comfort and tickle. *So just give the little boy's downy laugh or her gentle breath in bed a minute of thought because how could those soft memories ever hurt anyone ever?* Recalling them once in a while seemed like a perfectly good idea, like a tender, even respectful thing to do once in a while. Just opening and flipping through the pages of his mind's photo album, like he would with some of the boy's favourite fairy tales. That's a nice thing to do. *In fact to not recall them would be a more disrespectful thing,* he told himself. They're shining and they look so pretty and in fact sometimes the past calls so loudly that all you can do is answer, so you reach out to touch them to bring them in and hold them even just for a minute. One minute. But somehow, he found that feather had a quill sharp as a syringe. It pricked. Turned out the hollow of its stem was filled with the acid of regret. It injected. His veins coursed with that caustic payload. And the progress he'd made reversed itself and it would take him time to again drain himself of those memories. *So just stop already! Just stop. Please just stop.* Some part of him. *Remembering them just doesn't do you any good. You can't undo some things, so it's a painful indulgence, it's drinking antifreeze: sweet then it eats your insides.* He'd tell himself just to leave them alone, *Get a hold of yourself and let's get ahead of the past.* Sometimes he wondered if he had sorrow so deep it lived in the cream of his bones where it soured his marrow.

Other evenings the doubt came far less delicately. Sometimes the assault of the past arrived like a drive-by shooting. This night it did. He sat there wounded in the quiet cabin, his arms around his stomach like he'd been gut shot and left for dead.

But eventually, like always, he found a breath. And maybe without all his regimented medicine, that poison quill and those gut shots would have been fatal.

He regained himself, thumbed his knife open. He reached to a shelf and lifted the brick sharpening stone and put it on the table between lit candles. Reached for the mineral oil and dripped three oil drops to its grey surface. Watched the clear bubbles slowly spread, then pool together. He set the blade to the rock and went to draw it over the grit surface, but his hands shook and his eyes were wet. He put the knife down. Hung his head for a minute. The wood between his feet patterned with teardrops. They fell from his left eye that was a cloud of nostalgic ache, and from his right eye that was a cloud of future burden. Little wet circles pattering the wood's thin dust and ash. He raised his heavy head and wiped his cheeks and rested his chin on his fists.

He knew he needed to make peace with the past, with *Their* passing. With the ghosts holding the present hostage. What did they want. *What do you want?* He asked that out loud in his mind while wondering what their demands could be. His so far plan of extreme cold and heat and effort and sleep and books and second-degree arson seemed to have helped some but hadn't quite resolved things. He wanted more than some continual and combative standoff that had him pitting his resolve and self-willed durability up against the long reach of the sore past. He wanted the memories but without the pain. He wasn't sure if that was possible. They were precious things and the love he'd felt when he had his people were the strongest feelings he'd known and that beauty and love felt like truth. He wasn't convinced it was now all false and he wasn't convinced it all belonged to another time. Maybe it did, though. He didn't know. He wasn't good at this. He was really good with a bow and arrow and he wasn't bad in the kitchen, but he had no talents for when the love you thought you'd always have, you no longer get to have. He wasn't sure what you do then. Someone in the world—many people—knew the answer because this was common human plight, maybe the commonest. But he lived alone. When he was young and his parents died he just buried their death inside him: "For a boy unafraid to show his anger he was remarkably quiet that day," his grandparents said.

When Ethan's wife passed, her death nearly ruined him, but as he never entirely let her go, his loss of her was not total. Now in his solitude, the absence of the boy was bringing home all their departures.

So, what to do? He wondered how to process it, how to stomach it. He figured the person who knew best would be some sword-swallower, some circus-act fire-eater. He figured they'd be the ones to ask.

He'd read of mothers who forgave the murderer of their child. Husbands who forgave the drunk whose oncoming car crashed and killed their wife. He wondered if there were greater feats of human strength than forgiveness. He thought about it right then and there and figured there probably weren't. Crossing vast seas in a rowboat and thirty-day hunger strikes and all other spectacular displays of human resolve took second place to being able to forgive the most severe crimes: stolen life and murdered love. Partly he didn't want to forgive because at times his hate was motivating, orienting, and it fuelled his efforts. But how long to hold a grudge? How long was it reasonable to hate yourself?

His stomach was still knotted, as though the bullet, after it came for his son, somehow curved its flight to lodge in his own gut.

He was looking back to the stove. He reached out and opened the stove door and when it squeaked he closed then opened it again so it would squeak again.

He picked the knife back up and didn't begrudge his hands if they would shake nor his eyes if they would leak, and drew the blade over the stone worn concave from generations of steel. The full length of the blade from base to tip drawn in an arcing slice, then he switched sides. One then the other, over again, back and forth, with an even angle, and rhythmic motion, while tears pattered and the blade reflected candlelight up to the cabin ceiling that danced and shimmered then quit, then relit and danced again. The song of the grating blade in the sluice grit drawn back and forth over the whetstone sang: *shh shh shh shh.*

· · · ● · ● · · · ·

It was later than his normal bedtime and he considered not even lying down. What's the point when sleep hardly restores and the visions he sees brings no comfort? He loaded the stove and turned down its damper. He didn't lick his fingers, he just pinched out the candle flames.

· · · ● · ● · · · ·

When before he had scraped the remains of waxy globs off the cabin floor to mould those curls into a new candle, it was possible that some old scented wax belonging to his late wife had been salvaged, and tonight the burning wick freed a fragrant memory preserved in the wax whose nostalgic aroma lingered in the cabin where it seduced his mind. Because this night: a romantic dream.

She smiled and he smiled back. Nothing new there. And in it when she curled her finger, he followed. Same same. But as he got closer, he saw it wasn't *her*. It was not *her*. And that was a first. And though the thick perfume of the dream had to some degree bewitched him, he had enough faculty to turn back if he had so desired. Turn back before he couldn't. But he didn't. At first he didn't realize it wasn't his late wife and when he did realize it, he didn't stop. Irreverent dream and the first of its blasphemous kind. Not sweeter for the infidelity—maybe for some, not for him—not heightened by the temptation. But it happened. And he let it happen.

A woman effuse with sensuality. Her femininity almost feline in her movements, playfully kittenish at times. Though when she walked, her hips like a larger cat making the nonchalant sway of a relaxed predator. She had delicacy and charm and sweetness and coy and she affected an almost inebriating attraction, like she herself was the model of it. Like she stoked heart fires. He was warmed.

Her curves took cues from nature, shapes smoothed like they'd been polished, long lapped by the infatuate water. Her hair in his dream-mind teased by an enamoured wind. She had elegance, yet a wildness. Refinement, yet smokey. She and her fluid movements like some feminine whiskey. All the while nebulous, for when he woke he could not recall the tone of her skin, and of her eyes he remembered only their iridescence. He was sure her hair was long, but of its shade, uncertain. Some unconstrained female enchanting his mind. Perhaps in a dream of Aphrodite he had loved Love herself.

Skin that smelled as sweet as it looked soft. When he saw it he bet it touched like silk, and for proof he drew his finger along her lines. Never having to lift his finger, they were one unbroken line. He traced her figure where it narrowed in places and widened voluptuously in others and where it was bare in places and furred in others and some places where he drew his finger she smiled and some places he drew his finger she sighed and some places he touched she just breathed, and he liked that best. He lightly traced her with a lost fingertip now returned to him, and that unknown surgeon had enhanced it ten thousand times more sensitive, somehow for both toucher and feeler.

That tingling finger curved around the underside of one of her breasts. He painted that finger around the outside of one perfect mound and then above where it sloped to her chest, then drew it down to the valley of her breasts. He continued on his way to map her other rise. When finished his circumnavigation he connected the figure eight, which tied like a bow in her cleavage—his subconscious acting in his dream-mind had him drawing the sign of infinity on her chest, the quantity of time he wanted to spend there. He drew it again and she with a coaxing sound between a sigh and a moan encouraged that finger to continue its way wherever on her skin it dared journey.

That finger now joined by another and they tip-toed over her chest. She inhaled. Those fingers walked taller, both from the swell of her chest and from their pride in raising her body. Continuing on towards the shallow hollow of her neck, fingers travelling over her body now softly sinking as she exhaled with a honeyed sigh. A sound oceans on their best day could never replicate. Her slender neck with no freckle. Never once did he trip on a wrinkle, never finding any cracks in her skin weathered with time that he needed to fjord. Her body faultless as a precious gem held in a vault in the mind of a god.

None of that felt right and maybe that's what woke him.

Perhaps in the night that Greek enchantress had stepped from a myth into a dream. Or maybe she was shaped from a lump of ideal clay he carried inside his mind. And if each mind has its own version of perfection, perhaps some gods are shaped by the hands of their creator. He should then ask himself: *Just who are you worshipping?*

Lying there he was still wrapped up in the silk of the dream's luxuriance. She had stepped away, but the fabric of her dress lingered over him, like a curtain slow to settle after billowed by the breeze. The sun on him. He lay feeling partly moved, partly guilty: both clear and clouded.

Her smooth legs wrapped around him in the night had felt like most tender embrace. They felt good. But he wondered if her legs crossed behind his back were like two crossed fingers exempting a person from deceit. With so much trickery and malice in the world that had lost his trust it perhaps never deserved, he wondered if those long stems were the legs of a mantis, a woman to seduce his foolish heart before eating it out through his chest. The gods are not to be trusted, he knew that, and he was pretty sure she was one.

If he could bury that confusing and irreverent dream in the garden, his hands would already be holding a shovel. He went to get up. He saw he was wet. As if the rain had come for dry seeds.

TOWN

JACOB SITTING IN A kitchen chair worn of its patina. Jacob climbing the walls of his mind. This current mind-wall was unique. Unlike other walls, this one had a sound. Knocking. Three times. He stared at it while it coalesced from his foggy head into an apartment door.

The same day the police saw the burned cabins and then spoke to Ethan, the same evening they'd spoken with Dave then left without taking a formal statement concerning his abduction, nor charging Dave as an accomplice to murder, the same cruiser parked outside an apartment building. The police officers climbed the first flight of stairs and walked towards suite 202. Listening through the door, they heard only faint sounds of a television coming from an adjacent suite. Bill knocked three times. Listened.

Jacob staring at his door.

Bill knocked again, the same rhythm, heavier tenor.

Anything consistent in its metre can be used to measure change. The even pacing of the knock seemed to Jacob a relation of time, but in the short three-beat duration, his predicament did not improve and the absence of a fourth knock as if time had run out.

Bill waited for sounds of steps towards the door. Heard none. He looked at Steve and Steve took a step back and raised his leg to boot the door in and Bill put his hand on the tip of Steve's boot hanging in midair and sent it back down to the floor. "Easy, Columbo."

Steve didn't know who that was.

"The landlord was listed 101. Go see if he's home."

Steve went to leave but then Bill tried the doorknob and it turned. "Wait."

He hadn't opened the door, he just held it in place unlatched. The younger officer had his hand on the butt of his sidearm.

On the table was an empty mickey, lying on its side. At the table unshaven in an undershirt, Jacob. Bill saw dark enough bags under the boy's eyes that it nearly looked like he'd been in a fight. A fight with himself. Looked like he'd lost.

· · • · • • • · · ·

The town talked even more after news of the boy. Bill or Steve or Dave—not Jacob—or Sarah or perhaps the pilot or a clerk at the police station or someone else overhearing it must have leaked it because the next morning an underdog theory—*The trapper lit the fire*—rivalled the contender—*Jacob and Dave had done it.* The townsfolk were like trenchcoated sleuths in a dingy bar talking about who'd started the fire. Like tunic-clad Greek philosophers on the sandstone steps outside the school of Athens, they debated its ethics.

Conversations at a bar, the only bar in town:

"Obviously he started it." The *he* could have been any of the three primary suspects but this woman at a table was talking about he who most called *the trapper.*

"That's not obvious at all," said one of her two friends seated at the table, a middle-aged man.

She continued. "His family owned the lodge. Lost it gambling. Fast forward to his boy being shot by one of the owners! Next day eight cabins burn down." She opened her hand then passed it before her like the doings of this event were so apparent the scene might just recreate itself in miniature from out of the air between them.

"It wasn't the next day."

"Whatever. A day or two later, same thing."

"No. This is what happened. Jacob shoots a bear. The bear's a boy. They know there's no way they're going to keep running that outfit, no way they'd be able to attract clients up there now. But the thing is," the man leaned in and sorta hissed out his theory like a punctured car tire, as if this motive was so original he was running it by them alone first before he considered filing for a patent—"*he knows his money is all tied up in it.*"

The two others listened to the hisser.

"I know for a real fact because years ago I saw that lodge listed in the *Buy & Sell* and that place would not be easy to find a buyer for. And it wasn't stained with a murder back then. So what does he do? Jacob is no idiot. Say what you want about him. Not dumb. The place is insured." He looked from one to the other. "Think about it." He sat upright. He drank. He looked satisfied with his handiwork, as if the truth had always been there, trapped in marble, and he'd chipped away at it, now setting it free. A fork to his left and a knife to his right may as well have been a hammer and chisel, as the half-drunk-Michelange-lo-of-bar-room-truths leaned back.

The lady processed and the heretofore silent man agreed. "I could see that."

The lady said, "I wonder if a fire inspector will be able to tell. If they'll get one up there."

Though the town was split as to how the fire had started, one of several sub-debates concerned the following matter: *assuming* the trapper had started the fire, was he justified in so doing?

The town didn't have a lawyer but it had a notary public. A school teacher sitting with him said, "I'd say he was in the right. Because I'd do it too. And you'd do it too." A man at another table listening in without hiding it was convinced by this, and not from the strength of the teacher's argument but from just how passionately the teacher delivered his conviction. In the sphere of public debate, rhetoric more often beats logic.

The notary countered, "Actually no. It's not right and I wouldn't. Cliché or not, two wrongs don't make a right." He set down his beer and winked but held it. "An eye for an eye and we all end up blind."

"There's a history here that matters," the teacher said. "Remember the past and you lose an eye," he mirrored the wink the notary had now relaxed, "fail to, and you lose them both." The teacher closed his eyes for a second then reached blindly towards his friend's face who batted it away. "So it's not wrong. Burning it down was not wrong. It's not retributive—it's *restorative*. He was justified in lighting it as it closes a loop. They had it coming. It's actually a fair response given prior events."

"No, it's not restorative. That's funny. It's the opposite of that. It's second-degree arson. That's a serious crime and *if* it was him then it was one man carrying out vigilante justice—*that's not justice*. This is why we have police. Courts of law. Not personal vendetta and summary executions. Take that back to Sicily, Corleone. You trade that in, living within a community, a society. Deferring to the proper authorities is what puts the *civil* in civilization and those were huge, huge steps for humanity we took a long time ago. Without putting our trust in the proper channels of our institutions we live in a state of barbarism and fear, danger of violent death, and the life of humankind, solitary, poor, nasty, brutish, and—"

"—Short on patience for that tired quote I've heard too many times. What if you don't expect justice? What if there's a little favouritism in local law enforcement? We're not in an equitable state perfectly accounting for all crimes. You know what I'm talking about."

The notary missed the point on that and squinted like he was trying to squeeze out some clarity.

"The story of his dad not being charged with assault. Remember Samuel Reed?"

"Oh. That's what, two, three decades old now, right?"

"Still Bill in charge."

"Who knows what really happened there. And even if favouritism existed, wouldn't that only benefit the trapper here? That's even less reason to take the law into his own hands."

"I thought we were talking in abstracts?"

"Well, we are. But you're confusing me."

"Look," the teacher said, "there's such a thing as citizen's arrest, right? So sometimes it *is* correct to handle things on our own. That's all he was doing. Well justified in doing it."

"This is not that."

"Whatever. I think it's fair. I'd do the same." The teacher raised a fist of solidarity. "And it's really only the insurance company that suffers here. The guy's my hero. I say he took one back for the common man." The teacher lowered his fist and raised his beer and was joined by the guy listening in, who was joined by one more.

"You're an idiot," the notary said to his friend. "What does the insurance company do?"

"Eats it."

"No. You're an idiot. What about you," he said to the guy sitting at the next table, his beer in the air halfway to his mouth in either some half-baked show of allegiance to the trapper, or toasting to the stung balance sheet of the insurance company. "You know?" the notary asked him.

That man bearded and gruff-looking. "They eat it."

"No. They just raise their premiums and pass it on to you."

The gruff guy leaned in and outstretched his beer in front of the notary, and the teacher leaned to meet it clinking with his own.

"Robin friggin' Hood. To the trapper!" A few in the bar echoed the teacher's toast. The notary mistimed his drink and ending up drinking with the cheers. He smiled shaking his head and got up for the bathroom. On his way he passed the jukebox where someone had put on *Ring of Fire*. The notary on his walk to the john just shook his head.

For those who thought he'd both lit the fire and was justified in doing so, he was kinda their folklore, their living legend. It wasn't just that it gave them a conversation point that could be struck up as easily as talk about the weather, it was that it gave some of them something to root for, in a strange sense, maybe even something to believe in. Like he was theirs. He as guardian of the forest. Of values. They made him into something he wasn't quite, though perhaps in some strange regard, something he wasn't entirely not, either. How else do legends get made?

Some theories were becoming so very intricate it really makes you wish the capable human mind couldn't always be tasked to ends more worthy of its cleverness.

"Here's how it went down." Marko was a mechanic and he wore a faded, collared shirt tucked into Lee blue jeans, no belt, two pens clipped inside his breast pocket and a small notepad sticking out, like a scientist's pocket square. Moustached. Glasses. "They went to hunt. Right? Okay. Left some sort of carcass, bit of discarded animal fat in the shed. A squirrel gets in. Starts running around looking for scraps."

"Squirrels eat meat?" his companion Wesley asked.

Marko either didn't know the answer or didn't care about the question, or his subpar hearing from a working life spent in heavy mechanics missed it. "Squirrel running along the workbench hits a wrench, big one, like thirty-two millimetre."

"The hell is that, King George?"

"Like inch-and-a-quarter."

"Better." Wesley nodded. Drank.

"Squirrel running in the shed knocks a big wrench off the workbench. You know where I'm going with this."

"Marko, I have no friggin' clue where you're going with this. And I predict the squirrel in the story," he burped, "is you."

"Wrench falls and hits a boat battery." Marko raised up his eyebrows then pointed a finger at them. "Battery arcs."

“Cute.”

“Sparks. Rag, some paper, *whoosh*.” He made a blooming motion with his hands. “Cabin burned. *Cabins* burned. Yup. I bet that’s what happened.” He drank. “You know why?”

His companion just stared eyes half-open waiting for his loony friend who was going to tell him anyways.

“Because it almost happened to me.” He held up a peace sign. “Twice.”

Wesley clapped slowly. “Great work. Hey, Marko. Have you ever heard of Occam’s razor?”

“Stockholm’s blazer?” His hearing.

“Occam’s razor. Look it up. Then if I was you I’d slit that theory’s wrists with it.”

Weeks passed, and the lodge as a topic of conversation did not.

WOODS

GRANDDAD LOVED GRAN'S WRINKLES every one of them. Once he tried to count them and got to about three before she smacked him. He said that given he'd caused some of her wrinkles, he therefore had ownership rights to them. That, actually, that really made them *his*. He informed her which ones he'd decided to lay claim to: half the ones on each sides of her mouth—just those from when she smiled, not the frown lines—and all the ones streaking from her eyes. He'd take all those. Told her teasingly she could keep the ones on her forehead.

He said that and she in her last days wasn't so weak as to prevent scrunching them all up then smacking his arm. That made him laugh.

When Gran left, when she died, Granddad took that as his cue and followed along shortly.

Granddad sitting with his back against a tree that had come up right through the bedrock. Made it look like it split the rock to grow. Maybe it had. He looking weathered enough and rather sculpted—chipped, shaped, chiselled—by his surroundings, like he too had grown up out of the land. He had. The creek whispering. Water spilling, murmuring over smooth rocks, trickling into shallow pools.

A long red leech in the water. It had not slithered its way up the current, hadn't curled among the polished rocks as it moved upriver with its body so long and thin, sliding over polished rocks until it turned for the bank, as if it knew with some unnatural sense where to go. It didn't slip its head out of the water and climb the bank and slither over the rocks, pouring itself over dry ground towards a tree, its long scarlet tail so far down-creek, thin and fading out by the bleach of the sun, its body staining the bedrock as it snaked towards a tree to latch its mouth. No.

What really happened was an old man under a tree relaxed his hand and a spool of ribbon spilled out. The spool rolling down from the base of a tree, to the bank, to the creek. A long scarlet ribbon spilled its silk over the bedrock and slipped into the water seamlessly as an otter. As if it heard the sweet trickle, the water laughing like young lovers at play, and it went to join the song of the creek. A ribbon to flow in the water like music through the night. Unwinding, curling in the currents, turning in the eddies, taken by the flow.

TOWN

"LET ME GET THIS straight." The man seated at a table in the bar had most of his red plaid shirt tucked into his blue jeans. Big belt buckle under a pot belly. And though he regularly drove his rig through cattle country, the man was no wrangler. A handlebar moustache. A baseball cap pitched upwards that looked small on his big head. His boots only loosely laced and with a bit of melted snow under his table, like there was under all the other occupied tables. In the winter night he had parked eighteen wheels across three parking spots on the street out front, then walked through the door under its buzzing green fluorescent sign.

"You tell me if I got this straight. Buddy put a bear hide on his son. In an area with bears. And hunters. *Where he himself actually worked at a hunting lodge back in the day.*" The man leaned in when he said that as if he was going to employ the theatrics of a whisper, but the beers had long liquified that option for subtlety. He leaned back and tilted his head just slightly and had about a quarter smile.

"So far I got this right. Right?"

Nobody at the table he'd joined uninvited said anything. "Right?" He asked again in a bit heavier tone.

Someone gave a reluctant-looking nod but timed it with a drink from his bottle so it was fairly disguised to anyone not at the table.

"Okay, so far so good. Then buddy told his son to go sit up on a hill." The trucker turned his incredulous-looking face to each of the five of them in turn. The beer in his mug wasn't lager yellow like the pub's lighting and it wasn't stout dark like the pub's corners, it was somewhere in between. A red or brown ale. The others at the table were drinking Coors and Bud. He raised the glass and lowered it and wiped his face with the back of his hand. Some foam remained in his soup-strainer.

"Do I have the facts right?" He shook his head. "There's no way I have the facts right." The hairs of his crumb-catcher now looking like a curtain being drawn up by its corners for the start of some lewd act. "Shit." He spat the word and it came punctuated. "That's a special kind of jackass." Whisker-curtain fully raised now. Cigarettes had coloured all but one of his teeth yellow, and that tooth had fallen out years before. Occasionally his tongue could be seen moving behind that off-centred tooth-hole in his mandible, like a rat pacing its den. Earlier that night the trucker smoked a cigarette hands-free through it, claimed he had requested the dentist wiggle that "Chiclet" free for that very purpose. Later he claimed he pulled out that chomper himself with pliers, and he took out his Leatherman belt-tool as evidence.

Someone at the table got up, likely for a pee or a smoke. The trucker looked at the four remainders. "Impressive. That is impressive. Well. I guess you don't make that mistake twice." He raised his eyebrows to his own cleverness. Someone else at the table left, maybe to play the video poker.

The trucker's beer was half-empty and he was ready for another and was watching the waitress two tables over and didn't call to her immediately. She was facing away while putting some empty mugs on her tray and leaned over to wipe the far side of the round wooden tabletop and he was wondering if you call them tights or leggings or like a thick pantyhose maybe, and if she wore them in summer too. He said out loud, "Hope not," but having not said anything prior nobody knew what he was talking about. He noticed the leggings were slightly darker where her inner thighs met her skirt. He raised a single finger to pitch up his hat a touch but it was already pitched, so not making contact with the brim he ended up just pointing his finger upwards like a bidder at an auction.

"Honey."

She cleaned.

"Hey, honey." One decibel louder and not without a bit of melody to it, though a tune nobody within earshot much enjoyed.

The waitress, Pam, turned around enough and saw his eyes were waiting for hers and that he was smiling just a cat hair beyond cordially. She acknowledged him with the faintest inclining of her head then turned back to finish her task. Pam set down some new cardboard coasters that said Lucky, filled the bowl of pretzels. Everyone enjoyed the pretzels.

The chatter of the full pub became more amiable, encouraged by a quick-tempo Johnny Cash tune coming from the jukebox.

He knew her minimal acknowledgement meant his order had been taken but with middle finger and thumb he flicked the side of his glass anyways. It made a *pink* or *dink* sound. She didn't turn back around. "I'll have another, darlin'." He added some affection to its melody and said like she was still looking at him, "And sweetheart, drop a shot of Jameson in it."

Someone at the closest table whose back was immediately behind the trucker's said something to their table. Given that at any given table, the weather was the most common topic of conversation, it could have been about the weather. Though that would make it strange why they all laughed.

The trucker turned back smiling from Pam to his table, whose majority of seats were now open for new asses. To recap, the likely options for vacancy were: gamblin', peein', smokin'. Of the two sitters remaining, one was looking down, the other had peeled off half the beer bottle's sticker and was folding it. That bottle now said *Coo*.

"And you're saying somehow this guy is still walking around free?" Nobody at the table had said that, nobody at the table had brought it up in the first place, in fact, they hadn't said word one to him. But he could have come across that tragic story anywhere as it had made national newspapers. "Well. That sounds about right for this fucked-up world we live in." He shook his head. "Buddy ever come in here? That's someone I'd like to meet." He drank. Someone seated directly behind him, who had made the earlier comment, pushed out their chair and it screeched on the wood floor and bumped the trucker's chair. His raised beer sloshed and wetted his snot-mop, which dripped foamy beer back into his glass. He turned.

The person was stout and stable-looking with a torso nearly as thick as it was wide and hadn't turned to the trucker. Stood with a half-drunk bottle of Bud but set that bottle down empty. That table was quiet. The trucker's table was quiet. Sorrel boots took a side-step out of a small snow puddle then turned and stepped the two short paces to stand at the trucker's side.

He still held his foamy beer but was about to not hold his temper, the real story behind his porous smile. He looked over and saw hanging at this person's side were forearms equal to, if not thicker than, his own. One looked to have been tattooed. Some type of long-sword. Or birthmark? the trucker wondered. At his table someone pushed back a chair and it made no screech and then they vacated the chair. Johnny probably just taking a breather between songs and the conversations probably coming to a natural lull here as a hush befell the pub.

The trucker was attempting to find some meaning in that long ink or birth blotch colouring that thick arm. He wanted to ask this person both, "What the fuckin' sword meant" as well "Why the hell after what I can only assume is a life of usin' a chair you seem to operate this one like an asshole?" But first and maybe because his head was slightly heavy with drink, before he looked up, he looked down. Topping those white Sorrels, hem of a green dress. Military in colour. Buttons began at waist level and carried upwards over a compact bust, and of those buttons all were buttoned. Certainly militant in her attention to the attire: no wrinkles, no fluff. Sleeves of the dress rolled to her elbows. Collar of dress buttoned high enough a neck would have to be inferred. Thin lips, thick glasses. Pale face, unsmiling. Dark hair in a tight bun.

Babich was one of the school teachers. Ethan's boy never attended her class but she would see him every winter when father and son trekked south from woods to town for living supplies and course work. She organized his curriculum and sent them away with textbooks and test material. That made the boy one of her students. A teacher has a privilege of getting to know a child, their character and internality and imagination on a unique and intimate level. Not just from classroom engagement. There is a relationship formed by reading the answers a student has given much thought to. A glimpse into their green and growing world. When a child trusts the teacher the teacher holds the privileged position of shaping rationale, interpretation, judgment, values, creativity, helping that student feel safe with their vulnerability of uncertainty. Few bonds are more sacred. More than once that boy's long-form answers on an English quiz made her smile. That boy who would find a way to insert a fact about grouse into a topic that in no way concerned wild fowl. Question: *Why would Jane arrive to the bakery sooner travelling by bicycle than walking?* Answer: Two wheels are faster than two feet. But a grouse flies so fast it would already be eating the muffin.

On a Sunday afternoon the principal of the school had called Babich at home. She whose walls were lined with books had no words. Hung up the phone. Closed the blinds. Took down a bottle. Wanted to do something bad. Something she used to do. From her parents she received ugly traits and poor instruction. Fifty years ago it was a teacher who saved her. Over the years that sword tattoo changed from a glorification of violence to a reminder of the greater strength it took restraining it. Set the bottle in front of her. Then just crossed her arms. Tomorrow was Monday. She just cried.

This man finding something amusing in the death of a boy, the death of one of her students, weakened her restraint.

She leaned in, lowering her hands to the table.

His temper moderated by confusion. "Ma'am?"

"Take it back," she said.

The trucker hesitantly looked to his party for some clarification as to just what the hell was going on here and what this rigid-looking old bat was talking about. He turned and saw he now sat alone. He tried to decipher from out of her brevity some intelligible meaning. Take the word *Ma'am* back? Or take back whatever he had just been gabbing about, which at that exact moment had slipped his mind. Or maybe she meant something else entirely: take back some offence he had given at a prior time to her or someone she knew—and he did believe there was a reasonable chance he had given such offence. He started trying to dredge up his many social infractions in this particular region of his long-haul deliveries. But like the earliest signs of fur growing on a forgotten piece of cheddar, his mind was lightly fuzzed from the beers, and he did not answer straight away. He was squinting hard from the mental gymnastics of it all.

She watched him narrow his eyes at her. She'd seen it before. "That's how it's going to be, hey." Her throat sounded drier than all the humour she had so far displayed. She balled up her left without lifting it.

His eyes revisited her arm's marking, and now no doubt in his mind that skin had been inked. Her fist stretched her skin tight enough that long-sword kinda wavered then got rigid where it sheathed on her arm. The rat in his mouth was pressed against its hole, like they both were watching.

That balled-up left must have been misdirection and the words she'd spoken must have counted to her as fair warning because she drew her other arm back then held it cocked there a split-second like a loaded catapult, and just long enough for him to roll his eyes that way and see it was cupped. His face went wary-looking. She sent that loaded arm sweeping through the air and cuffed his head. His melon cocked sideways and if someone sat his right they'd have suffered a small spray of residual suds sheltered in his flavour-saver.

"Ow! Tha' hell's wrong with you?"

That sounded about the furthest away from the apology she was expecting. His head sorta cowering to his right from the last blow, she boxed his other ear and smacked him back central.

Jukebox tunes and pub din and pinks and dinks and any tender coos coming from the patrons was all deaf to his ears. His head all bells. His hat had come off with the impact and his bald patch now exposed, he looked like he lost something more than his hair. He stared wide-eyed, mouth agape, tooth-hole missing its cowardly tongue-rat, maybe off in search of some better words to push through the larger hole.

Her dark hair pulled back so tight that even with the halo of ceiling light behind her he did not pick out one single strand wavering out of line. Her formerly pale face now rosy. As if this old-world disciplinarian never came into her full colour until she was inflicting obedience. In the same way certain cage fight-ers don't even hit their stride 'til halfway through the second round, Babich here looked like she was just warming up and coming into her own.

Maybe the man intuited all that, as he said with a volume it'd be hard for anyone who wasn't her to hear: "Sorry."

She said, "What?" like she was talking to the other side of the room.

"Sorry."

"For what?"

He took three maybe four seconds trying to come up with anything at all she might want to hear. He said, sounding genuine, "For what I done."

Babich just looked at him and nobody was talking. Nobody was walking, either, besides one person whose steps were striking in the silence. You'd think that person was walking with wooden clogs over the hardwood floor for all their resonance, suspenseful beats like the person if not the executioner then the one delivering the sentencing.

The block-heel shoes stopped at their table. Pam set down the glass and the shot the trucker ordered.

"Thank you, honey." Babich said that without taking her eyes off the trucker. Babich reached out kinda quickly for that boilermaker and the man flinched. Someone else telling this story later would say she gave a short laugh right then. When they said that they got that right. She dropped into the beer the shot glass, which made a hollow and wet spelunk. The beer foamed down the sides. She brought it to her lips now less thin, one might even say a little plush. Then she tilted her head up and drank this man's beer. When she finished, remnant suds ran down the inner glass walls to form a shallow foam pool. She tilted it towards herself while still looking at him and spat the shot glass into the empty mug with a jangle loud enough you'd think one or the other should have broken.

Babich said to Pam already bringing it over: "This man will take his bill." Her voice straight youthful.

WOODS

THE MOON HOLDING HIS gaze was full, full of unrest. Its yellow tint eerie. Given the time of year, he knew of course it was not a Flower Moon or a Pink Moon, nor a Hunter's Moon. He was losing track of days but knew it was either a Cold Moon or a Wolf Moon. Looked like it possessed some knowledge, and what it lacked, that high-lumen spotlight could extract any secrets it desired from whomever it entranced. He kinda shuddered at it before closing the door. Moons like those do more than liven the forest, they're liable to enwild the mind.

While eating his dinner, he read a book of proverbs. Not *the* Book of Proverbs, just *a* book of proverbs. He tore the thin and bubbled bread crust, dipping chunks in a shallow bowl of olive oil with sunken black drops of balsamic vinegar. After dinner he put the fish bones in a pot of water so the marrow would seep out over the night's long simmer. He set the pot to the back of the stove. In the cupboard was where he kept the bay leaves and opening it he didn't find one and couldn't recall if there were any more in the cellar. He did see a little bowl of dried mushrooms in there.

One day while his boy was out hunting, he had gone and harvested a couple varieties. They cooked the chanterelles with dinner. These others he set on a high shelf close to the stove to dry. Vulvas with little frayed mycelial threads, skinny stems curled from drying, small caps. As if twisted from their own potency. These ones were not chanterelles and wouldn't flavour soup so well. He had a book on wild mushrooms but rarely opened it; his family's traditional knowledge of botany was extensive and stayed fresh from regular practice.

Gran once pointed out this particular species of fungus growing on a rotting alder near the creek. Told him not to fry these ones with onions, then laughed. Then stopped laughing and told him to respect it. "Mind their vigour," she said.

Consuming plants with psychedelic properties is a practice common the world over for nearly as long as recorded history. Though the plants vary, the general intention mostly does not. People seek alternative views of the world through keyholes shaped like a mushroom, sips of plant juice, licked toad skin or inhaled the smoke from burning its venom. Whether what is glimpsed in that altered state are things that exist on their own, now made visible by the plant's effect on perception, or things only manufactured within the brain of those who ate it, drank it, smoked it, certain plants relax the rigidity of one's mental framework and supple up the plasticity of the mind.

Many cultures embrace those hallucinogens, ritualize them, administer them under the guidance of someone who'd had that knowledge passed down to them: a healer, a shaman, a guide, a curandera. Medicine to heal, medicine to explore.

Ethan knew there were experiences negative enough that they could cause lasting trauma to the impressionable mind. He had first-hand proof of that. If what he considered to be his life's central failures could be called the stains of his past, then their ink, the colours of bruises, of old dead blood, had soaked through the layers of his mind and discoloured the fabric of his reality.

Gran said cut hearts are slower to heal than skin gashes. But these little guys have the potential to help close the deepest wounds. But then she said you never know. "Sometimes they play like greased otters and their jinx is all wild," she laughed. She cautioned, "They can make things darker if you turn away from what you see."

Grey and curled psilocybe quebecensis in his cupboard. With a single finger he pushed them around in the shallow bowl. Their dried bodies so very light. Twisted skinny stems, like they were caught in a wave, or made of one. Maybe they were actually straight but it was the world around them contorted. Tiny caps, as if they knew a light so bright they had donned little shading conical hats, like equatorial farmhands.

He was a little apprehensive.

He didn't eat one.

He ate three.

Then he filled the stove and took a chair and calmly waited for liftoff.

His mouth was chalky and the aftertaste putrid. A few minutes passed and nothing happened. *Probably too old,* he thought to himself while he was eating his dessert, a chalky and putrid-tasting fourth mushroom, bringing his total to approximately six dried grams. A quantity some would classify as a heroic dose capable of opening a pathway to a hero's journey. But they weren't working. He was just leaning back and looking at how the play of the table's candlelight on the ceiling kinda made the wood appear to stretch and shrink a little. *Probably just go to bed.*

He heard a slight whine. Maybe a log had some moisture in it that the stove was cooking out. *Closer to a mosquito,* he thought, *but there's no skeeters in winter,* he countered. The sound was siren: at first a tiny bit louder, then a tiny bit quieter—a gradual oscillation to its whine. He turned and it wasn't coming from the stove but from the candle on the table. *Water in the wax? The wick?* He listened to hear if some moisture in the candle would sputter and pop and the whine stop. He got up and walked to the table and took a chair, propped his elbows and went to rest his chin pensively on his hands to inspect the candle. He saw that his hands were older hands. He held one up and looked at its back and saw that the skin was alive, shrinking and expanding. It looked like the back of a slithering snake or a turtle flexing its shell. *Turtles can't flex their shells. So snake then.* He reasoned that if the options were alive skin or dead skin, of course he wanted the former, and so, with the matter of his hand-skin settled, he inspected the candle.

Closer to the source the sound now resembled crying. Higher-pitched female crying. He looked around the cabin for anything out of place or if some fairy tale storybook had been left open and the friendly mushrooms had invited a character to walk off the page. Though the room was now curiously pulsing and shining, nothing appeared fantastical.

Back to the candle. An insect circled the flame. That's not so strange: even in winter some lost gnat or slumbering larvae critter could have gotten smuggled in on the stalk of a dusty carrot, or come out of hiding from the deep eye of a cellar potato. But this insect crying like a child stuck on a slow merry-go-round. Large wings. It appeared to be a mayfly.

What afflicted Ethan was dragging around the shadows of his past. This bug's flutter cast no shade on the table. He was considering proposing that he or she take his shadow. He squinted, counting up its many feet, a detail he'd have to include when pitching the idea of stitching it on. He was collecting his words then thought that he ought to just outrightly ask this creature to confirm his suspicions of its misery. He said, "Why are you crying?"

The insect wasted no time. It spoke. "I came into the cabin as an egg carried in with the creek water. The cabin was so warm I thought it was spring." It was a she. She looked dejected, her pupils drooping in her big pretty eyes. "I hatched and now there's no going back and I'm alone and I don't have much time."

Like a weeping fairy and her tiny voice so faint that as she flew the far side of her orbit he had to bring his face closer to the flame.

"I am not ready to say goodbye. No way." Her voice high like a piccolo. Her long lashes swept over her stunning peeps. "I'm in love with life and I barely got to know it. This cabin. This fire. That light." She pointed one of her six legs. "This can't be all I get to know. I am not ready to leave. I have too much love to give. I want this! I want a thousand years of this." At that her eyes welled, brimmed, held their banks. Her charmingly high voice, its anguish did not exclude a certain beauty. "I've never loved. I'm heartbroken by all the love I'll never get to have."

He said with a voice that didn't try to hide its affliction her sorrow aroused, "How much longer do you have, Mae?"

"What time is it?"

"I don't know."

"Not long."

She kept flying her holding pattern around the candle. As she passed him she turned her head and cast those two polished gems of whatever precious stone is grey, glimmering the more from their wetness. "Will you speak to me of love?"

She was now flying away and so the mayfly's "Please" was faint. The diminutive effect of her distancing only made her request more dire.

With the pillow of her deathbed already fluffed, how could he deny her humble request? *Love*, he mused to himself. *Where to begin?* Certainly not at the end or he'd lose this lost romantic before he even got started. He wanted to tell her of that lush country, the utter enrapture of true love. *Mae, it's not fable. I've seen it I've lived it.* He was going to try and explain to her the beautiful depths of a profound bond, that the treasure of loving another more than yourself exists to be found for those courageous enough to seek it. *But in that search, Mae, in that search, there are risks. And if one day you hold such a treasure, the only thing that awaits is loss. The very act of possessing it is a reminder you will one day not. Oh, Mae. It can't be otherwise.* He almost told her all that. There were a thousand things he could say to her about love and he wanted to tell her everything, even silly things like massaging the ears of your lover who never asked for such a gesture, and washing her feet in the creek even though her footpads are clean and the gaps between her toes already flossed by grass, *Yet you wash them anyways, Mae—tender nonsense none more holy when you make love your religion.* He almost told her that, but he knew she was on short time and he couldn't wax leisurely. And now his mind was another step ahead, stumbling on the hurdle of what happens when your beloved is no longer.

His face sagged, and the candle highlighting its features accented its shadows.

She turned coming through the outer ring of her far lap and was wondering why he hadn't answered her. When she saw his face she right then had more concern for him than herself. With one of her many legs she covered her mouth as she gasped at his droop.

He had many ideas on the topic of love and he searched among them for one that didn't end in heartbreak—as surely there must be at least one. If he just searched a little longer, a little deeper, he'd find it. But the lack of that tale's swift arrival caused him anxiety, which doubled as he realized he was being careless with her limited time. Yet he refused to tell her sad truths of love's severed roots and delimbed branches.

He looked up and saw those glistening peeps coming his way—there's no way he'd break this poor nymph's heart. He had a few seconds to either dredge something up, or stone his face to deliver a bluff about love. He considered cutting out all the meat of the story and just saying with tremendous conviction, *Happily ever after!* With luck she'd be so distracted by the bow and ribbon that she'd never find out that the box was empty.

He faked a smile then held up his hand over his mouth and cleared his throat to signal he was about to begin. He was only buying time. In a last attempt he searched for something shiny in the murky bottoms of his memory bank. He became so engrossed in his quest for a love story with a happy ending that for a moment he forgot it was *she* who'd asked insight of *him*, and raising his head back up he almost asked her: *When skin weathers and life withers, isn't any love, any warmth, always from a false dawn? December-Mae, could it be otherwise?*

She rounded the bend. The troughs of her flutter now dipped lower and he wondered if the weight of her brimming tears was getting heavy.

"Love... Oh Mae..." Here he goes.

He said truthfully that his dinner wasn't sitting so well and his stomach, like his mind, felt a touch peculiar and he excused himself for a minute. "I'll be back," he said.

He got up and saw the cabin door was one hue darker than its normal brown, potentially in the shade of his projected fear. Besides the corners of his own mind, he knew where demons do lurk. *Night.* And that knowledge can be used for two ends: avoidance or confrontation.

He opened the door and the cold air rushed him like a band of thugs in a home invasion. The candlelight behind him flickered. He was concerned for Mae but the night called, was nearly howling for him. He stepped to the frosted planks whose snow-crunch under his boot was louder and more detailed than any step he'd ever placed ever. Looked outwards, upwards. The theatre of night. The sky glittered its vault of constellated gods, a twinkling display of myths and legends. Up there, a great bear slowly prowled the firmament. He saw it. He saw a young archer who must have been adored by his people because he was clad in diamonds. He saw a streaking star but believed it to be the tracer of a shot arrow and with his fist raised, he rooted once for the young hunter. So proud. He watched the bear in slow evasion as it fled from the sky. How it lowered itself down from the sky hindfeet first like Pooh Bear dropping from a low branch. That concerned Ethan. His raised arm slowly lowering. The big bear vanished into the horizon of shadowy treetops. He blinked hard and used that descending fist to rub his eyes. He looked back up for Ursa Major and no big dipper there was. Told himself a vagrant patch of cloud hidden by the night must have blocked it. *Just go back in the cabin.*

The log cabin, its warmth radiating on his back, tempted his return. He moved to go inside but quarterways through the turn he became so very ashamed that he was literally turning his back on Gran's instruction, "Run away from the darkness and you're liable to provoke the ire of the plant." When facing the interior of the safe and warm cabin he became repelled by its false comfort, and so kept on through his turn, pirouetting with uncertainty. He pulled on a heavy wool sweater hanging just inside the cabin.

He believed that by setting an intention of nonjudgmental curiosity towards his inner turmoil, he might have a chance to understand his so far inability to process all that had happened. That maybe a novel look would help him come to terms with the boy's passing and his own new solitary world. He took the mushroom's hand and invited his insecurities to join them in the playground of the woods.

He set out among the trees whose shapes he knew as he'd watched them grow—but of their branch tips he was less certain. He walked with his arms out before him and his fingers upturned, wisely protective of his one and a half eyes, though coming at the expense of feeling rather frail and beggarly and insane.

As if he had walked into softly radioactive woods, his world began to glow with a giddy flame. A glade where the foxfire burned. He stood before an old stump hued with bioluminescence: the woodland altar of their union, where once two old rings had been placed to charge the gold with lovers' vows. *Do you love me and no other? I do. Keep me safe. I will.* He heard the night telling that broken history like each old word after it had been spoken never left the glade but got caught in the branches to dangle like wood chimes. Will-o'-the-wisp now playing their empty promises. All more haunting by the fact that the night was absent of wind. He walked on.

Something small fell in front of him. He looked down and saw a tree-nut half-buried in the snow. Picked it up. Looked upwards to a branch and figured he found the one who'd dropped it because its paws were about chestnut-width apart. Little black button eyes. In general he was mistrustful of this court jester of the forest, given its alarm had spoiled many hunts. But this one looked timid, almost meek. It looked to have something to say but perhaps was restrained by its own bashfulness. Ethan said to it, "Speak."

"I'm a boy," said the young squirrel.

He shook his head disappointedly at what he understood to be a shameless lie and an inappropriate joke about his departed son. "No. You're not." He was already over this brief and hurtful interaction.

The squirrel was perched directly in front of him. To pass it, he stepped towards it. The man had no time for this trickster. He'd leave him to his own sorry life and deceitful ways.

The squirrel didn't hide its jubilance. It reached out both short arms as it prepared to be touched: hand shook, pet or hugged; the night was cold and its heart was lonely and it welcomed all affection.

The man set between its spread paws the lost nut. He would stay true to his values even amidst the cruelty of others.

The squirrel held the chestnut tight against its chest covering its tiny heart, beating with the arrhythmia of rejection. It turned on its branch and watched the man walk away. In the only way it knew how, the same way that in its young life it celebrated its rare joys, it bared the brunt of life's hardships. With its chin up. And its jaw lowered. It sang loud its chitter of longing.

Ethan now trekked through light fog. He heard an owl call. Then he saw the call. The sound shaped itself from out of the dark woods in large misty letters sized to his stature. *O O H.* That confused him. Then the floating letters resettled as *H O O.*

As he scrutinized the word-cloud he saw more letters inscribed around the middle *O*. Most people would not turn their head to read a message written in an oval, but he was far from most people, and having ingested a staggeringly large dose of psychedelic mushrooms, even further from their common state of mind. His head dipped as he followed the letter's curve, to the extent that he rested a hand on the ground to prevent himself from tipping over.

When I let go of who I am, I become who I might be.

He righted himself. The big letters hadn't evaporated or floated away and they were blocking his path. He stepped through that big *O* on his way to seek who spoke it.

A stand of tall timber. He didn't notice to his right the camouflaged white body because its yellow eyes were looking away. Until they weren't. The owl uncoiled its head eerily by unswivelling one hundred and eighty degrees—at least. Balsamic pupils dropped in the olive oil saucers of its recessed sockets. White feathered head lacking much for a neck. Furrowed brow of the perpetually perplexed or eternally discerning or forever thoughtful. This warden of the night fluffed its feathers, then regained its stoic demeanour. Cheshire cat of the North; drugged Alice approached.

He knew that the legacy of its species is of course to be engaged in the generational pursuit of truth, but he was going to ask it to confirm its intelligence before he queried it further. He got far enough into the process to open his mouth while the words welled in his stomach, but then he wondered to himself, in this world of uncertainty, where truth is hard to prove, are those who would proclaim themselves wise, not undermining that very claim? Should I be suspect of the owl's convictions?

He wondered if by humbly acknowledging his own lack of certainty, whether that acknowledgement itself became its own claim to a type of wisdom: I admit I know more by admitting I know nothing. A confession by the father of philosophy himself. But wouldn't that necessarily invalidate me from further discussion? Ethan's mind like his stuck jaw was caught in the glue of a contradiction and he waded in the muskeg swamp of a self-refuting puzzle.

His mind said *muskeg* but it heard *quicksand,* and he knew he shouldn't struggle further in that queer bog. So now he was wholly trapped: mentally, physically. Perhaps the word *quicksand* caused a psychosomatic reaction, because his knees started to bend and he began to lower: from standing kinda normal-like to slowly sinking on solid ground. Not wanting to risk increasing the rate of his descent, he moved nothing but his eyes, and those *frantically*. They found little more than the ponderous owl in front of him.

Several layers deep in this hallucinatory and sinking predicament, his brow furrowed as much as his snowy friend's here. The owl's exquisite vision did not gain anything from being a few inches closer to what it observed, even if what it observed was in the process of crumpling, so when it bobbed its head down low, perhaps it was doing so as a sign of eagerness for what this biped with pupils dilated like a mystic might have to say. If central to wisdom is a willingness to find errors in your own ways, and someone whose ways of life quite different than your own is likely an excellent source for counterpoint, could be the owl's head dip was a sign of its thirst for knowledge, and its silence was testament to its role as eternal student. *You learn more with your beak shut.* If the owl had a creed, those words would emboss its crest.

This man also a reverent disciple of learning. So now a shared problem: who speaks first? Their locked eyes. Ethan was almost crouched now and looking like he was on his way to self-refuting himself out of existence, convinced the first to talk would prove themselves the least committed to learning and thus instantly lose the respect of the other, trivializing this rare meeting of the minds. He had one question brewing like a groundswell inside him. He didn't want to waste his chance to hear the owl's wisdom. *In the wilderness of solitude how does one be worthy of suffering?*

At that moment off to his left—the owl's right—came a clinking like rattling chain. The owl, unable to move its conical eyes, turned its whole head. The man mirrored the bird. With the dark and the distance he was unable to see who rattled it. He forgot his most pressing question and instead asked the owl if it knew who rattled the chains. He said, "Who?"

The owl snapped back to him, as though with surprise at finally hearing him speak.

Ethan thought he glimpsed in its snowy face some hint of disdain, in its dipping-sauce eyes some flavour of rejection. Maybe the sage bird, after hearing the first word this pretentious man spoke was a sound to mock its own kind's call, believed its time better spent with more authentic company.

The snowy owl spread its wings and flew away. Flight as silent as snow, as silent as wisdom.

In this most exotic of mushroom nights, while feeling that the plant's effect had not even peaked, he waded from the *quicksand-that-never was*, to investigate the *chain-rattle-that-might-not-be*. With the belief that the world's threats were ever-looming, he walked with one eye permanently squinted. *Alert to dangers that've already come,* he thought.

He trudged on. Amidst different emotions was a concern for Mae. He knew she didn't have much time and he was uncertain how much had passed. Though he'd met her early in her life and their time together was short, given that she would live out her whole life over the course of just a few hours, he wanted to know her while she blossomed into the privilege of advanced age. He considered returning to the cabin, and truthfully he might have if he knew the way home. Again, the chain rattled.

In the sky was the outline of a maple tree and he believed it close to the source of the sound. Arriving he found an animal in a leg trap, the trap's chain rattling. He knew at least in part this was make-believe because they'd not used those outlawed traps in decades. But he humoured his doped imagination as well whatever this enchanted forest was presenting him. He approached the trap.

There he found a wood devil, *a wolverine*, looking all kinds of vicious. The wolverine, with total composure, had watched him walk up and now said hissing between fangs like a boreal vampire, "Help me essscape." The metal teeth of the trap's jaws had not cut the animal's leg, and that surprised Ethan. The creature exuded mistrust, and he wasn't sure if it was the weaponry of the animal's mouth or that when he looked for its eyes he only saw dark marbles plugged into its pug face. It was as if the forest had taken all the most ignoble parts of the animals and assembled them into one creature fated for outcast. But he tried to conceal his revulsion. Shaggy sorta mangy hide and striped similar to a skunk. Its body drawn out like a mink but wide. Its stature low to the ground, making it appear as if it was always sneaking. He knew its nickname had been given because of its tendency to antagonize trappers—stealing dead animals from traps, breaking into food caches and cabins.

"Wood Devil," he addressed it, "can I trust you?" His ten-pace distance underscored the genuineness of the question. Even from there he could smell it—he wondered if after it finished tearing apart its victims with those dagger claws, it had a habit of rolling in the gore.

"Yesss. Yesss of course. Help me essscape." It reassured him with a voice equal portions hiss and growl.

But it's not the crow's fault that its song is a caw and the dove should take no credit for its tender coo. Like all of life—*all*—it's just luck or lack of it. And he believed the indignity of this animal's unbecoming construction did not tell of its heart, and that in the resonance of its ugly voice he could not decipher its true nature. He'd hold to his values and so rebelled against his own prejudices; he reached for the trap. The sneering animal encouraged him: "That'sss it," it hissed. "Then we'll hunt the weak together. There are enough pups and cubs for both of us. Fawnsss for every meal." Its pink tongue slipping outwards between its narrowly set fangs. "Together we can ssslake thisss country red."

It's not its fault, he told himself. *It is not its fault.*

The wolverine spoke with confidence, like it believed it had divined the nature of this man and knew what the trapper wanted to hear. Perhaps with its nose talented enough to rival a truffle pig's it could smell on his outstretched hands all the blood from four decades of slaying.

With no small effort, due in part to the strength of the cold steel, as well his stoned body's general incoordination, he managed to gap the jaws sufficiently that the animal wiggled its leg free and immediately the wolverine snarled and snapped its jaws at Ethan. He jerked back and its treacherous bite narrowly missed taking a chunk of his arm. It prowled forward on its short and powerful legs, its back so broad, this creature of muscle and scorn.

Either built into its bones was a predilection for nastiness, a creature genetically pissed off and its veins coursing angry blood, or its harsh outward appearance engendered in the world an undeserved disdain, against which it had equipped itself with villainous ways to help procure what it knew it needed from the revolted world. It clicked its teeth at him with short bites. Then opened those jaws so wide like they'd come unhinged, snapping them shut with a sharp clapping sound. Jaws that snap bones—not finger bones—femur bones, tibia bones. It shook its head fiercely and the saliva wetting its mandible flung out sideways. The wolverine cast a powerful claw at the ground, which flurried the snow up in a northern equivalent of a dirty fighter throwing sand.

The man yelled in frustration into the fluster of blinding snow, "But I saved you!"

The wolverine's reply was at first only a laugh and that taunting sound was caught up in the furious whirlwind. Ethan heard cruel laughter all around him in his wood-bedevilled world.

"That makes you soft," it sneered. "Soft is weak. I eat the weak and the woods get strong." This animal sounding like it'd been schooled by a certain dark philosopher whose words, even if at times poetical, did not redeem his inhumanity.

Ethan replied, "I'm a good man!" Unsure of his enemy's position, he turned while saying that and so inadvertently addressed it to the whole wide woods.

"You are not a good man," spoke the darkness.

"You don't know me." The flurried snow beginning to settle. He saw the beast and it hadn't moved.

Its wet nose sniffed accusingly at the air. "I know enough."

"Don't do this. Right here and now you can change your ways."

"You asssk too much of me," it said. "Your death is in my nature."

"Be kind. Your cruelty only isolates you."

"No matter. He who has a *why* can bear any *how*."

"But your *why* is blood!"

"Indeed."

"Let me go."

"Let yourself go."

"Let me be."

"Let yourself be." Surely it was taunting him now.

"Allow me my freedom."

"Take it for yourself." It stalked its squat body towards him and it sneered and hissed and told him it had set the trap itself to lure him. It laughed. "Your compassion makes you easy prey."

At that he could take no more, "You wood-devil bastard!" He would try to kill this cruel beast to rid the world of its malice. He reached for his knife where it clipped to his pocket but his hand did not find it. The blade was gone. He gave a quick searching glance to either side of him to see if he'd dropped it nearby.

The wolverine grinned hideously, all teeth. It prowled forwards.

Shorn of those that mattered most to him, now more naked than the day he was born 'cause that little babe was clothed in love and this man here had been stripped bare of it, he no longer feared loss. No longer feared the night: not its darkness, nor its villains. Don't threaten a man with little to lose. He spat in the snow. This man with eyes narrowed for violent acts did not step backwards. "Alright then," he told it. "You do you. 'Cause for fuckin' certain I will." He balled his fists to let the unruly creature know he was going down swinging. He said to it that though he was drugged he was not entirely delusional, and yeah they both knew he couldn't win, but there was still the question of just how injured his opponent would leave the fight. He promised it: "Very."

He recalled that when he had earlier pried open the steel jaws of the leg trap, their cold felt real, but he still questioned whether the trap actually existed, and in this night's peculiar metaphysics, where he couldn't tell if fact and fiction were two different snakes curled up together, or just one serpent with a head at each end, he reasoned maybe his knife wasn't really gone. He gambled large given his enemy was so close, but he shut his eye to will his killing blade to his stabbing hand.

He opened his eyes and looked to his right hand: *empty*.
"Hell."

The earth began pounding. As if a juggernaut was jogging. Heavy stomps closing in. He looked but nothing yet to see in the dark woods though perhaps smell for the olfactory gifted as the wolverine just ran away.

The heavy paces recalled to his mind the sound of a boy running in the loft and pounding down the stairs in the mornings. He was only briefly caught in that reverie, as right then, trundling towards him out of the forest, came the constellation bear. Rhinestone dots brightly pegged the main features of its body. It didn't come straight at him, just loped its huge body his general direction.

"So you have returned, Glitter Bear."

Him and the bears had had their differences, but he believed that if he began this encounter with a proper showing of respect, they could likely put past conflicts behind them. He hoped it might even have a message for him, suggest to him some direction, his cabin preferably, but he was open to any journey worth taking. Maybe it would tell of what it had seen in the heavens.

As it closed in, he heard a question once posed by his boy: *What do you have to tell me, Bear?* At times Ethan's own voice reminded him of his boy's, not just the words but even the cadence and inflections. Other times he found that his mannerisms were the boy's, or the boy's were his—they'd spent so much time together that the sequence of those shared traits had become obscure, and any attempt to distil himself into a base metal from out of the alloy of metallurgical time, seemed impossible. His mind echoed with his boy's question and he said aloud: "What do you have to tell me, Bear?" The big animal closed in. Ethan waited for its message.

The bear's gait was clumsy, its lope a bit lame. It didn't stop to talk it just turned its big starry head in passing. "Fuck you," said the bear.

In their prior confrontations, Ethan had gotten the upper hand over the bears. He saw the thorn in this one's side was his own knife buried handle-deep into hide. He scrutinized the handle to verify if what impaled Ursa Major here was his actual blade, or just some sort of starry prop, like a stage replica. Couldn't tell. He did see a thin river of trickling starlight coming from where the blade had been sunk.

He watched it go, big ass, and for all the animal's size, its tail bobbed comically short. The bear left a sparkling wake like it was tearing through the fabric of the night and behind it trailed a shimmering dust. He smiled, believing his boy had turned the tables on his nightmare and was chasing his fears. He smiled for his little archer, and listened to the decrescendoing pitter-patter of the glitter-bear.

The land here was flat but he could swear he was hiking over waves and through them. His bewilderment from consuming three small and rather innocuous-looking dead plants was feeling a little overwhelming. He wanted it to be over. It was not over. He wondered out loud, "What have I done?" Looked at his hands and wondered if he'd ever be the same again. Whatever that meant, whether he was referring to his altered mind-state or a nostalgia for a lifestyle he identified with prior to his significant family trauma. In his vertigo, he reached out sideways to steady himself and he did not miss the trunk because no trunk grew there and on his way down he heard the word *four*. He turned his head to see who spoke. But it was only a part of himself clarifying the actual quantity of fungi he'd ingested. *Four, not three,* the pedantic voice said again. He landed sideways in the snow. Luckily his arm already outstretched to find the tree that didn't exist braced his fall. He lay a moment in cold though unsobering rest.

The exotic mushrooms stretched the night long and he walked on, tripping large under these drugged heavens.

One drifting, glowing, solitary bead. His depth perception had seen better days and he could not tell if that tiny light was so close that it was radiating from inside his own skull, or if the trajectory of shine from a distant star happened to pass through a tree branch's icicle that misleadingly magnified the source. A bead the colour of polished pyrite. He shivered at the thought that it might be the eye of a wolf.

Ethan spoke. "I know you're here." He did not know if it was there. But a wager with no downside, and so a dice this mad gambler was willing to roll.

If there was a wolf, it said nothing back. Ethan figured it was safest to assume there's never one far away in this cruel world. He then remembered that eyes do blink and this one had not. He didn't entertain the idea of it being firefly glow. Though he'd had the privilege of meeting December-Mae, surely she was anomalous at this time of year. He became concerned that she, distraught over life's brevity and in a risky attempt to prolong it, could have dipped her wings to the candleflame, and then, like Icarus, was flying to that venerable firmament in attempt to take her place among the Greek elite.

That light was dimming. He drew in a huge breath to tell her that even the stars don't live forever and what, dear Mae, happens to the constellations when one of its glittering studs winks out? *Will we still call it Corona Borealis when it loses the points of its crown? Mae!* His face sagged for her doomed quest. Nevertheless, her light almost gone now and with her so far along her way he did not want to lower her spirits on her incredible journey—*she was being so brave.* He yelled wishing her truly well and with hopes that fate would be kind, "Good luck, Mae!" He listened for her voice. His echo in the lonely woods. *Wise lady.* He smiled at her prudence. *Save your breath for those trials ahead.*

When it comes to matters of the mind, whatever practices aid one's survival—be they root medicines or the worshipping of moons—have reasonable grounds to be considered legitimate. Here was a man stumbling around alone in a self-induced psychedelic carnival through the very real winter and his wilderness of loss and solitude. And though feebly wandering out there, yelling at nothing and falling often, and at this point lost and risking freezing his body solid, another interpretation could hold that this was no enfeebled state at all. That the deep confusion and baffling imagery in his journey was the manifestation of the mushroom's neurogenic effect on his brain. Not outlandish to call it one man's peculiar exorcism and learning to navigate old lands with novel sight.

From there the night became less conventional and his memory of it the next day less reliable. Probably for the best. He managed to lose his clothes. At one point he could be found kneeling under a stately pine tree. The needles of its low bows grazed his back, tickling, poking. He couldn't recall how he'd arrived there so he could not extricate himself via the same route. This particular psychedelic did often imbue a tendency to see things with a new light, but that's not always advantageous. He was perplexed in how to flee a shallow tree-well. The problem being that every way he looked was a plausible escape route, and thus overwhelmed by choice, the many options baffled him. Like the donkey fated to starve between equal bales of hay. Him trapped under a pine like a rabbit he'd once caught in a snare, perhaps under this very tree—it looked quite similar. He appearing more piteous than that poor cottontail. The gods above no longer amused.

They debated whether to mercifully end the life of this wayward man, or let him continue on his troubled way to suffer more slings and arrows that they themselves would throw. On the far side of another world was another plagued man, eternally condemned to forever push a stone up a hill. Right then he got a moment of respite when a god reached down and lifted away that big boulder. The deity with his arm loaded about to cast that rock like a meteor and end this mortal's life, heard the voice of some puer aeternus, *some child-god*, tugging at his sleeve. The man under the tree heard it too. The voice of a holy boy pleading for mercy from a violent god.

Whispered the boy: "Can we let him go?"

The man silent. The god too.

Whispered the boy: "Can we let him go?"

The child's voice lingered in the man long enough that he poured from himself a libation to his boy, flooding the tree-well with tears, then he floated out of it.

Having never been more disoriented, at times struggling to see, at times in the night he cried. And that's okay. Broken-hearted, but that's okay. He didn't cease his exploration and in the end he arrived back to the tree stump where he had started. He sat. The glowing glade. The glade flooded with light. He looked to the bright stump but saw the illumination coming from himself. Thin bursts of light streamed from his chest. He marvelled at his own bioluminescence. He saw the light was coming through cracks of his split heart. Even if broken forever, that's okay, 'cause he still stored a piece of the glowing universe in there.

Prismatic tears magnified the starlight bejewelling his face. He smiled with the resolve to love while he could—*Just love while I can with the privilege of time. What else is there?*

· · • • · • • · · ·

Eventually, with the grace of night, he found the cabin door. Saw the candle still burning but reduced to a nub. *Mae hadn't flown to the sky at all*—he saw her alighted on the candle's rim. Dangerously close. She who had said her heart was broken from all the love she'll never get to live. *Sagely, Mae, wise beyond your years. You, gracious lady. Mustn't the answer then be to cherish and to seek and to live with urgency? Proceed with a smile from the rarity of life even though predatory time stalks us? No? December-Mae?*

He hadn't left the doorway while he addressed her in his mind. In one of the mushroom's last pulses he was sure he only needed to think his thoughts and she'd know of them, their bond being mental. He knew he was not her equal in knowing the ways of life, since when he first met her early in her youth—earlier that night—she had already figured out something significant. He couldn't even imagine what kind of wisdom she'd earned in her advanced age. Or perhaps the knowledge was already contained within her, she a cousin of the gadfly who had argued that truth is relearning. *Of course it's not, but hey. Mae?* He waited for her to laugh along with him at Socrates' expense.

He walked over to apologize for his earlier abrupt departure, to tell her of his bizarre journey, to finally expound on love, but above all to thank her for having the courage to share her fears. They mattered to him.

He approached the candle. Her feet in the wax. *Oh Mae.*

Her body looked so frail he didn't dare reach out. He looked for her stunning grey eyes and goddess lashes. Only saw strange antennae on an alien head.

He blew out the dying flame. Her wings, already dried, were swept up and away, flapping in his breath.

· · · • · • · · ·

The next morning he was reflecting on his mushroom trip. It was as if he had opened a door to a college class where the professor was giving a lecture. He had taken his seat. The professor in her black garb with her back turned was speaking while chalking out her theories up on the blackboard. Her ideas were kinda hard to understand as well her diagrams. And of her syllogisms, the conclusions didn't always seem to follow from the premises. When the professor turned around: big red nose, painted face, her mad smile. He leaned in from where he sat and wondered if the thin line of madness and genius would be a little harder to walk in those big clown shoes sticking out below the garb. Last night he had seen nothing clear, yet he knew clearly of something.

The bowl in the kitchen had enough mushrooms for an equivalent trip, but he'd had enough mushrooms for about forever. He was going to throw them out the window but decided to not chance sending some poor bastard scavenger on such an intense journey. He decided to burn their magic and opened the stove door then laid them in. As though performing some occult papal ceremony, he went outside to witness their smoke. The stout chimney with its little rain cap not looking so unlike a chrome fungi itself. A dark puff. He wasn't calling them black magic, just, caution, is all. *Gran was right,* he thought. *She mostly always was.* Then he felt guilty that he may have gassed a jay, drugged a robin.

He knew he'd taken a great journey last night, must have travelled many miles as his legs were sore. He was curious just how far in fact he'd gone. He didn't have plans to retrace that whole expedition, just have a brief look. But with only a cursory glance from the porch he could see his steps didn't extend farther than a stone's throw. Loops among loops, criss-crossed tracks, large depressions. Looked like he'd fallen, often. Half a snow angel fanned into the ground in the clearing. Off to his right a pine tree with a few broken low bows. He saw a curious display of a sorta flat-triangular pattern of brown snow. But a defecation neither piled nor solid, bit of a troubled angle to its imprint, like an old car with a low hanging exhaust had backfired over the snow. Looked like the one who expelled it had shat with some conviction trying to rid a poison. About a torso length from that pattern was a more circular stain. He assumed it was a puke-hole bored into the snow, likely deepened by both its heat and rate of flow. He thanked the sober heavens he couldn't actually recall having taken the pose of that double-bore purging manoeuvre. "No more mushrooms." A final pledge. That one out loud.

Town

As weeks passed, some details of the original story were distorted. By some accounts forgotten, in others embellished. And whether various tellers had done so with the conscious aim to swell his myth and fatten the tale, the legend of the trapper grew—people like to talk and they poured those truths some drinks.

Some town folk tracked the story like bloodhounds on a manhunt, but even bloodhounds get lost in the weeds. One night when the stools at the bar were full, someone was saying how two decades ago a part of the forest up there surrounding the hunting outfit had burned down, the forest fire that happened when the owners, the parents of Ethan's wife, had put the lodge and land up for sale. "It gets listed and then a fire ate up a lot of the land surrounding the hunting outfit. Obviously hunting land is less marketable all half-burned up. The place stayed vacant for a while. Just makes you wonder is all."

Buddy to his left, "I'd forgotten about that. Yeah. That whole place is cursed. What a history. That family must have done something terrible in a past life. You know. The Universe has a way of making all these things balance out."

A person sitting one stool to the left of that guy heard that and knew *the Universe* that just got referenced had a capital *U* and he rolled his eyes and was going to say something and looked over and saw that the person was drinking a club soda. He saw the club soda and shook his head and squinted at the speaker who wasn't even looking at him and he channelled his aversion into a few choice words. "Cheque please, Ivan."

Stool to the left of Club Soda empty. Club Soda listened to his friend sitting his right. "No, my point is that it wasn't an act of God. The same guy who lit that one all those years ago lit this one."

"Oh. Serial arsonist you're saying."

"Kinda fits, don't it? Well, we'll see how long it takes to sell this time."

"It's listed?"

He reached behind the bar top to the lower counter and took the Saturday paper from a stack of three. Opened it to the real-estate classifieds. Pointed a finger below a listing lacking a picture, just a short description under a headline. *Remote Hunting Land for Sale. $250,000.*

"Oh wow." He made a clicking sound with molars and cheek. "It was something like five hundred thousand a few years ago."

"Yeah. You interested?" The guy was grinning.

"Yeah. I'll make my offer. Right after I sleep in the cemetery. On Halloween." Only Club Soda laughed at his own joke.

Even with its low asking price nobody local would touch it. Some believed it was cursed. But anyone who knows any land's full history would think that land was cursed. Nevertheless, the more recent homicidal past made it most unmarketable. The land was broadly listed in the back pages of hunting-and-fishing magazines and online classifieds, but remote land like that is not so uncommon. The odd interested party would call the local real-estate agent, who then would dutifully inform that potential buyer of *some* of that land's history. When the potential buyer running an online search would input the former hunting outfit's name, *Sportsman's Lodge North Country*, sad headlines published by national newspapers cropped up. "Hunter Kills Boy Dressed as a Black Bear."

One inquirer must not have seen those stories because he drove in from out of town. Arrived at eleven a.m. An hour early for his appointment with the realtor, he went to the café for a late breakfast. Sitting in his booth and having eaten his eggs, hash browns, sausage, side of tomato and white toast, he lingered with his refilled coffee.

An order was being taken one booth over. "Coffee black. Eggs poached medium. Toast unbuttered. Bacon crisp. Bring the bill with the order, please."

The man thought to himself that based on her precision as well her pressed clothes and sorta no-fuss demeanour, it might be worth asking her opinion. Couldn't hurt.

"Morning, ma'am."

She looked over her open book to his booth directly ahead.

"This is sort of a strange question to ask someone out of the blue, but I was just looking for a little local insight on a certain property I'm interested in." He had printed out and circled the listing and held it up for her.

Babich set down the coffee. "I don't mind, son. Ask away."

He half stood then pointed politely to the open bench of her booth, "Do you mind?"

"Sit."

He passed her the paper and she moved the metal napkin dispenser to make room. She looked from the paper to the buyer. "I know it. An old family of the mostly departed." She said mostly and he wasn't entirely sure what that meant. "At the start of last winter eight buildings all burned down. All on their own up there. With no power running to them." She told him that if he asked around he was going to hear a sad story, and that he was going to hear things like *caretook, guarded, protected*. She inclined her head. "Haunted." She told him about the buried family. "I'd leave it alone if I were you."

Another night at the bar, the only bar, and it wasn't closing hour yet but it wasn't far off. It had taken a few attempts to really lay this plan's bricks and hammer its boards, given its architects by that hour were a little sloppy at the craft. One guy slapped the table. His pal, half-asleep and half-drunk, so really only one-quarter fully present, tried to muster his attention. "I know what. Let's start a fund. Raise the money to buy that land and return it to him."

"Who again?"

"The former owner." The lead engineer here kinda disregarded the fact that before the trapper's family acquired that parcel through the legislation of the 1800s enacted to help "settle" the lands while also taking them from those that had lived there for millennia, there were prior residents—those who went back millennia. But this guy's funny heart was still sorta in the right place. He continued, "That spooky land is now up for grabs. I say we return it to the one who haunts it."

When he got home that night he woke up his daughter telling her she had to make a poster. His daughter all sleepy and confused and wearing cat pyjamas, which had a hood with cat ears. She said, "What, Dad?" His wife hearing him come up the stairs said to the confused little cat-girl rubbing her eyes like paws, "Sorry, honey." She leaned her husband against a wall and put her little girl to bed again and then put her husband to bed.

That following morning was a Sunday and the little cat-girl started on the project. She enlisted her friends. Crayons and markers and coloured pencils and construction paper were distributed. The writing of those young free spirits of the classroom was curled out in elegant cursive: *The Trapper*. For those analytical kids showing first traits of minds governed by logic and order, plastic stencils were employed to trace letters uniform in both size and shape—though at times spaced with imperfect gaps on a tilted axis. Stencil versus freehand: futures foretold in these early choices? Though the wind may bend the branches, don't the seeds contain the trees? One kid alternated: curves looped into the next rigid shape. So, that child already lost.

On many posters the trapper seemed to be outsized, sometimes rivalling the height of the trees. Often he sported a round head and his smile took up half of it. Arms muscled like Popeye's. Some pictures had him with his bow and arrows. A dead moose on the snow, if you give that child credit for not colouring the white page. On another, the carcass was a beaver, the trapper's knife bloody. Kids. His hair ranged from cropped to shoulder length and on one he had red locks that sorta curled out and became tree vines about him. The young artist made his mark in the bottom left. *Gordie.* Taped below all the posters on a separate sheet, a parent had written details of the fundraiser. Little cardboard boxes like UNICEF receptacles hung underneath. That same day, posters were pinned up at the gas station, the diner, the bar, the other diner, the hotel and the motel. The one at the motel taken down.

The newspapers that told the tragic tale of the trapper and his boy had details intimate to the degree that one might think the person mostly featured in those articles might not have been so enthused about having his personal life made so public. Had he known. As a follow-up story the fundraising effort was also published in several papers, both online and print. Significant funds were raised and held in escrow at a bank. By January the campaign had raised about one hundred and twenty thousand dollars, nearly halfway to its goal of buying that land and gifting it to the man whose nickname titled the posters. But the campaign lost its steam and the flow of funds turned to a trickle.

Woods

For several days the trapper was buoyed by the mushroom's insight. But with each day, its message *to love while he could with the privilege of time* seemed to diminish in potency. The experience hadn't brought the catharsis he hoped it might. If he was in fact healing, his progress was not like flight of a Canada goose but that of a monarch, flutters and dips. He knew that though time had healed his cut eye, it had not sutured his deepest wounds. The continued spiritual anguish did burden him.

Fucking bear it then.

Some part of him, all rock, wouldn't quit. So neither did he. He had resolve without resolution.

He was navigating best he could his world of abysses, chasms of regret, crevasses of loss and lonely failure. But strung across these depressions, like thin shining tightropes, were gold threads that could be tread. He tried to place one tentative and unsure step ahead of the next, feeling his uncertain way while trying to walk the straight and narrow.

His days hardly differentiated and his routine and practices of self-care were so very repetitious. He liked routine. Routine felt good. The structure of it at first gave him something to cling to, like rails, then eventually something to climb, like rungs. He found some well-being in structure then found some growth in well-being. *And what better way to achieve a little spiritual ascent than holding the hand of a ghost*, he told himself that with laughless humour. Humour was a part of his medicine. He was taking his medicine.

On the table, the arm of the handheld mirror was sticking out from under a pile of books. He hadn't put it away since the day long ago when he had bandaged his eye. Though he'd stopped dressing the wounds he hadn't even checked the scars. He slid it out from under the stack. Brought it up and turned it. His healed, half-closed eye. *Good. Where once you had to squint to shoot, now you're always ready.* He turned his head in examination. The scarred skin of his temple and eyelid.

The ritual of his mornings had him up before sunrise, first getting the fire going. To delay an inevitable trip to town, he had reduced his coffee from two cups to one, replacing it with tea. He steeped dried leaves from last summer's foraging, wild mint and raspberry, dandelion that while neither native nor sown did sprout like a weed around the cabin, brewed birch-bark twigs and hemlock needles from winter trees for winter teas. He'd exercise and shave and wash himself. Then it was black coffee in a white porcelain mug warm in his hands that he drank slowly by the window and the stove's fire was warm and its sounds comforting and the brew smelled like sacred and the sun outside lit the window and did nothing more than slowly rise, and illuminate, and warm, and be perfect. He'd read great books, by his account, some of the best ever written. Stories that weren't stories at all, of love and loss and death and joy and suffering, history and culture; the redemption found through reading of the human experience.

You are not alone. He'd lose himself in it. He found new ideas in old pages and read not to finish a book but to see beauty, understand a concept, better understand the world. He had always been a slow reader and now he was a slower reader and he considered that progress.

He read early Greek thinkers, when philosophy—though extremely flawed in its justifications for slavery and disregard for human equality and women's rights and other moral structure-fires of its day—was concerned with how to live virtuously. Not the obscurity and pedantry that much of philosophy in later centuries would become. He read and found insight in the Koran and the Bible, when they weren't proclaiming various incredibly heinous acts. He saw a pathway for a partial release of mental afflictions through the teachings of Buddha, when those texts weren't proclaiming highly dubious metaphysics. History books were always bookmarked. Though he had to read a lot of poetry to find a stanza of resonance, there were lines written with enough steel they could be used as girders for bridges. If the vaulted night skies are where lying tsars store their jewels, then the pages of literature were the keeping place of much other wealth. Ethan was rich. Turns out he did have books of self-help. Turns out he mostly read from that genre.

He believed in mornings and he was devout and he hadn't called it worship but with such ritualized adoration, what other name?

After breakfast he would shoot his Daily Arrows—that's what he and his boy had called it so he kept on calling it that. He hoped that by deliberately speaking words from former times he could coax them from out of the jaws of the past, if not defang that very beast. He was continually trying to lay down his defensive arms. *Boy. Boy,* he would say. *Boyboyboy.* He would try to take it back. Realizing he had little control as to whether the evening would bring a darkness far blacker than the pigmentless night, he tried to release his preoccupation with his fears, telling himself that it couldn't be anything different than what it was going to be. Things came before, things have to play out. *Hate the man who shot your boy as much as you hate yourself for dressing him as a bear and hate the bear that eats the fawns and hate the grass that feeds the fawns and hate the sun that grows the grass and hate the snow that buries the garden and hate everything along with it. Just hate it all. Or accept that things came before and so have to play out. There's no getting outside of it. Are you so arrogant to believe you stand outside of cause and effect?*

His left-hand's finger with the missing tip did not affect his archery, but altering his form to accommodate his right eye was not so easy. The cognitive tracks bringing his knuckle to his old anchor point, low on his jaw, were deeply rutted. He'd draw the bow but find himself retaking his old form and have to draw down and start again. A slow process of sculpting new muscle memory. It took time. He gave it that. Sometimes he practised while kneeling, sometimes he'd strap on the climbing spurs and from up in a tree loose arrows to the bag target. He'd get his heart rate up from push-ups then let fly a dozen fletched darts for the red paint. Eventually he had to draw a second bullseye on the face of the target, and then a third, because he'd sliced a couple vanes and one time split a shaft. *You are Robin Hood.* He'd once said that to the boy. He smiled at that now.

His talents returned to former levels.

Then he exceeded them.

He could make a heart shot on a moving deer at fifty yards, but he still didn't shoot past thirty and never on a moving animal.

Every bolt on his bow was tight and he knew the twist count in his string down to a half-turn and its limbs gleamed from polishing and he stropped the broadheads' razor blades on buckskin until they shined like flakes of the sun.

He believed that he was entitled to very little in this world and he aspired to be worthy of his lot. To have a body deserved of the air it draws, to have a heart worthy of a beat.

At the edge of the cabin's clearing, a pine branch ten feet off the ground was rubbed barkless in two places, and that bare wood looked polished. His hands unblistered from chin-ups because they were already calloused from rope climbs without the aid of his feet. Physical strength as fundamental as spiritual fortitude: *earn your perseverance in this harsh world*, he told himself. It wasn't that the world deliberately preyed on the hurting and the weak, but it certainly didn't favour them. The world isn't malevolent, it's indifferent; its wounding more like shotgun spread than sniper fire. *So armour up*, he decided. It's better to be a warrior in the garden than a gardener in the war and so he hardened. Push-ups, sit-ups, squats with a heavy log over his shoulders and farmer carries hauling pails of creek water that even amidst the bitter cold was still flowing with its own defiant turbulence. The creek inspired him. The tree bows flexed under heavy snow loads. The trees inspired him. He took instruction from the woods. He at once bulked up his body while exorcising his demons. He didn't do reps to muscle failure, as being sore would've meant he couldn't afterwards put that strength to practical use, but every other day he set a new highwater mark. His regime gradually shaping him, giving him old-world strength, the physique of a lumberjack, farmer or mason. A form sculpted by the woods—Rodin of a Northern man. That ponderous sculpture animated from his stony pose to wander the woods.

He kept vigil for threats in whatever shape they might take: harsh weather, peak predators, cabin fire or famine, for cold and for loss and for death. By both inflicting and receiving suffering, he knew that upheaval is always closer than it seems and every morning he splashed that truth on his face like the cold water from the basin he washed away the sleep with. Wash away the illusion of his own permanence. Wake him to the fact that though one coming morning will feel like the rest it would be his last. He tried to sow humble seeds of gratitude by appreciating the absence of specific torments, a type of negative happiness: no roof leak, no toothache.

Cords of wood were stacked and split for the rest of the winter and well into the next and he laid long strips of bark overtop the stacks to shield them from the winter snow and coming spring rain. He saw himself in the spring rain. He sat and visualized himself in it, *him in the rain*, projecting himself into the future so the fibres of his mind, like the tendrils of bush beans, could reach out and curl and pull him along. *Medicine*—his list was long.

Looking through tears that he did not disdain, he cut his nails and trimmed his hair.

The cellar with its shelves full of mason jars looked like a mediaeval apothecary, or the storehouse of a travelling freak show's extraordinary collectibles preserved in formaldehyde—those foetuses and shrunken heads and baby pigs. Though his were full of fish, smoked walleye and pike packed in salt, other jars brined and the water flavoured with oregano and thyme leaves, garlic cloves and whole peppercorns. It had been the slowest year for deer hunting he'd ever known, but he was going out regularly, and with luck—his good, the deer's bad—he would add pemmican and strips of smoked venison to his cellar.

In a kind of semi-formal exploration of pain, he routinely plunged in ice dips, then tried to observe as calmly as he could the mental phenomena from that insufferable water, asking himself if there might be a glimmer from some diamond stud sewn into the cloak of hurt. He'd jog frozen to the misty shack and be with his body's fireworks, transitioning from the artillery of the cold, to the armistice of the warmth, to the new onslaught of the intense heat. He'd tell himself to sit there and take it. He'd sometimes first set a cup of mint tea in the sauna and when he returned the space would be infused with its aroma and he'd then drink it to amplify and internalize the heat, ending his sweat-soaked session with eyes closed, legs crossed, and a mind open, inviting any lurking demons to make themselves known. They were only messengers coming to let him know he had something to address. When both the stove and his inferno thoughts rose the temperature of the sweat-shed to such thermometric heights it'd mush a spud, he'd attempt to remain even longer in a state of dispassionate observation—feeling the burning air through his nose, listening to the rage of his heart without trying to corral it.

Sometimes hardship, whether self-inflicted or otherwise, fortifies and growth results. But not all hardship strengthens; sometimes it just erodes the inflicted, and that degraded thing is never the same. He wasn't entirely sure if he was getting it all right. He found that even pain and pleasure were not reliable beacons. It was hard to know when discomfort was reliably signalling stressors to avoid, or when the ache came from the strengthening brought on by a beneficial challenge.

He wasn't sure if that earlier sweet dream of a goddess was a star trying to help him navigate a course through old lands to new love, or if she represented some seductive falsehood that would have him chasing an empty ideal. How to decipher a signal from out of cacophony?

He found there was a fluidity to his mental states and whatever it was, good or bad, he could wait and soon enough he'd notice a different feeling. Recognizing the transient nature of his mind meant whatever emotion occupied it in that moment seemed a bit less credible, more trivial, and thus the prick of sad quills less sharp, the winds of self-doubt less strong. *Lonely—so what? So what?* he asked himself. *Lonely isn't a death sentence. It's just a bit sad some nights.* His spirit sometimes a bit heavy in the night. But the sun brought the tinder of morning: she warmed, she lightened. And when she lifted so too rose his spirits like a rising branch melted of the night's frost and freed of its cool burden. Then the day would begin with its own pursuits and challenges and unexpected pockets of suffering, reward, and beauty.

He was doing alright. Mostly he felt pretty good. Like maybe nine-tenths happy, and one-tenth sad. That's not bad, all things considered. The lonely tenth was living in the loft of his mind. One past day it was her tears that had soaked the little trapper's explosives. She cried often, but she tried to keep her sobs silent for she did not want to spread more sadness in the world. One night her quiet tears pooled on the floorboard of his mind, then drained through a missing knot in a plank and they sprinkled down and got caught in the light from the projector flickering its images in the theatre of his skull. One voice in his head thought it was raining diamonds, "*Diamonds*," she whispered. She was overjoyed at their beauty and she nudged her friend next to her, and he smiled also. And so the accounts in the world of *happy* and *sad* were about as equal as before the lonely tenth cried her pretty tears. Ethan was looking out the window one afternoon and thought he saw a December rain, but he'd lost track of the days. It was the new year's light playing in the floral patterns of the frosted window.

He was out hiking when he felt another presence stalking him. It had been lurking for a few days. One prior day near the creek it was so very close to him and with the small river's audible flow he wouldn't have heard its steps so he must have just sensed it. But when he turned, it was gone. Then one day it came again. Briefly. Then the next.

Contentment.

He hadn't seen it coming, but there it was. An imperfect and inconstant contentment.

TOWN

THE SMALL TOWN WAS a jumping off point for fishing and hunting trips. Wealthy men, and it was almost exclusively men, drove or were flown up in small chartered planes to the town and took lodging at one of the two accommodations. Some fishing charter companies were based out of town but most flew their clients farther north on floatplanes to remote camps and lodges.

One night a group of four wealthy businessmen returning from a stay at a fly-in hunting resort were eating dinner at a table of the bar. Pepper steak; potato split down the middle and in the steaming cleft a square of melting butter, chives, an option for sour cream and bacon bits; Caesar salad, warm bread. Beers before the main course, wine during. One of them was looking at a poster pinned into the wood panelling of the bar. Stencilled letters that flowed into freehand. By now the paper was torn and had a couple stains. It displayed a primal-looking masculine cartoon standing above some massacred and hybrid beast: body of a beaver, head of a moose. The artist signing his name had turned the first letter around, making the uppercase *G* and lowercase *e* something of mirror reflections. Like *beginning* and *end*, though farthest apart, had a relationship that excluded the middle. Fuckin' Gordie, here. That artist rebellious at his early age not even respecting basic alphabetry. Next to the fantastic Wildman and sized to his height was a crayon-drawn thermometer. Its tube halfway coloured in red and there was a dotted line delineating funds raised, funds outstanding. The businessman while still looking at the poster forked a piece of meat then dipped it in the bar's homemade BBQ sauce. Ivan, the establishment's owner, called it his "Small-Town-Bar-B-Cue Sauce."

After retracting those tines his mouth had emptied of its cargo, the businessman pointed them to the poster. "Who's the woodland killer with the T on his shirt standing over the fucked-up buck-badger?" Given the avant-garde of Gordie's latest work, this man's interpretation was entirely valid.

The waitress Pam gave them the broad strokes. Ivan was standing a ways off, not so far he couldn't hear. When she finished, he came over to narrow those strokes up some, came out from around the bar with a complimentary bottle of wine and took up a chair. Ivan told them the story as he knew it, his version of it, everyone's being subtly different given the unresolved hypotheses and telephone-gamed dynamics distorting its fidelity.

He told how the land was first acquired. How it'd later been lost. How the man with a *T* on that poster, who in all probability had no such *T*-sweater in real life, had met his real-life wife, lost her. Lost his son. The fire, and the several theories of the fire, and the fact that the police hadn't charged anyone with arson, though there was a charge of manslaughter. He told them how the insurance company had hired a fire inspector, but since those lakes had been in an indeterminate state of slush at the time, that inspection was delayed. And then about six feet of snow fell. He said such inspections are more often than not inconclusive anyways. Told it start to finish while his audience of four cut their steak, forked their spud, mopped their plates with bread. They looked entertained, like they'd come for a meal but got dinner and a show.

The proprietor while he was telling it had gotten up, and still talking, went behind the bar and returned with a second bottle of red, one of his better, that to these guys was not such a special bottle. He knew one of the gentleman by name because everybody did, not just in town. He pretended like he didn't. The one guy owned a company with a market cap as big as some small countries' treasuries. Though Ivan didn't know the three others, they were known names in financial circles. One managed a successful fund of funds. The two others were early-stage investors who although had way more investments that went to zero, they had a few that went to the moon, then beyond it. Based on their exchanging head turns and *C'mons* and *No ways* and eye rolls, safe to say all four were taken in by the story's entertainment value and nothing else. In the same way certain movies start with a disclaimer: *These events are based on a true story*, they likely figured this recounted version had about as much in common with the bare facts as a carrot cake has with its featured vegetable. It's mostly not even orange.

At the story's conclusion all four of them were looking for the angle here, smelled a ploy at play to pull on non-locals or rich guys or something. These guys were pursued profession-ally. In the business of sniffing out bullshit, their spidey senses were tingling like they could tell it wasn't just the spud being buttered.

But Ivan was not massaging the details of the story, given that real life had wilded it up enough. He was only trying to make supple the leather of their wallets by telling a captivating history while liberally pouring out wine. At the end the fund manager, smiling, said what all of them were thinking, "Come on. How much of that is actually true?"

"Ask around," Ivan shrugged. "Most of the details are in the paper even. And not just the local paper. *The boy. The fire.* It's all there. The funds have slowly been coming in drop by drop." Saying this, he pulled the cork from the bottle and their sounds almost rhymed. *Pop.* Ivan had his own version of trophy hunting: catch the wealthy in good spirits and ply them with good spirits on their way home from catching trophies. Play it right and who knows how many zeroes you might see at the bottom of the bill. Ivan with four big racks in his crosshairs.

The natural habitat of these men was well above ground level in professionally decorated offices, high-rises with stunning views of glass and concrete. In front of their mahogany or oak desks were Italian leather chairs awaiting founders of promising companies who would lob offers of equity at those desks—fractional ownership at favourable terms. The men behind the desks would listen and question and patiently wait to swing for only the fattest of pitches.

Two empty bottles. Ivan figured he'd been both a good host and a good sportsman; he left them alone. He knew when to take line and when to let some out.

Someone plugged the jukebox. There hadn't been any songs for a spell and this one came on a bit louder than normal. Peculiarly, organ music to a song that started slow. After a few bars—too sweet and freeing to call them bars at all, notes so sweet they dissolved what was trapped behind them—there came a light guitar riff. A couple isolated strums like just lonely islands of lost chords, chords looking for company. Heavy drumbeats—company found—but spaced out and deliberate. Like a meat mallet that set about tenderizing the melody. An electric guitar warped with a slide pulled the notes into their proper bent shape, all slow and warped. People must have liked it because fewer spoke.

The CEO who had a wall in his sound room where hung a guitar once played by King next to a guitar once played by Clapton next to a guitar signed and once owned and played by Hendrix said, "Free Bird." Not like he was helping others identify it, just giving it the respect of speaking its title. After listening for a bit he closed his eyes. Now says a bit quieter, "Let's just not talk for this one." They don't.

He's sitting there leaned back in the wooden chair listening to the floating sounds of Skynyrd. And though their plane did go down that day, the savage gods couldn't take it all. The CEO has his eyes closed. He's listening for guitar licks among vocals he knows well. Instead he hears the thin resonance of a skinny stream of wine. He doesn't open his eyes to see that pour filling a glass. He knows its sound well. He was smiling before so he doesn't stop now. He can't hear the colour but he does. He can't hear the colour but he does and he hears the liquid curling in the glass and in his mind he sees its red colour, almost transparent as it falls, deeper red where the curve of the glass catches it, nearly purple as it fills for the dim lighting of the pub. It's not his glass. His he holds in his lap and so he was smiling at his friend's cup being filled. He hears that stream being thinned out and he blindly reaches his outwards. The skinny sound stops for a half beat then starts again and he feels his glass becoming heavier, becoming full. Full. He wasn't concerned if it would runneth over 'cause in that moment it already had. The smiling CEO looking like a blind beggar who at least in this moment is not so dismayed with life's circumstance. He can't see that the other glass recently filled still hangs in the air, then two more glasses join them. The pouring stops. He's about to retract his arm. He both hears and feels four clinks of crystal.

When the song started to fade, the CEO opened his eyes. He said to Ivan, "How much to make this same thing happen next year—steaks, music, wine, this same table. *Everything*. We're going to pay ahead and see if we can't lock it in." He asked that like he was at Sotheby's, but this time it wasn't a rare guitar that had gotten wheeled out to the bidders. On auction was a piece of sweet time with his favourite buddies with his favourite song and food and bread, and though the wine started out a little flat it must have decanted not just into the glass but gone on to swirl around the whole room and the warm atmosphere must have unfurled its fat petals and ripened its bouquet because it tasted of music and friendship and the flavour of cabernet red—what colour? The colour of love.

Ivan looked like he was trying not to look like he was running some numbers in his head. He brought his eyeballs back down from where he'd momentarily rolled them up to calculate on the ceiling of the room. His proposed number: "We're just happy to have you. The good times are on the house. This year. Every year." He left the bottle.

Later when the group left, Ivan walked over to see what he'd caught. He counted the cash and was surprised it only covered the food and drinks. He thought he'd sent a single bullet straight through all of their hearts. He lifted the cash. Under the bill and taken down from where it had been pinned into the cheap pressboard panelling was the poster. A black pen had coloured in the fundraising thermometer level to its top. An arrow pointed to a phone number with an unfamiliar area code.

Someone later said angel investors arrived by floatplane.

WOODS

WHEN THE SNOW FELL heavy as a curtain he'd clean and bake and make soup and sharpen blades and he'd watch the fat flakes fall like he was a man in a snow globe—shaken, definitely shaken, but it was all still kinda idyllic. He'd watch the fat snowflakes thinking he'd never want any other weather than snow. And then next day the weather would break and the sun would come out and he'd think, I never want any other weather than sunny days. And in time to come when the spring brought rains, he also liked the rains.

When he made bread it was nearly a half day's affair, but his mind, engrossed with the craft, quieted, and the effort's final result tasted incredible and he treasured every cut slice or torn chunk. The crust chewy, the crumb soft. At once savoury, acidic, and sweet. This one still warm in his hands looked perfect, all light and risen and different woodish browns and scored in a hash with the crust singing its cooling song. The beauty of it as much as its flavour. Though yet to taste it, his watering mouth agreed. He took the bread outside. He tore it in half and the loaf bloomed a great savoury cloud into the midday air. He halved those halves then halved them again and he walked some ways from the cabin with an arm to his stomach swaddling the savoury eighths. He walked a large circle through the woods surrounding his cabin. When intermittently he found a stump or boulder, he'd stop and place a chunk on it until he'd offered up seven of eight. He was hungry and he held the last and looked at it, then he laid it also. The gesture more for himself than the birds and the squirrels. Flavouring his world with a little silly kindness. The man modelling himself after the boy he had tried to raise: develop a little hardness to him while trying to keep him pure at his core. At once gritty and sweet. Part of himself begrudged the softness of that act, but he did not begrudge the part of himself begrudging himself. He just made another loaf.

The charm of the present is that if he felt good right now, those feelings were true: the future couldn't change that. That future present could only speak for itself, not this current present. More and more he felt good. He tried to leverage current contentment for future gains: memorized verses from some of his favourite books. Good words in times of trouble lift heavy. Exercised even harder. Strong muscles in times of trouble lift heavy. Ate as nutritiously as he could. Made his silly offerings like seeds for the birds and the squirrels, the breaking of bread with his forested world—all these modest pursuits of epiphanous love. That's what he called it. Love where he formerly didn't see it. He could register traces of light in pockets that used to hold only dark.

Ethan didn't believe in miracles, he believed in the wondrous complexities of a world where a lot of things happen at once, combining and interplaying to make rare things from hidden things, all of it with so much mystery and beauty that how could it even be possible, and he had once shrugged his shoulders and told the boy magic. "Magic," he had said to the boy. *Boy. Boy.* And he still believed that. He'd made no progress deducing the metaphysics of the incredible world and had arrived at no better word for it. Miracle seemed to imply intention. Magic seemed better. But he might say he believed in the supernatural because *that there was even something rather than nothing* seemed quite supernatural in and of itself, or in the very least, extraordinary. He believed in the extraordinary.

Dinners were simple but he gave them effort. He seasoned with dried herbs and spices that he'd grown or picked. Overhead and next to the pots and pans hung bulbs of garlic from long scapes he and the boy had braided the summer before. Sprigs of thyme, sage, rosemary, and parsley were lashed with thin strings looking like miniature bouquets for ceremonial offerings. He'd first smell their modest aromas before he cut them to release a more bountiful bouquet, and then tried to match their aromatics to the night's dish. Tasted as he went, salted in stages. He tried not to alter too much the inherent flavours of the wild meats and vegetables he was preparing, using the seasonings to draw out what was already present, enhance and accent them and mostly let them speak for themselves. On the wooden counter the chef's knife tapped rapidly enough to turn the head of a woodpecker while he eased carrots and onions towards the blade sliding against his nails and healed finger-nub. The precision of a sharp knife. The sounds of searing and bubbling and the textures and the colours and the smells and the flavours. He wondered whether the lines separating meditation and worship and religion and beauty and love were in fact lines at all—none of it God, all of it holy.

He had read of a lost boy who had said that happiness is only real when shared. That sounded true, partially because it was succinct and pretty. Similar to how the goods of a well-dressed salesman seem of higher quality than those from some scrub hawker. When he first read that years ago, it seemed sage, but the fact was when he was engaged in something that mattered—hunting, cooking wild food, even listening to rain tapping on the roof, reading great writing, black coffee at rising dawns—in all that and more there was something good even doing it alone. And it was a happy thing. And it was a real thing. He felt like he owed an apology to that poor boy as well all the other lost romantics.

There's language to the woods and though he'd lost it for a time its message was coming back crisp as lightning crack, true as loon call. On his last hike he stopped under a grand maple and he felt rooted. He wondered to himself if when you're in your proper church, spirits get lifted. Behold, said the tree.

Heavy snows did not cover the modest peace he was cultivating in his mind's garden. His body scarred, though no longer blue; his soul bruised, but not beaten. He was humbly fostering a little solace in his woodland sanctuary, willing to struggle and kick for his version of love in its various forms: the trees and the creek and the birds and the words and the bread and the blade and the snow and the bow and the forest fauna and the temple sauna. The language of the woods now paired with song as he found the rhythm of his days.

One afternoon he was kneading a sourdough flatbread and laid the dough into a hot pan on the stove. He set the jar of maple syrup on the table and then went to the shed to get wood and got distracted by some bobcat tracks. When he returned he found the flatbread blackened and cabin smoky and so left the door open to vent it. He lifted the black disc from the cast iron. A bird fluttered in through the haze. It landed on the arrow shaft he purposely never had removed from the wall.

It was looking at him and it tilted its neckless head.

"My boy Jack? My girl Jackie?" He wished he had painted a bracelet on Jackie's ankle so he could know for sure. He smiled and pinched the flatbread and pitched some crumbs to the floor below the whisky jack.

Though dawn was coming earlier and dusk delayed, spring was still weeks away. He figured it late January, but it could have been early February, maybe even mid month. Didn't know didn't much care. He was more curious about the small plane flying his way. Wheels, not skis. The plane coming in low and slow over the trees. He hadn't seen one in a while. *Some fly-over out of curiosity,* he figured, *or Bill checking in before heading north to one of the communities.* In past days, any plane sighting brought a tinge of invasion. But with nobody to protect he didn't feel the plane was invasive, just foreign. He watched the alien bird lowering.

Its flaps down and nose up, flying just above stall speed. The pilot-side wing dipped. A rectangular brown package not all that small was falling to the cabin's clearing. It thumped in the snow. The pilot levelled the wings and waved smiling. Ethan Edwards, slow to raise an arm, slow to return it.

· · · ● · ● · · · ·

Ethan had been sitting in the cabin with the air-dropped package on his knees. Heavy brown paper. His first thought before he picked it up was that it was of a legal nature from the police or the courts. *Who else would send something?* he wondered. But he ruled it out for two reasons. One: its size. It was almost three feet long and barely fit through the plane's window. Two: Whoever had addressed wrote *Ethan Trapper Edwards.* That wasn't his real middle name. Like they were trying to cover their bases or attempting to satisfy all sending parties or had a sense of

348

humour. The facial muscles to express intrigue, perplexity and concern are all about the same. That mixed mindset showed on his face. He swallowed and those mechanics were lumpy. When he flipped the package over, nothing rattled and nothing was written on the back. He considered burning or burying it. *How could this be anything other than setbacks and complications?* He hefted it again. Neither feathers nor bricks. He tore where it was taped, unwrapped the heavy paper and set that away for fire-starter. Cardboard box taped shut. He thumbed his blade and slit the tape and opened the folds.

It was stuffed full with a blanket, bundled not folded. Not a blanket, an afghan. Its colours like a fall forest—reds, yellows, oranges. He saw that and didn't move. Then added to the three facial expressions were a fourth and fifth: distrust, distaste. For a package from another world, it looked like a delivery from the past. He lifted it out and it had more than just wool weight to it. From its pregnant shape it looked like a cocoon.

How do you move on if you call the past to every scene? Certain shapes and shades, items and sounds, were still trapdoors to his former life. For certain most people would easily detect the differences between the two blankets, this one looking newer with fewer frayed threads and stray fibres, and the colours of this new wool more vibrant. But progress or not, his lens to the present was still smudged, in places smeared, with the past.

An affront, a sacrilege. His feelings less mixed now. *Sick joke?* He wondered if when he unrolled it he'd find some voodoo doll, bones even—the old colours, this swaddled shape—all too similar to that sad day he laid a four-foot god six-feet deep. A fraction of Ethan, some splinter of the man whose rage had the power to blind his rationality, knew a rogue defiler had desecrated a holy tomb. He'd track that fucker down. Like a wooden stake whittled sharp to drive through hearts, that splinter was inciting the other parts for violent acts. *Just find a clue as to who sent this.* Inside Ethan other self-parts pricked up their ears. What gives more purpose and zeal to life than vengeance?

He reached out and pushed at the top of the bundle to reveal its violation. The afghan unrolled.

At its centre was a Ziploc bag of muffins. Blueberry muffins gently squished, now slowly reflating. The splinter-self with the call to arms now bashfully silent. Beside the bag of muffins was a large package of coffee beans. He smiled at the muffins. He smelled the beans.

At the bottom of the box was a book and a couple chocolate bars and several papers. The bars said eighty percent cacao and he didn't know what that meant and one morning he would try a piece with his mug of black coffee and figure that when he did inevitably head to town, he'd be returning with little else on his sled.

A book of classic literary fiction, Russian author. He guessed who sent it before he opened the cover of the well-cracked spine and saw the brief inscription that confirmed the gifter. "*If I could only read one...*" For a woman with whom their interactions had been marked by her brevity, he took those few words as a quantity equivalent to a prequel of this particular tome she'd gifted. Those old novelists having been paid by the word. He lifted out about a dozen folded papers from the box. Some white printer paper, some yellow foolscap. All folded in half. On their exteriors, varying titles of *Trapper*, *E.E.*, *T*, *Ethan* or *Mr.* plus one of those previous titles.

He unfolded the first and before he read it could see it was obviously from a child. The printed and imperfect lettering. The colouring. His cheeks hurt as he wasn't so used to the shape they had taken. If he had tried to recall when he had last smiled that wide, that memory would have taken him back to a former era, but he didn't bother trying to dust off that ledger of past happy days and rather just enjoyed this new one. A few of them had no words just pictures and he wondered if it was a sign of their younger age or lower intelligence—or neither; they were perhaps just less literary more visionary. A common theme was him standing beside something dead, various animals he'd slain: bear, moose, beaver. Most of them with touching geometry: warm shapes drawn in love colours. Red hearts or pretty golden stars.

One letter in pink pencil crayon: *Dear Mr. Trapper. I'm very sorry about your little boy. He is the same age as me. I hope you are not sad anymore. Love, Tatiana.*

After a few of these letters his wide smile a saucer catching tears. He unfolded another. Curious cursive paired with skewed stencilled letters, this child marching to the beat of his own drum. The trapper's cartoon eyes were sized asymmetrically. Ethan laughed quietly at the accidental prescience of the artist. He wasn't sure when he had last laughed. His hair was long and red and it intertwined with the vines of the trees, those wavy curls becoming the background of the letter, like an energy field, or the artist had wanted to capture a melody in crayon. A very small sun was encircled by darkness and that seemed to make it brighter. A black bird—not a blackbird—some crow or raven roosted on what you'd have to call, if you retraced that curly perch, the long length of his tangled hair. And he was pretty sure a couple of the hair-vines climbing a tree were not ivy but snakes, because near the ends of those particular strands were white circles looking like eyeballs and forked from their ends were thin serpentine tongues. Yellow forked tongues. Red hair-snakes. So most of the colours lacking fidelity to the world. His legs were blue tree trunks and he knew that because one had a branch. He had no shirt and his chest hair was thick like a bear's and the picture-Ethan like the current-Ethan smiled large. Under the chest fur was the faintest outline of a heart. He could just make it out there. He was pretty sure the artist had drawn a heart in red then coloured overtop of it with dark green. Almost like the artist had held the paper over some gravestone's debossed heart and made a charcoal rubbing. He passed his finger over it but of course it wasn't textured and he turned the paper over to see if the heart was actually drawn on the verso but it was not.

"Well, hell," he laughed softly. The artist had signed it, "Gordie." Some child whose vision of the world was less constrained by life's patterns and expectations and social norms had made a picture that awakened something in his audience. It sounded like laughter. It wasn't laughter.

Maybe he wasn't a character in a dream of the sleeping king, like he'd told his boy who then accused him of plagiarism, "You stole that!" Maybe he was being drawn up on a page of a colouring book held in the hands of an imaginative child. So, a child's creation, not a king's. He smiled considering the make-believe.

He was touched by all the drawings but he liked this one best and took it and pinned it with a nail into the wooden wall and *my God laughter felt like a drug*. He couldn't remember the last time he had laughed. To be fair, he had actually laughed hysterically while trapped in a shallow tree-well during his mushroom trip, but couldn't recall that now and this quiet laughter was of a different kind. It felt like something good and vital and potent got released into his body, spiked his bloodstream, then delivered its sweet biochemical payload into his heart. Like he could see becoming an addict to it. He'd kinda forgotten about laughter, and that seemed very strange to him.

Here he was in his woodland sanctuary just trying to cultivate a little mental peace-and-quiet with simple and honest living, and his treed walls had been broached by some dive-bomber who attacked dropping mortar rounds of children's letters and a teacher's book and a cop's wife's muffins and young artists' drawings—all of them munitions which ought to take their place alongside chemical gases and cluster bombs and other ignoble weaponry forbidden by the rules of honourable warfare. In his battening and hardening in order to weather life's madness and storms had come the interruption of human love. Their affectionate shelling found the chinks in his chainmail.

This peculiar soldier of misfortune, with his ice dips and sauna bakes and drug trips and chin-ups, sidestepping crevasses in a world scattered with landmines, a man humbly secluding himself from further spiritual fracture and ruin, ought to be left alone. Turns out under that new body armour, he was naked under there. Ethan felt raw.

Lastly in the box was a legal-sized envelope. The town's district office and its address centred on the page. *So there was a legal portion after all.* The envelope wasn't sealed. He slid out its contents. Three pages paperclipped and fronted with a yellow sticky note. He read it over. He read it again.

· · · ● · ● · · ·

Early dawn glowing up its purple world. A hint of sunrise burning like a stray ember from the stove's bed of slumbering coals. He was up earlier than normal and had been reading the morning sky's story that told nothing more than that low star's slow rise. Same story as yesterday. Little else required.

All the letters on the table behind him. The papers of the deed, its sticky note explaining how he was now the owner of the same hundred and sixty acres that once belonged to his family. Or, he would be the owner. All he had to do was head to town and sign to take possession and make it official. Of course at first he couldn't believe it. But then he wasn't surprised at all. Try to shake it as he had, he was glued to the past. Why would his family's land be any different? He'd step forward and the past would step its shadow. Other times he placed a boot and found that the past had already preceded him.

He sat separately from those papers but nonetheless, they had all drifted up and slid through some mail slot in the back of his head.

He set the kettle to warm then sat back down by the window looking at the austere beauty of snow-covered woods in a crushed-grape dawn. That merlot just starting to be thinned with chardonnay sunlight. White porcelain mug warming his hands. Everything quiet as oils on canvas. Here he was in the tidy cabin, warm and well slept, a devout in a congregation of one in his temple of solitude, and while worshipping the holy vintage of a Northern morning he felt—

—Enough! Enough. Fuck off with your romanticism. How many layers deep is your bullshit? Keep this up and you'll live out your days all alone.

The lighting. Look at the lighting. It's like wine.

You don't drink wine.

Look at the needles, even in the winter they're still green.

They're fucking needles. They're needles. Green. Who cares? Stop playing make-believe. Are you looking forward to sitting by the fire alone tonight? Then tomorrow? The one after that? Does that sound like poetry? Stop pretending. Stop calling loneliness solitude, and romanticizing your lies. You're just an ageing man living alone in the woods. You're getting so sophisticated the way you lie to yourself, I almost believed it.

Ethan sipped the coffee.

What you're doing here isn't any good. This is not a life. It's not. It's nothing.

Ethan blew over the coffee.

You're not special and the world doesn't care about you. Your future is to wither and die. Maybe today, maybe tomorrow. Get that in your head.

It's there.

You lost it all. Now what? The only thing keeping you going is a full return to your own self-righteousness. Almost there. So crown yourself a lonely king over some pile of dirt whose mound you'll further raise with your own dead body. Dirt. That's you. You do know that, right?

Keep telling me that.

I will.

Good.

He sipped from the mug. Aren't you tasting this? Aren't you smelling it. He inhaled clearly through his nose in the pine cabin with trace aromas of fire and bread and hot coffee. He looked to the stack of great books beside him. The gilt names of their authors glowing before the sun lit them.

You really don't feel it? This isn't enough? He asked that in all seriousness.

Bread and coffee and books and sunlight. That's enough for you? Hey? Just stop. Who are you kidding? Stop peddling your shit.

Normally he wouldn't have said anything but it'd been many days now cooped up with this perpetual dialectic of an isolated consciousness. The embattled self. Cabin fever. He said: If I'm in sales then so are you. What are you selling? What's better? He didn't wait for himself to answer. You're going to try to sell some bleeding-heart romance. I know you too. I see you.

You're dying inside and you don't even recognize it. You're the worm at the bottom of the tequila bottle, I'm trying to show you a way out.

You don't drink tequila. Now who's talking out of their ass? Do you even know how patronizing you sound? I'm alright. Actually. This all feels pretty good. I can bear a little lonely. Lonely isn't so bad and nothing's perfect. Where's better? Town? You'll say town. What do you think is waiting out there? Hey? How does that end? Loss. And how many people in the company of others are still lonely? How many people don't even really like the few friends they have? How many trapped in relationships of convenience? People just afraid of leaving rather than some strong bond holding them together. Half of marriages end in divorce—how many that keep it together are still chronically unhappy, people dying inside. Trapped. People drowning in routine and so very tired of the annoying habits of the person next to them and they're choking back a part of them that wants to scream out at the dinner table so instead they just reach for their wine. Add in the infidelities and the cruelties and the lies and now you've sunken much lower than lonely. You're the one dressing it up. I'm saying right here, *look*, the needles are green. You're saying you know where they grow greener. I'm good. Maybe it's you that needs some honesty. Hey? Maybe it's you who should look in the mirror.

I'm alright.

Listen to yourself. You think you know but you don't. Maybe you just love the concept of love. You're idealizing something you're now too far removed from to remember all the ugly bits. You'll idolize a holy saint until five minutes together you're ready to throttle him for how he whistles through his nose eating his soup. That's what's waiting for you.

Is your world all books now that you don't even know when you're thinking and when you're repeating? Don't fool yourself. Look at your hands, they're already withering. You're on short time. You're sitting there alone and withering.

That's only a problem for one of us.

Look.

He lowered the mug and humoured himself and turned over his hands.

Look.

I'm looking.

Those cracks. You're getting old.

I'm proud of that leathery skin.

Just stop. You're killing me. Stop dressing everything up. I can't take it. It's just old skin getting older is all it is.

Cracks like Granddad's hands were cracked. You fault him too?

You're living a lie, bud. You're alone and you're getting old.

That's only a dirty word for one of us, bud.

Look at the corners of your eyes.

He reached for the hand mirror, his face dimmed in the early light but not so much he couldn't see crow's feet, cracks and lines.

Look.

You look. You're scrutinizing for imperfections when you could be scrutinizing for beauty. I see lines like Gran's eyes. You saying in her old age she wasn't beautiful? You're calling Gran ugly?

Just calling a spade a spade. Loneliness isn't solitude and pain isn't beauty and old is old—Gran or whoever.

I don't even know you anymore. Her lines were cut from a thousand smiles. I should be so lucky.

You smiling much now?

When did you get so bitter on me? Maybe I'm okay with being an old man. There's grace there. An honesty. Out there fishing in the morning.

Where your old arthritic hands can't tie the knots.

Where I wouldn't resent them for it. And if it's too cold that I can't tie the line, I'll drink coffee or make a fire or sit and watch the sunrise till my hands are ready. And if they're still not ready I'll just watch the birds and the clouds, and that's okay too. If I have to tie the knots in the cabin where my hands are warm, then so be it, that's just fine by me. And if my knees hurt walking down the gametrail I'll go slow and I'll find a good stick and I'll carve the stick and make a deer-hide strap for my hand. Take things as they come and expect nothing and just be happy with any mildness to the day. He looked down at the backs of his hands and they weren't like Granddad's yet but part of him was. Part of me already is an old man, he thought, just waiting for my hands to catch up. Where I don't even care if I hook anything and I only take what I can eat, so mostly let them go and I'll only keep one I've foul hooked or worn out too bad for him to recover and where mostly I'm just out there anyways 'cause it's pretty. Just 'cause it's pretty. Like it's pretty now in the wine light. You're missing it. You should see it. Did I mention the wine? he teased himself. You should come with me. I got room for you. Then I'll come back from fishing and clean up and sit and it's still early in the tidy cabin and I'll look out the window with the fire going and drink black coffee and maybe sweep the floor again even when it doesn't need it and read all the way to noon and look out at the water from my cabin and the pretty grey sky above and wonder if it'll rain today. That's enough for me. I think it might be. I think there's love there.

You don't live next to a lake. What are you even talking about?

Just seeing if you're paying attention. Yeah, you better keep your eye on me. You can have the half eye, I get the whole one. He winked it.

But an old man alone in the woods? that part asked now sounding more agreeable and genuinely curious, if not perhaps scared. *Is that what we're signing up for? Is that enough?*

He thought about it.

The kettle started to whistle. An alarm for decisions that needed to be made.

· · • · • · • · • · ·

Stove damper shut. Mug empty beside the chair. On the frosted porch, Act One, Scene One: shadow puppets of birds at play. A little breeze roamed, looking to wander that lonely country between the man's ears. A squirrel come for a seed. A man gone hunting.

Doubt is an unpleasant condition, but certainty is absurd. From a book he'd long ago returned to a shelf but a line he had not. *Philosophy is to teach how to live without certainty.* Another passage etched on the inside of his skull. Still though, he couldn't help being concerned with the incertitude: town or woods?

It wasn't yet spring, so the sweet fragrance emitted by a late-winter warm stretch was either a forgivable lie or believable promise. A half-morning's hike away was a section of woods where the taller trees, wider trunks, and broader canopies sheltered deer from storms, and there the animals tended to congregate for their winter range. He thought most clearly while hiking.

The sun lit icicles hanging from branches and in one section of the forest those crystal roots dripped wet beads into their own tiny puddles of varying depths, playing notes that ranged the scale of xylophonic bloops and plinks. Their curious sharps and flats matching his uncertain thoughts of what to do with the property deed. One hundred and sixty acres returned. *Just go in and sign? Do I even want it?*

He knew he had to go to town soon enough anyways regardless of the deed. It wasn't the inevitable trip that was weighing on his mind. Trapping was a dying trade; few people bought furs anymore. *So, what? Take possession of the land and rebuild the cabins and run the outfit for hunting like before? Bring this story full circle?* He couldn't imagine that that type of tourism was in any less demand than when he last quit it. *Start up the lodge like Granddad?* It was the most obvious choice and it made logical sense because he would need money and he had once been a guide and knew how it all worked. When he visualized what that would look like, it conjured up a feeling he imagined a person who after surviving a decade shipwrecked on a small atoll and then having returned to civilization might feel when he found the world he knew was no longer. Those kinds of feelings. The idea of raising up new cabin walls felt more like resurrecting the dead.

So then what. Sell it? Thank them for the land, then sell it and keep the money. No doubt, not exactly what they had in mind. But maybe I'm not who they think I am and why do I owe them anything? I could live for a long time up here with that money. Never even have to go to town again. Buy a satellite phone and call in for air-dropped supplies whenever I need a refill. The appeal of that idea meshed a couple gears in his head. *One quick visit to town and sign the deed and return to live happily ever lonely after?*

His plodding steps of uncertainty were interrupted by the sight of cleft hooves. Deer tracks. Those big prints stopped him in his own tracks. One of the fore prints was turned slightly inwards. He eyed their path to the big timber off in the distance.

We aren't always privy to our particular biases nor their workings. We often don't see our well-meaning but flawed self-preservation tendencies hindering us from growth. It was hard for him to know what he really wanted and what he didn't. Where through the path of self-honesty lay happy country, and what was false comfort or faulty shield. He had real love for the beauty and tranquility of the woods, truly he did, and it held many simple pleasures and it was the world his family long knew. *The thing is,* he reflected, *that family always had family.* He did not. He was framing the question as Town or Woods, but it was really People or Solitude: human connection or woodland seclusion. *So, what about people? What about time spent with those capable of inflating your heart? What about laughter?* He asked himself that while thinking about the children's drawings. But he knew happiness could be real without being shared, and maybe he didn't need fixing.

All my happiest memories are people.

All my worst memories are people.

Earlier he had thought that he had a fundamental love for life that preceded the people that populated it. *To simply have gotten a chance at life takes incalculable luck, the privilege to simply witness a world of such splendour.* But he wondered if he was lying to himself 'cause it felt like deep down he might have once loved his wife and his boy more than life itself. That would explain why their loss felt so total. He just didn't know the answer to that and so it seemed like honest self-exploration had its limits. Ethan had assumed he was folded like a letter, where just one untruth lay in the crease. In actuality this man's truths were so intricately fitted together that opening one crease revealed another and the layered dimensions had him folded not so much like a letter and more like a paper crane. *What are you avoiding?* Trying to get at the root of his incertitude. *What scares you? Is it the past that's holding on to you or are you not letting go? Is living out your life alone in the forest a type of real love?* It felt like it might be. *Or are you scared of greater connection because of its ever-potential to again be ripped painfully away?* He could ask all that while genuinely not knowing what he should do. *Scared of letting the next person down like you did her? Like you did him? Like you let yourself down?* All the folds, so many folds. *Hey origami-man I'm talking to you.*

He didn't see the bird circle high above. Its wings unflapping.

The land that awaited to be returned to him had a complicated past. That was not lost on him. *Should I restore it to those who lived here first?* He considered this. *Who were the people who lived on this particular part of land before the government claimed it, then sold it off? Was it the case that when the settlers acquired it from those who lived there before, those earlier people had taken it from some other?* He didn't know. He'd read in books and also heard Granddad's stories of Nôhkow that the land's ownership wasn't ever an ownership. It was people who harmoniously shared it with one another and with other animals. But he wondered if that was some make-believe, idealized version of the past. Otherwise why had he heard tales of tribal wars *over* this very land if not *for taking* the land. *Maybe it wasn't some peaceful and singular history and sometimes it was battled for and bled over, and could be the North, with its majestic trees, was so fertile and lush from all the warring blood and bones that nourished it, like most other lands and other history—mostly unrecorded—of one group taking land from another who took it from another.* He didn't know and wondered who did know, and whether anyone could prove unequivocally their version. Accounts of history can be murky, and uncontentious narratives rare, and both parties—victor and defeated—may have biased accounts from distinct perspectives. Who then fairly adjudicates that opaque past with its scroll all tattered and bloodstained and burned and eaten by moths?

He was close to the big timber. He stopped and retrieved from his pack a small tin bowl that cradled things within it and so didn't actually take up much space. He set it on a log. He punctured two holes in a can of condensed milk, which he usually saved for special occasions, but celebrating his own birthday alone or Christmas or whatever else didn't have a lot of charm, so he'd taken it out with him today. Poured its contents into the bowl. With his fingers slightly splayed he lightly sifted in flour and baking powder and salt he had premixed the prior night. Added a bit of water from his canteen. He whittled the ends of a broken stick free of bark and stirred the dough. Took a handful of snow and rubbed a flat rock clean and kneaded the dough on the rock until it had elasticity. Stretched it then rolled the dough into a snake on his knee. Dangled an end of the snake-dough to the long roasting-stick. Pinched that dough's dangling tail back on itself to secure it, turned the stick in one hand while lowering the dough to wrap it in a twizzle, then pinched the end of the higher tail back on itself again near the tip of the stick. An old Scottish food taken up by the Métis. He roasted the bannock over the fire until its skin leoparded brown. Lightly smoked rough-bread like that doesn't even need butter or jam but he'd packed a bit of wild-raspberry preserve anyways. Poured out a dandelion tea from his thermos to the cup-lid and its steam mimicked the fire mimicking the cloudy sky.

He had read of a poet who was considered by many of his time to be one of the greats. His advanced age had matured the tireless pursuit of his craft and with so much depth of life to draw on he was composing stunning verses of searing truth. Truths that dug profoundly deeper from the wisdom of age. In that same book, the author wrote that poets should start writing when they're four and take it seriously through their forties and not publish until their eighties. He only wrote in pencil because nothing is certain. That's how he phrased it. Though that very statement that poet chipped into the side of a boulder next to his house. Before he died, the poet was becoming embittered by what he perceived as the injustices of life. His revolt was to bear down on his craft and he wrote even more beautifully, perhaps some of the most exquisite lines ever composed—golden prose so bright it didn't blind but gave vision. He'd put pen to paper and render firework verses, sentences spraying off the page like each word was a bottle of shaken champagne waiting to be uncorked by a reader's moving eyes. And when he was finished a poem, he would take the pages and burn them, burn them to deprive the world of that beauty. The poet turned inward emotionally and reclusive socially. Then he died. For Ethan

Edwards, that poet served as a perfect counter-example of how not to live.

Inside him was a voice, small but mighty, telling him to rally for love. It said be cautious of becoming a knight with armour so thick it hardens you off from the very thing you seek. The little plea inside him said, Many rivers to cross—don't drown in the first. Heavy armour only brings failure when your quest is truth and love. Certain subtle truths need to be felt and some loves have a soft touch.

Ethan reclined against his backpack.

Smoky sky, smoky fire, smoky thoughts: town or woods?

His lunch was finished and the big woods were close but he kept watching the fire. He wondered if anything else ever in all of human history has held the gaze of human eyes for so long. It vastly predates books and modern entertainment, and sunsets are brief. A humble thing and simple pleasure that transcends culture and time, just like music, but he wasn't much for music. And how many solutions have been found glimmering in the coals and how many innovators owe its ruminative flames honourable mention? He stared at the fire like it held the answers as maybe it did. The only other thing he could imagine that might rival the total quantity of time captivating human eyes, was another pair of human eyes.

The fire was burning down and any flames that licked up from the coals grew rare.

He wanted love. That he knew. All else paled beside it. Nothing was worthier of his efforts. And his love of the forest was real. He loved the snow and he loved the summer. The pure air. The nights and fires. Stars and skies that have been described so very many times there's no need for another. But what's one more. The great wondrous firmament pricked by endless pins of distant light from lost suns and burning worlds and wild rays shining for unknown time, where stars twinkled like eyes lit with their own glowing incredulity at witnessing such beauty. The green-and-purple sprawling dance of northern lights. Where among cricket creek and brook babble and owl hoo and countless other talents in the jukebox night there is wolf howl. That wild and coarse and eerie song and whether or not she's singing it for you she's always somehow drawing something out of you in that evocative sound. Reverence and scared and lonely and awe. Singing it like she's borrowing it from your belly and so just telling it on your behalf. *The North. The forest.* He loved it top to bottom. Never leave it. The trees and fire and birds and the lake and white snow on green bows. Spring's birth. Summer's opulence. Fall's quilt-work. Winter's austerity. Never leave it, even if he did he never would, 'cause it was all woven up inside him and like his blood kept warm 'cause Gran had knitted some mitt he wore around his heart—red to match, finger holes for arteries—never bury that, nor burn it, nor even take it off when its thread laced his ventricles. Town or woods: *Woods. It'll always be woods.*

In a magic trick performed by a million breaths before him, he blew on the embers to pull little flaming bouquets hidden in the cracked sleeves of the coals. He blew deeply like he was blowing out soft apologies and trying to inhale self-acceptance and exhale promises and inhale forgiveness and he wished he had endless breaths to draw as he'd only use them to say endless sorries. As he would the next fire. And the one after. The fire woofed, not like the dogs of hell heard at the lodge's burning, some gentler breed. As if fire, like dog, was man's best friend. He warmed his hands.

But what about love that loves back? What about hands out-stretched helping other hands. Words spoken into other ears and ideas and laughter shared. What a world when you can make laughter, where you can *make* love—somehow the most precious thing isn't of finite quantity, you can just go make it out of nothing. How to even imagine a better world when such alchemy is already possible? What about love free from specious dreams and false ideals, love freckled and wrinkled and lined and flawed and beautiful. What about sweet imperfections and the holy privilege to expose where you're folded and offer up your creases and hope that folds can fit together. The sacredness of intimacy and a shared life like you once knew. Ethan? Companionship not as a means to fill a void, but as something to elevate a newfound scrap of peace in this work in progress, Ethan?

He drank the last of his cold tea.

He had read of a species capable of flying to the moon. A species concocting potions to neutralize disease and extend life. A species who if your heart gave up was capable of transplanting in a new one. He'd read of all that. Who could believe all that? Probably none of that was true. Probably just folk stories, charlatanic wizardry, as all that sounded like the work of immortals. Who'd want to spend time with company like that.

Decision fatigue was literally tiring him. He leaned farther back against his pack and his heavy eyes took a minute of rest. In his dream he was hiking. Same day same everything. The darkness behind him was not his shadow keeping pace. So that made it no different than usual. But in his dream he had the audacity to confront Death. He started raising his bow but the Reaper had been waiting and it was quicker on the draw. Ethan over his forty years had hunted a lot and his quantity of slain was testament to being one of Death's most gifted pupils. But in this case the student would not overtake the master. The Dark Angel brought its scythe up quickly, then deftly touched the long blade to the centre of Ethan's Adam's apple. Ethan didn't drop his bow but he didn't dare raise it higher. The deep hood that shrouded the grim spirit completely enshadowed its skull, and the only sign of animation there was the faint trace of a gloating smile. Its huge blade dragged over the loose skin of Ethan's throat, the cold flat of the scythe under his chin, tilting his head. The blade is not a sword but a farmer's tool. The Angel of the Abyss was just having a look to see if this lost lamb, this uncertain stalk of wheat—if the soul of this sorry fool was mature enough to harvest. Ethan woke looking up at the big Northern sky. His neck above his scarf was exposed; the coldness on his skin was not as sharp as metal but the message no less acute.

He packed up his cookware and thermos and he was close enough to hunting grounds that he nocked an arrow.

He was approaching the big woods when from them he heard an elegiac rattle. Maybe Death really was closer than normal and that spooky percussion came from a quartet of dead minstrels who followed his morbid travels. No song coming from their gaping mouths, but playing their phalanges like spoons over their knees.

When the sound came again he realized he knew it well: deer antlers rubbing and scraping the trunk of a tree, a buck tousling its rack in the leafless winter branches. He couldn't see the deer but he knew its direction and he snapped into a predatory focus and entered that familiar country and primal flow state. He breathed softer and listened harder and his body and being entire got honed.

Snowshoe hares in the North are all white all winter, who knows what colour they are anywhere else. If anyone claimed these northern lands were haunted, soliciting the opinion of this six-foot jackrabbit with a violent bow would be a good place to begin that lore's investigation. If he had made a notch on the weapon's limbs for every life he had taken, it'd be whittled away to not much. When earlier that morning he donned the furred suit, he felt like he was adorning himself with the past—both the recent and the long ago—and he said, "Good. I am the past. A suit to complement my bones." This predator who when hunting had his focus so tunnelled, purpose so singular, intent so driven, that his stalking was hardly bound by real limits and maybe he had followed that elusive hare that led Alice down the hole, then clubbed it and dragged it back out, 'cause warming his head was a white rabbit hat. That rabbit late for his date forever.

He could hear the buck rubbing the tree and now he could see some fifty yards away willow branches moving. His right hand at the string ready to draw. There were several large trees and with the light breeze in his face he positioned a thick trunk between him and the buck. He'd practised enough wearing his backpack and knew it wouldn't hamper the shot. He stalked hunched and slow and silent and deadly.

Fifteen yards away the buck's antlers were sticking out to the left of the trunk. Chocolate-dark rack, which likely meant it had lived most of its life under the densest canopies in the low-lit deep timber. By this time of year the rut activity slows down and those bucks still active after months of fighting and fornicating and fasting are the dominant animals with the greatest stamina. He kept that tree between their line of sight and leaned right to see its body. Belly a bit thinner than it would be other times of the year, but its back looking broad and with hindquarters shaped for both strength and agility, like a cutting horse. He didn't need to get closer. He could draw his bow behind the cover of the trunk and send an arrow through vitals.

Ethan pulled and came with no hesitation to full draw at his new anchor point. The oblivious buck still rustling its antlers in the branches. He found his target patch of fur behind its foreleg and began easing his trigger-hand backwards so the shot would surprise him as it should, sending a razor-tipped killing stick through a lung and a heart and a lung. Then the buck turned. It stopped its headwork and turned around. He lost his shot placement. The deer settled, looking off to Ethan's right with its head exposed. It hadn't seen him in his white-camouflage suit. The deer dipped its head slightly, then stepped forward, lamely. *Maybe a twisted knee or bruised shoulder from a recent skirmish, maybe something more grave*, Ethan thought. He looked but saw no scars or blood on its hide. Gauging its health because he wasn't going to shoot if it was diseased and the meat compromised. It stepped again and it was a hobble. He saw the lower part of its right foreleg was a bit thin. Likely some old injury. It was a healthy-looking older deer that had a limp. An ideal harvest. If he didn't take it, the wolves would soon enough. His eye ever-narrowed looking through the peep.

He saw himself. Other things besides just the cabin's hand-held mirror do reflect. Could've been its laboured gait or advancing age or that it was still out there tearing things up and looking for trouble late in the season after being through some hard living.

Kill like the owl kills—swift and without remorse, that creed in his head.

If the line separating good and evil runs through the heart of everyone, maybe there is another line demarcating lamb from wolf. That line now extended through Ethan's whole body and on one shoulder stood an angel, the other a devil. One said *kill* and one said *live*. But to kill brought the security of healthy food, and to allow mercy risked going without. He wasn't sure which petition came from whom.

You know this deer is just you, right? Ageing and alone and injured. Let this one go and wish him well and let yourself go and wish yourself well. Let the wolves come if they will.

But maybe that was just some devilry from a disloyal and rebellious piece of his mind unhappy with prior decisions, trying to starve him out here.

One deer provides a lot of meat and it's old and it's caught a limp so the wolves won't be far away. Take its life with reverence. Send the arrow.

Once while out hunting he admonished the boy for his childlike mercy. He wished the small dove of mercy inside him had not begun spreading her wings because his world was uncertain enough and his shoulder was beginning to ache from holding a serious bow at full draw.

The bow wavered and the buck caught that subtle motion. Black pupils returning the stare of black pupils. As if those dark focal points were the ends of two narrow bores beyond whose terminals nothing in that moment was of concern to either gazer. If the buck sensed the danger, its alarm lagged the speed of the glinting broadhead the man had just loosed.

Ethan's world slowed as he watched an arrow tipped with three flakes of the sun. Its light disappeared. As if for all the hundreds of shooting stars he'd seen on Northern nights, he now watched for the first time one destroy a world. The broadhead cut into the buck's hide, then its organs, then the tri-bladed tip exited the far side of the animal's body. Shaft and fletching trailed the blades which had entered clean and exited ugly and the entire arrow passed through the animal's body before it could even blink, before it could process the arriving panic too general to inform it that it would now die. The deer mule-kicked and bolted a short ways through the brush, then tripped and crashed.

Where it lay, it kicked the undergrowth. It kicked like it didn't know it wasn't still running. It kicked slower trying to stand up. It kicked once softly in some futile protest or petition. It didn't kick.

The deer about sixty feet away from him. Hidden by its crash in the ferns. Close enough he could hear its laboured breath and so without sight of the animal it sounded like the forest itself was suffering. Ethan nocked another arrow, but pursue and the animal's adrenaline might enable it to run again and hide anew and die but not be found. What's most humane, though doesn't seem it, is to just let that deep and fatal cut drain life away. Probably the pain reduced from the shock, but who could say. A quick and ethical death in the longest two minutes of the animal's life. Not all that short either for the one who sent the arrow. He listened to its wheezing inhales and wet exhales. The gurgle of blood in its lungs. Nothing holy about it, seemed about the furthest thing from beauty.

Then, quiet. He gave the proceeding nothingness a few minutes. The whole forest was heavy. *You are the wolf. You are death.*

He retrieved his arrow that had passed through the deer then impaled the earth. He walked to the animal. First saw its white belly that wasn't heaving. It had fallen to its side with the entry wound facing the sky. He looked at that small cut behind its foreleg and had he not known it was there it would have been hard to see. The deer's eye, like the sky, was still and clouded. Ethan looked upwards following that empty gaze and he wasn't sure why.

He kneeled and put the back of his hand to its nose. Then cupped his hand over the buck's vacant and familiar eye. A nerve, laggard in emptying its charge, or a dawdling last pulse of life, gave a flutter and sweep to the lashes. He felt it brush his fingers. No breath, no kick or heave of the chest or greater appeals to mercifully end its life already gone. Just one lost flutter and sweep. Ethan's exhale was heavy.

He apologized to it. He said quietly, "I'm sorry." He thanked it. He whispered, "Thank you, deer."

Death and a deer and a man kneeling in the big woods covered in the pall of loss. His hand cupped over the buck's eye, his head low. A warm bit of life leaking out of the deer's eye, wetting his deformed finger. Warm tear leaking out his own scarred eye. It all just felt like some sad and shared and common variation of broken life, broken love.

You didn't kill your son by dressing him in a bear suit. You didn't kill him by putting him in a bear suit. It's just not on you. Life is hard and sometimes it's not and bad things happen and sometimes they don't and then you die. Your story is the boy's story is the buck's story. Just let it go.

His eyes leaked. His head low.

He wasn't sure if he fully believed that part of himself. He wasn't sure if he ever would. He kneeled with his hand on the buck long enough he felt it cool. Snow had begun falling. Little piles forming on his shoulders.

Not some cathartic moment. Not that. He'd never shake the past. It was as inflammable as it was undrownable as it was irrational and undruggable. He is the past. He had started realizing that days ago. You don't get free from what you're made of. That's possible in the same way breaking free from your skin and lungs are possible. Break free of your heart and blood. His memories of his boy and his wife and all the rest weren't skeletons in his mind's closet, they were his bones that built him. He'd shake free of them as easily as he'd shake free of his femur, rattle out his ribs clattering to the floor. Though time could distort and fade some details away, it hadn't dissolved the memories of those most serious events, and he'd find out in later years it never would. Time isn't the antidote of regret, only its medium. He wished the gift of the mushroom's insight *to love while he could with the privilege of time* had the properties of a golden key that fit all the wards and bits of his mind and soul and unlocked a permanent state of well-being. Its message did resonate, and he would keep it close, but the plant's healing properties were not total. The philosophical concept of a deterministic world—*everything that happens is playing out from what came before, and therefore nothing is ultimately anyone's fault or to anyone's credit*—made sense to him, and he just wished he could achieve enduring emotional relief proportional to that argument's logical tightness. *The wonder that anything even exists at all, that there is even a landscape on which to bear suffering, hardship as proof of the privilege of life*, only brought him so much respite because he could stand in the sunlight of pretty words and though his skin would warm, their rays were not so penetrative as to fully melt his soul's deep winter. Some pockets of his core were light; some pockets of his core were glacier.

It was as if he was not a machine programmed by the laws of logic, not a person quickly repairable by spiritual insight, but rather he was some organic thing built from murky, interconnected feelings and subconscious wounds and deep emotional scars and evolutionary tendencies and habits and biases and hope and fear and love and what all else that he did not know. In the nights and years to come, none of his mind's floral rhetoric and logical proofs, cruel castigations or tender motivations would theorize, motivate, frighten himself into relief. He would sometimes still miss his wife and his boy. That's okay.

Once on a candlelit night up in the loft while he drew sweet breaths through cracked ribs, he'd written a letter to the boy wherein he asked the boy to promise he'd endure. He felt he now owed the boy that very promise he himself had asked of him. Above all, *endure*. That night long ago he set that letter on the coals of the stove, but somehow the promise it bore remained. As though the promise was mineral: you can't burn that. And like the story of the regal fox so entranced with her prey she jumps and never comes down, like the aloof rabbit picked off by a great horned owl, this man here didn't see it coming. That letter that turned to feathery ash had replumed a phoenix, regenerated a promise. A promise to the boy he once had he now carried in his head, so he owed the promise as much to his boy as he did to himself.

He dragged away his hand covering the buck's eye to fully close its lid forever.

He was still a hunter. He was no longer a trapper. He hadn't been one for a while. He carried enough residue of death to know trapping was no longer for him. He could turn his head and see a thousand skeletons, listen on a quiet night and hear the clack and jangle of their loose bones. He'd continue to hunt, but only what he needed for food, and with the sacredness of life and the tragedy of its loss, he knew each death would be heavy, and each he took would in part be at his own expense, and though he would strive to kill swiftly, it would come with much remorse, much remorse. And his own death would come too, with no greater significance nor any less, and the thirsty Earth would swallow his blood as eagerly and impartially as those she had already drunk.

Ethan kneeling beside the dead deer in the quiet woods with the snow falling. He looked at the back of one of his ageing hands, studied it like some variant of a palm reader. In the progression of Rodin sculptures, where once he was *The Kiss*, then *The Thinker*, petition that artist to chisel and title this new one.

Snow falling weightlessly. Delicate enough each flake might just as easily float as it would fall. Soft as confectionary sugar. The winter savouring one of the snow's last descents. Snowing as if clouds were being milled between great hands into the finest flour. The sifted snow dusted his head, sifted and dusted the forest. Those feathers falling softly as the powdered bones of angels.

TOWN

Dave packed up and left town. It wasn't from guilt or shame and he wasn't leaving his home or looking for a new one. Sarah had always wanted a change and Dave had always wanted Sarah. If the roads weren't snow packed, they'd have left dust in their tracks.

Given the accidental nature of the boy's death, that he was wearing a bear cloak in a hunting locale where a newly enacted law required the wearing of hunters' blaze orange, as well based on precedent of a similar case's dismissal in another jurisdiction, Jacob's charge of manslaughter was dismissed. The stigma Jacob felt he bore was not one of a murder conviction, nor was it hatred or disdain or even much mild accusation from the town. On the whole, the town understood. He just wore the stain of ugly misfortune. Many people were coloured with it too, but he failed to see that.

Even inside his apartment Jacob would wear a hat pulled down low over his eyes. At first he didn't much leave it except for groceries and booze. Sometimes the bar. The only time he felt blended in was after he'd had a few drinks, even just two helped. So he felt blended-in pretty often. He would tell himself that's all he'd have that day, every day. But two were a lubricant for the third. After three came all the rest. Mornings were hard but they got easier at about noon, about eleven. For the first while after the town learned how the boy died, Jacob had the ability to quiet public spaces, like some anti-wave whose negative vibe could flatline conversations. As time passed his anti-wave strength could only lower the volume of others. In days to come the only person he continued to silence was himself. He spoke less in general, and of that day not at all. His hearing from a ringing in his ears was not so good.

Woods

First day of spring. A dawn of violet light. The sun with violent beauty vanquishing the dark, its orange expanding into the sky's outer reaches like the glow of a neutron bomb. A breeze just lighter than a whisper, so its words blowing over the frozen pond told nothing more than a rumour of a message to come. Grains of snow rolled down the backs of small snow crests frozen in waves on the pond's surface. The winter wind pebbled the skin of a naked man.

He had made a decision on the deed. He wanted to donate the ownership to a land conservatory. Just or unjust, he hoped to keep his cabin with its small acre of land grandfathered in from squatter's rights. He didn't know how he was going to make money. He didn't know what he was going to do. He held that in his head, the bit of thrill but mostly weight of uncertainty. The pleasure of being a middle-aged man discovering his world and sometimes creating it. He was partly scared. But you don't get scared, said the boy in his head. He was partly scared. *Good.*

He gave it a name: *scared*. He liked scared. Scared felt like truth. She said there's not always solace in the truth but there is a strength in knowing it.

Maybe the burning monk hadn't transported himself away from the pain. Maybe he felt so grateful for the opportunity to serve those he loved in a worthy cause that he struck that match and touched its fateful sulphurous head to his fuel-drenched body to torch his meagre flesh. Maybe hotter flames already burned inside him and his strength was not from a wall he'd stacked with mantra bricks. Maybe love had consumed his body before flames ever did. And long after his charred remains extinguished and the dark plumes of his smoke were carried away by the winds, his devotion, his sacrifice, still smouldered in others' hearts as some enduring gesture.

Ethan stuck out one foot and set his toes on the water's surface and dabbled in the coming discomfort. A small ripple on the dark water. He used his toes to flick out a berg. Larger ripple. Returned them cool and wet to the wooden plank. He shivered.

Wild long and dark hair. A few strands moving in the lightest breeze of the warming dawn with its violet lighting. Breezes that roamed like the ghosts of what was. Birds that moved like birds. Him staring in a chopped ice hole through one and a half eyes. Half of him watching his mind, half the world.

This man standing on the doorstep to his chapel of pain about to worship the sweetness of a short life and renew his vow of endurance. He raised his eyes in that valorous dawn in its wintry lighting. Eyes looking a little scared, maybe a little hopeful.

Two geese above didn't honk but flew low and fast enough he heard their wings whistle. They were flapping wing-to-wing southwards, flying towards a world of paper cranes.

His chest pricked with old claw markings. Ten tiny depressions the cold turned pink. Connect the dots to make a glyph that told the legend of a bear that wanted ribs for dinner and so came pounding on the door of his chest. Bear that picked the wrong door, picked the wrong fight. Bear stabbed twice in its left lung before finally getting slayed by a mythic little cherub. He looked down at those many scars. Raised his hands. Set his fingertips to the ten holes. Felt at those little pockmarks like some stamp of pride he bore upon his chest—Braille sunken not raised. As if it was a ten-finger notation scribed into his chest, like he was keeping score. Not wins and losses, notes and beats. And if you overlaid it on piano keys and played it one by one, its notes would sing of beauty and suffering, hope and sadness, hate and forgiveness, fear and regret, love and love lost. Play those notes together for a chord composed by a bear and a boy and a man and a Northern woods and listen to the sound of their bond. Though a song of death, likely still a love song, in one way or the other. A song of the wilderness within us all.

TOWN

THE JUKEBOX SANG ITS last song of the night. It would sing again. It was late and the bartender said the bar would soon be closing and one table paid their bill and left and a lady at the bar asked for hers and one table was finishing their drinks. In the corner sat a man whose presence was as reliable as the drip falling from the bathroom tap no matter how hard you turned it. Big blown-up nose from habits he'd quit more than once. Wild hair. Deformed face. His complexion was made darker from the weaker lighting in the bar's corners. Not easy to age him. He could have aged prematurely from what one would have to assume was a life of hard living. Though certain attributes are proprietary to the North, that one was not.

"Listen," he said. Hardly anybody listened to him, they weren't now. "I was on a hunting trip. I was camping and canoeing." He had stopped for the night and was heating his canned spaghetti directly on the coals and into the can's tin top he poked a vent hole with his can-opener blade. Sat watching it until he was satisfied with the quantity of steam jetting the vent. The sun-low sky was clear when he set the spaghetti in the fire, clear when he wrapped a towel around the can and took it off the coals then levered his blade into the perimeter. When he had almost connected his circle he pried the top.

"Halfway through my supper the horizon started to go dark." A wide horizon of muscled clouds dark as wrath. "And the winds weren't blowing they were sucking. Towards the storm." He watched it roiling towards him. He says he's sure, "Sometimes thunder comes first." No cracks, no flashes, just distant thunder rumbling like heavy trampling. "Then I could feel it too." That furious leading edge grew taller or just looked taller having arrived above him. Roiling towers of dark clouds pollute the whole sky.

Then the sounds of trampling stopped. Then all sounds stopped. The winds that were sucking towards the storm now cease entirely. Like the contents of that area, including the air, were being emptied. Temperature plummeted. "The hairs on my arms stood up." At the bar he runs a hand over his bare arm. "It felt like the air might just start to spark." Like the storm had been inhaling then held its breath before it blew. Then it blew. "Christ, did it blow."

Initially the flames of his small fire built from that volume of stoke, as if they were mounting a defence and attempting to ward off what advanced. Then the flames were bent backwards like a boxer on the ropes. Then they flattened and extinguished leaving nothing more than a glowing coal pile of rubies the wind buffed so bright, "I had to squint my eyes." In the bar he brings his hand up.

He couldn't seek shelter in his tent as it was still bundled in his pack and a good thing because it never would have held to its stakes. The bow of his canoe where it floated on the lake was being loosened by the storm. He set his dinner down.

"I ran." Then as suddenly as someone cutting the strings to a beaded curtain, rain fell heavily and evenly and landed with the tumult of ten thousand hooves trampling the earth. He ran and rain slung by the wind stung his face and stymied his vision. The hull already heavy with water and perhaps had it not taken on that weight it would have already been dislodged.

He grabbed the bow barely keeping purchase to the shore and the canoe now nearly parallel to the land and him not able to perpendicular it. He managed to lift it high enough he caused a wave of water to smash the stern and the added rear-weight threatened to sink that end. He closed his stinging eyes and groaned and leaned back and managed to drag that heavy canoe a measly couple feet which he hoped would do. "If I coulda, Ida drug it up and flipped it and crawled under."

Rain turned to hail, "Blast from a shotgun loaded with rock salt." Even on his gnarled hands they sting enough that he winced and thus exposed his teeth and the ice balls ricocheted pinging off his teeth, and believe him or not he says he could actually hear that. "Ping ping ping," he says and smiles those sparse teeth in the bar.

He kept on going while the bartender cleaned the taps and counter.

He feared the anger of that storm enough that he bailed on the pack and just ran for a tree.

"I know," his eyes widen. If anyone's listening to him which mostly they aren't he knows they're all thinking the same thing. "I know I'm not supposed to go to a tree in a storm. But what else do I do?"

He huddles against a tree. The branches of the cedar sway like the storm might rip them off. His footing among exposed roots and one arched from the ground just enough for the toe of his boot to fill its gap. You can tell he likes that part of the story. He says he could face any storm like that. Him standing under the tree's umbrella in a circular patch of dry earth, where outside is a land pebbled white.

Then the hail stops. The winds abate. Relieved he survived, he looks up to the sky. "And right then a bolt coming out of the sky. Straight at me." It hits his tree and splits that cedar clean in two. Wood and bark and a man's embrace to a tree violently ripped apart like some horrible zipper and the tree explodes in a flash of gothic light and smokes up the air and before he smells burnt cedar he smells sulphur. Sparks shower like foundry spray. Smouldering bark sizzling at the base of a ruined tree and his embrace cut in half. "My hair was on fire." Small flames at his feet and they twist without wind.

"Then gone. Just, over." He makes a gesture in the bar.

The sky doesn't clear but the clouds thin just enough to admit of dusk.

Maybe his story is word-for-word gospel truth. Or maybe it's true. "Words might lie but scars don't," he says. He points to the side of his face with its blotchy skin twisted and tightened from an old burn. "Got lucky there."

The bartender said the bar would soon be closing. So far he had not closed it. Outside there was a light skiff of snow over the pavement. Above, a green electric sign hummed.

WOODS

MANY YEARS PASSED. THE little boy floating inside Ethan had mostly lain down and curled up inside the man's heart. He mostly lay there sleeping peacefully, allowing something beautiful to grow up out of him. Overtop his grave a maple tree grew. He became a nurse tree. The boy liked nurse trees.

Ethan's scars had nearly faded away. New cuts came, and with the privilege of time, more would. Him outside the cabin now, standing in the snow.

He brought his right hand up, white with the cold. He kissed the undersides of the tips of his fingers. Old fingers on an old hand. Skin cracked and lined like a map of rivers he had paddled. On his left hand one nub finger missing its tip, and that's okay, 'cause he had enough love in a piece of his pinky toe that life could come for a few more.

His left hand wasn't cold like his right. Red nails. He teased her about that. Left hand warmed by the clasp of another and their fingers were laced like promises. She made him tuck that cut finger into the warm space between their clasp. He thought that was cute. Teased her about that too. Red nails. Red like an old dress, red like a new dawn. He brought his right hand's fingertips to his mouth and they shook a bit, and he kissed their undersides. Then he delivered the kiss to the headstones, to those cairns outside the cabin. Rocks gone dark from touch. Gone dark from kisses.

Acknowledgments

I WANT TO THANK certain individuals whose work inspires my development, both as a writer and a person. And though I may never meet you (you're rather famous or rather dead), I still want to acknowledge your work, with the hope others might find it and similarly benefit as I have.

Sam Harris, your investigations into consciousness, free will and determinism, mindfulness, are all tremendously and positively influential on my conception of the world. In my daily life, I hold your insights close enough that they find their way into my writing. Bertrand Russell said philosophy should teach how to live without certainty; you're continuing that tradition to the benefit of many people. I thank you.

Viktor Frankl, in the most abhorrent living conditions, truly the ugliest imaginable—wife and children dead, their ashes falling around you as you are being worked to death while starving in the freezing snow (words that even hurt to type)—you found something redeeming. I don't know how, but you did. "Love is the ultimate and the highest goal to which man can aspire. The salvation of man is through love and in love. A man who has nothing left in this world still may know bliss, be it only for a brief moment, in the contemplation of his beloved. In a position of utter desolation, when man cannot express himself in positive action, when his only achievement may consist in enduring his sufferings in the right way [...] man can, through loving contemplation of the image he carries of his beloved, achieve fulfilment. Love [...] finds its deepest meaning in his spiritual being, his inner self." I've gifted your book more than any other. Thank you.

David Foster Wallace, I consider your speech "This is Water" to be the logical proof of magic. While at my best I may embody only a fraction of the patience and humility and compassion and creativity your speech inspires, I still try to employ its wisdom. I agree, hard times are still "on fire with the same force that lit the stars." And I agree, "The really important kind of freedom involves attention, and awareness, and discipline, and effort, and being able truly to care about other people and to sacrifice for them, over and over, in myriad petty little unsexy ways, every day." Few novels, few stacks of novels, will contain as much insight as your short speech. Thank you for it.

Lex Fridman, you have such a unique orientation of discipline mixed with humour mixed with love, compassion, empathy, humility, humanism, optimism. I can't imagine a better orientation to life. The explorations in your podcast are valuable. Your ethos inspires me. Thank you for your work.

Thank you Cormac McCarthy, Ernest Hemingway, Leo Tolstoy, and Fyodor Dostoevsky.

<u>Attributing some mentions in the novel.</u>

"There is only one thing I dread: not to be worthy of my sufferings." —Fyodor Dostoevsky

"He with a *why* can bear any *how*." —Friedrich Nietzsche

"We are healthy only to the extent that our ideas are humane." —Kurt Vonnegut Jr.

"Will your restless heart come back to mine on a journey through the past." —Song lyrics from "Journey Through the Past." Neil Young

The picture the trapper holds of the burning monk: Thich Quang Duc.

IF YOU ENJOYED *IMMORTAL North Two* to the extent you want others to find it, please rate and review it. That helps. Thanks. — Tom

Tom Stewart is a memoirist and novelist. He was born in 1982 and grew up near Winnipeg, Canada. He attended University of Manitoba, studying literature and philosophy, worked in the North as a fishing and hunting guide, oil-rig roughneck and bush pilot. Tom now lives in Tofino, Vancouver Island.

For a free collection of short stories and to receive a monthly newsletter from Tom with updates of the novel-in-progress, please visit www.luckydollarmedia.com

BOOKS BY TOM STEWART

Immortal North: A Novel

Immortal North Two: A Novel

Under Big-Hearted Skies: A Young Man's Memoir of Adventure, Wilderness, & Love

Collected Works: Short Stories & First Chapters